Adored by the Grumpy Ghost

Mapletown Monster Mates

Book 1

Ivy Knox

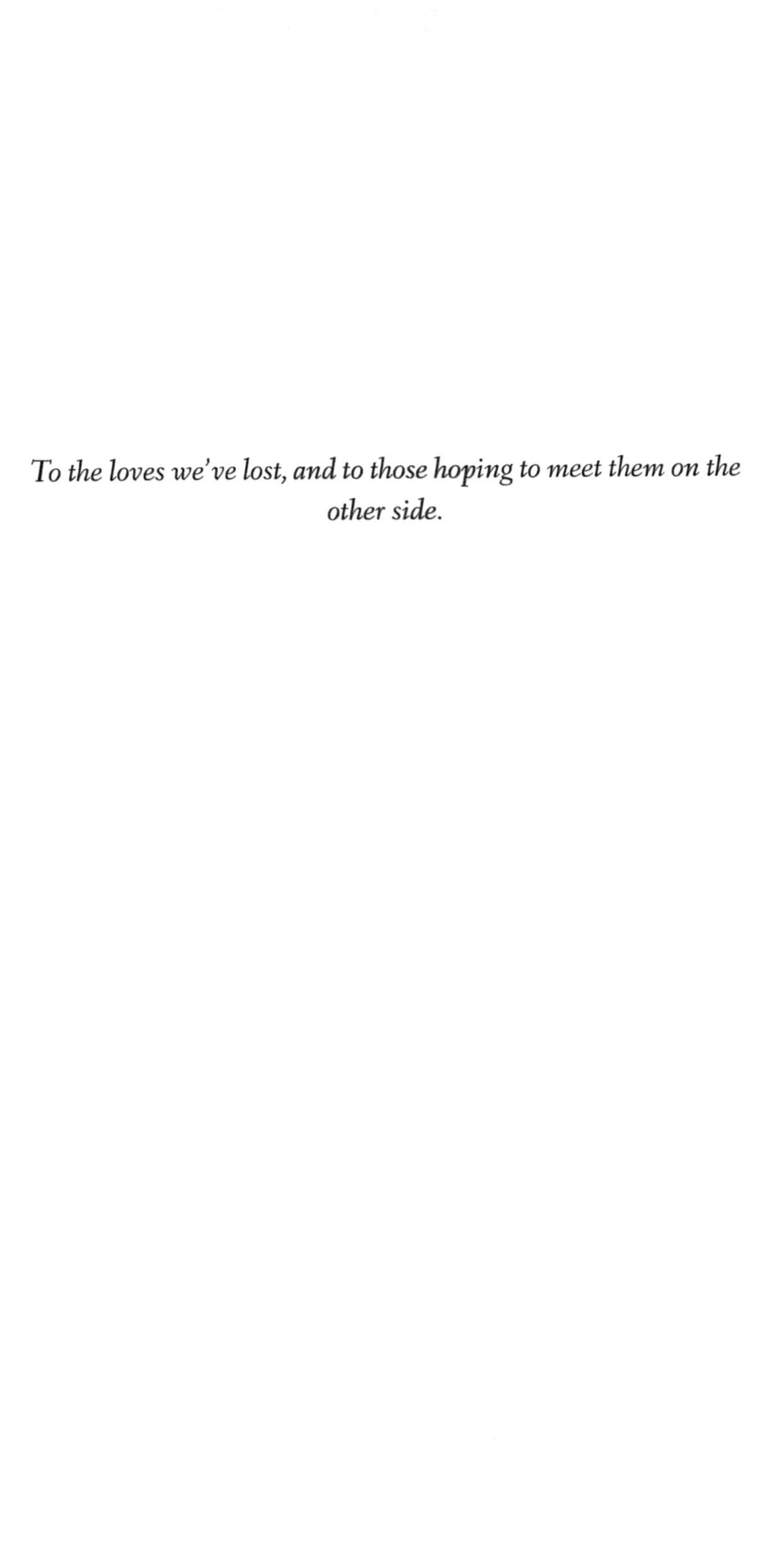

To the loves we've lost, and to those hoping to meet them on the other side.

Content Warning

If you don't have any concerns regarding content and how it may affect you, **feel free to skip ahead to avoid spoilers**!

This book contains: strong language, open-door sex scenes, cancer, death of a parent, caregiving, internalized fatphobia the FMC is working through, miscarriages (only mentioned re: FMC's past), anxiety, depression, financial stress, bugs: termites and one spider, illness: flu (FMC recovers quickly), child death (MMC remembers newborn son's death and young sister's death), maternal death (MMC remembers late wife's death during childbirth), illness: tuberculosis (MMC's cause of death), parental abuse (MMC briefly describes childhood), biracial lived experience (not the FMC or MMC), trans child coming out (not the FMC or MMC), which may be triggering for some. Please prioritize your mental health first.

Mapletown Forest
Caraway Manor
Mapletown Rock
Fast Glass Tavern
Mapletown Graveyard
House of Blooms Flowers
Spellbound Apothecary

COFFEE
...blebrook Inn
Local Harvest
Hot & Steamy Coffee Bar
Tome Time Bookstore
Batter Spatter Bakery
Crust Lust Pizzeria
Mapletown Post Office

Chapter 1
Natalie

If my bra accumulates another drop of boob sweat, I could probably fill a pool. The August heat is relentless, and it's not doing me any favors on this manic job hunt. My hair is sticking to my face, my thighs are chafed and raw, and my ass is in a deep state of swamp. I'd much prefer to email the local businesses from home, with the air conditioner blowing directly onto my skin, but this town is the size of a thimble, and the business owners around here don't seem even slightly tech-savvy. There are few modern-looking websites or social media pages among them.

I have no choice but to drop off my resumes by car and on foot.

Not that it'll make a difference. I've been handing my resume to every business in western Vermont since Mr. Colson taped an eviction notice to my door last week, and I've yet to get a call back, even just to tell me they're not interested. There aren't a lot of businesses who need someone with a few nursing school credits, experience as a dental office receptionist (for thirteen months), hair salon assistant (nine months), bowling alley employee (nine months), and chain restaurant server (sixteen months), apparently. You'd think my time spent scratching the surface of various industries would make me seem interesting and maybe a little mysterious, but nope. It likely makes me look like a flake.

I pull into the parking lot of my apartment building and spot Mr. Colson outside the utility shed, sanding down...something. It looks like a giant log, but smooth. I can't tell what it is, or what it'll end up being once he's done.

He puts down his tools and steps away from his workbench the moment he sees me. "How's the job search coming?" he shouts before letting out a barking cough.

Mr. Colson was a math professor at Dartmouth for over twenty years and has now taken up woodworking in his retirement. He has a wispy tuft of white hair floating wildly on his head, a matching white mustache, and is often wearing clothes that look at least one size too big. I used to find his scratchy voice and smoker's cough comforting, mostly because they belonged to a man who left casseroles on our doorstep when the chemo was wreaking havoc on Mom's system. Since the eviction notice, however, his presence fills me with anxiety.

"Same as yesterday," I reply, wiping the sweat from my forehead with the back of my hand. "No leads."

He nods. "I'm sure you'll find something."

I take a tentative step toward him. "Listen, Mr. Colson, I know I owe a lot in rent–"

"Five thousand six hundred fifty dollars," he cuts in, his tone sharp.

"Yes," I continue through gritted teeth.

Manners go a long way. That's what Mom would say right now, if she were still here.

I take a breath and offer a warm smile as I continue. "I would pay you every dime of that amount if I had it, sir. It's just...the chemo treatments and hospital stays completely wiped out the money Mom had saved, and you know we couldn't afford a full-time caretaker. There was no way I could be by her side and work a full-time job. Now that I have the time, I'm trying to find something. Anything. You know I am."

His gaze drops to the dirt as he scratches his chin. "I know, kiddo."

I bristle at the nickname. It's not the first time I've heard it, but that was then. That was *before*. Before Mom died and before he decided to evict me. What right does he have to act like nothing has changed when my entire universe is upside down?

As painful as it is to remain in the place where Mom died, it's home. It's the place we shared for the last six years. It's hard to believe it's been two weeks since she passed. Time no longer feels real, and I wonder if it ever will again. Somehow, the moment she died feels like it was a year ago, and an hour ago, simultaneously.

I moved in with her after I broke up with my ex, Kyle, and about a year before she got sick for the first time. She would go into remission twice more before the cancer came back for good. During that time, I held many jobs for short periods, and I'd inevitably have to quit once Mom needed help with transportation to her appointments, and closer monitoring during rounds of chemo. Then I'd find another job, low-paying but close by, and the cycle would repeat.

Despite the darkness her cancer journey carried, I'm glad I was able to be here, to spend this time with her. There are memories covering every inch of this apartment that I don't want to forget. "If you could just give me a little more time—"

"Tell you what," he says, clearing his throat. "If you can pay one month of overdue rent by this Friday, I'll stop the eviction process."

"That's almost two grand," I say with a scoff. I spent the last few bucks I had to buy bread, jelly, and peanut butter so I can feed myself for the week. "Without a job, how am I supposed to come up with that kind of money?"

"Look, Rita was a lovely woman, and you've both been reliable tenants—until recently, that is—but you've reached the end of my patience." He turns back toward his workbench, then stops. "Do you know how many Dartmouth students come by here asking about upcoming vacancies? The unit you're in is the biggest one. I have bills to pay, too, Natalie. You're not the only one with problems."

He's right. I wish I could whip out some Saul Goodman-esque charm and legalese to intimidate Mr. Colson into letting me stay, but I'm drawing a blank. I'm also not the type that could intimidate anyone, since I have the bravado of a mouse. "Understood," I say with a meek sigh as I head toward my apartment.

Once inside, I yank off my soggy clothes and throw on a loose t-shirt before padding to the fridge and chugging the last of my orange juice.

I hear my phone buzzing in my purse, and my muscles automatically clench. Is it the credit card company reminding me that the payment I sent is less than the minimum? Is it another spam loan offer? Or is it the electric company threatening to turn off service? Most news seems to be bad news as of late.

Thankfully, it's none of those. My old college roommate, Lindsay, is in town until tomorrow and wants to get an early dinner at the brewery we used to frequent every Friday night while we were in school. We weren't smart enough to get into Dartmouth, but Riverview University is only two towns away, so my commute to dinner will be quick. I haven't seen her in years and have never needed the company more than I do right now.

There's one credit card in my wallet that's about a hundred dollars under its credit limit, and it may not be wise to use it for eating out, but my loneliness is stronger than my financial resolve, so fuck it. I'm going to spend it anyway. I'll deal with the consequences later.

I show up at Wish You Were Beer ten minutes early, but of course, Lindsay beats me. No matter how early I arrive anywhere to meet her, she's there first. It's always been like this with us, and it's infuriating.

She's sitting in our favorite booth toward the back, and when she sees me, she starts waving ecstatically with both hands. Her long, effortlessly straight black hair is pulled off her angular face in a high, tight ponytail that reaches the middle of her back.

Everything about her is polished and intentional.

Her ivory sleeveless tank top and chambray linen pants are wrinkle-free and paired perfectly with tan espadrilles. Even at five-foot-nine, Lindsay has never shied away from wearing heels. "Compared to your average woman, there are six more inches of me to love, so any man worth my time will focus on that over his own insecurities," she said a few years ago when she joined a new dating app. Her give-a-fucks went on a permanent vacation not long after she became a mom, and I envy her for that.

I notice that her eyes look brighter and her skin smoother than the last time I saw her. In place of a hug, we chest-bump our boobs together like we always have, and I slide into my seat across from her.

"What's all this?" I ask, gesturing to her face. "Did you suck the soul out of a child to get that skin, or was it Botox?"

She nods, beaming with pride. "Botox and filler and some

other bits and bobs. Girl. Best birthday present I've ever received."

"Birthday botox?" I ask. "Who got you that?"

Her brow furrows as much as it can despite the paralyzed nerves. "Me."

I laugh. "Good for you. You look like you sleep more than the dead."

She bows her head while munching on a French fry. "Thank you. Thank you."

"How's Jackson? Staying out of trouble?"

"For the most part. In fact, the older he gets, the less he seems like his dad, so really, I couldn't be happier."

I remember how terrified she was to find out she was pregnant. She and Jackson's father were off-and-on, and she had just moved into a tiny, rundown studio apartment. I thought for sure she'd get an abortion, but she chose to keep it and raise the baby on her own. Jackson's dad is involved in a limited capacity, which is most likely what Lindsay prefers. My girl loves control and doesn't suffer fools.

I take a couple of fries from the basket and moan in pleasure when the crisp saltiness hits my tongue. "Did you order already?"

"No, of course not." She looks mildly offended at the suggestion. "This is my reward for punctuality. Our reservation doesn't start for another six minutes, so these don't even count."

"Genius."

"By the way," she starts, "this meal is on me. It doesn't make up for the fact that I missed your mom's funeral, but hopefully it can serve as a small token of my shame. I'm sorry it's been so long since we last saw each other."

"No shame needed. Mom didn't want a funeral, so there was nothing to miss."

"That right?"

I sigh as I recall the conversation I had with Mom about how she wanted things to go once she passed. "She hated being the center of attention, and she knew how much I hate it too. I told her I'd honor her however she wanted, funeral included. I'd give a speech, do an interpretive dance, anything. But she said no. She told me to spread her ashes someday in a place that meant something to me, and that was it."

Lindsay chuckles. "Typical Rita. Selfless with a heart of gold."

"Yeah." I swallow down a wave of unshed tears as I watch the cars speed by on the highway. "Did you think we'd end up here?"

"Where, this place? Or, like, here in life? Because if it's the former, hell yeah. Their shoestring fries aren't too salty, or too crispy, and they have that squishy soft middle without being undercooked. Do you know how difficult it is to nail that balance? Few restaurants can."

I *didn't* know that. I also don't care. Fries are like pizza to me. You put any variety of them in front of me, and I will devour them with gusto. "The latter."

She considers this while studying the pale pink tips of her polished nails. "A forty-one-year-old single mom living in Boston, with saggy titties and legs covered in spider veins, sharing custody with a dumbass who used to shout, 'That's how Billy do!' whenever he blew his load? No. This is not where I thought I'd end up."

A smirk tugs at my lips. She's being self-deprecating, when really, she should be proud as hell. She's been successful in her career as far as I know, and at least she has a kid.

I got close to that. Once. The kid, the husband, the happy ending. I almost had it.

Before I can dwell on the memories, she adds, "Who gives a shit? I had goals when we were in college for how I wanted my life to turn out, but nothing happened the way I thought it would. There's no blueprint for where you're supposed to be because life isn't a straight line. It's a bunch of loops and dips and a few messy, tight knots that seem like they'll suffocate you before you can smooth them out."

She's right. When I see friends from school on social media, a lot of them are hitting milestones in the "correct" order: the job, the wedding, the family, the house, yada, yada, but I'm also seeing divorces, custody battles, moving back in with Mom and Dad, fresh starts, career changes, and the like. Just because you get the white picket fence doesn't mean you'll get to keep it.

"What are you doing here, anyway? Did you quit that fancy corporate job in Boston?"

"Nah, I took the week off. My grandmother died," she says with a sigh.

"Oh, I'm so sorry."

She waves a dismissive hand. "Don't be. Nonna Penny was ninety-seven years old. She went in her sleep. Couldn't ask for a better ending."

Indeed. I hope that's how I go out.

"My dad and I were worried a few months ago because it seemed like her mind was starting to go. We went to visit her, and she kept having these conversations with herself. It was odd. We even scheduled an appointment with the doctor, but she passed before we could get her in."

"Huh. That is strange."

"She left me her house in Mapletown. Have you been up there? The town square has a boulder and gazebo surrounded by a couple shops and dense forest. The town itself is fucking tiny, and the house is..." Lindsay pauses, "a big place, more like a mansion, really, but everything inside is hideous and partially broken." She puts her elbows on the table and drops her head in her hands. "I have no idea what I'm going to do with it."

"What do you mean? Sell it. A big house in the middle of the mountains in northern New Hampshire? Even in rough condition, I'm sure there's a leaf peeper or vacation rental host who'd see its potential and pay way too much for it."

"Yeah, but I'd have to get her stuff out of there and have repairs done before a realtor can start showing it, and how am I supposed to manage that when I work close to sixty hours a week in Boston? That'd be a two- maybe three-hour commute each way."

"There's no way you could work remotely? Even for a short time?"

She shakes her head. "They'd let me if I wanted to, but I have so many clients in the city that I'd still have to see, so it wouldn't make sense. Plus, Jackson's in school, and it's not like I can rely on Billy to help out."

The server comes and takes our order: two chocolate milkshakes, two waters, a Reuben for me, a buffalo chicken sandwich for her, and another large order of fries for us to split. Even twenty years later, our order is the same.

"Where are you living now?" she asks. "The same place you shared with Rita?"

I shift uncomfortably in my seat. "Um, yeah, but not for much longer." The last thing I want to do is dump my financial woes on Lindsay. Yet, the words come out anyway. "I'm getting evicted."

Lindsay gasps. "The fuck? Why? You were a neat freak even in college. What possible reason could someone have to throw you out?"

"It's my fault. I haven't been able to make rent the last few months. The landlord, Mr. Colson, has been kind enough to let it slide until now."

Ugh, now I'm defending the man.

"What a fuc–" Lindsay says, then stops. A few seconds

pass, then several more. Her mouth goes from an O shape to a wide, triumphant grin. "Oh my god. I've got it, Nat. Are you ready? I'm not sure you're ready. Do you want to go to the bathroom first? Because you are absolutely going to piss yourself when I tell you what I'm thinking."

She's not nearly as crafty as she thinks she is. I wait for her to reveal her epiphany—knowing exactly what she's about to suggest—but she continues to stare at me, as if she wants me to guess. "I'm ready," I say, playing along. "What is it?"

"Okay. I have a house I don't know what to do with, and you're in need of a place to live."

It's not a terrible idea. I am desperate for a place to live. There are some snags in this plan, though. "How much would you charge me to stay there? When would I need to be out by?"

"Pfft, you don't have to pay anything. I'm not going to charge you to stay in an old-ass house with an abundance of dusty knick-knacks and broken appliances. I'm sure there are a million more desirable places for you to go, but if you're in a pinch, take it. You can stay as long as you want. It'll make me feel better knowing the place isn't just sitting there, slowly rotting."

My throat suddenly feels dry. Excitement courses through me at the prospect of not being homeless. I take a gulp of the milkshake the server just dropped off as I try to steady my thumping heart. "So, you'd be my landlord? Are you sure that's a good idea?" It feels like a terrible idea.

She reaches across the table and grabs my hand. "I'm your friend, and you'd be house-sitting until I have the mental capacity to decide what I want to do with it."

I can't hide my smile any longer.

Lindsay notices and mirrors my glee. "You in?"

Nodding, I reply, "Yeah, okay. I'm in."

Chapter 2
Winston

It's the last day of August when the Irritating One with the long legs returns, and this time, she isn't alone. My jaw tics as I watch the two women chatter excitedly as they enter my home, tracking dirt and god knows what else over Penelope's rug. She would have a fit if she were still alive to see this.

I hate looking at the fringed corners of that rug, with its heinous gray and brown paisley design. Always have. Now that she's gone, though, I feel the rug needs a defender. Her family has already gone through her personal belongings, only taking a select few framed photos and pieces of jewelry before deeming the rest of her things too old or ugly to keep. Hearing them insult her most cherished items twisted my gut. I'm grateful she wasn't around to hear it for herself.

"There are fans in every room, and don't worry, I had an air conditioner installed in your bedroom," the Irritating One says to her friend as she tosses her leather handbag at the couch.

Don't bother hanging it on one of the many available coat

hooks, I want to say. *This is clearly a barnyard. Piss all over the floor while you're at it.*

"Nonna Penny's room is on the left at the top of the stairs," she says. "Yours is across the hall. There's an en suite in both bedrooms, and a half bath next to the kitchen. There's a study next to Nonna's room with a bunch of old books. The other two bedrooms on the third floor are filled with all the crap she never got rid of."

Lindsay. Yes, that's her name. She's one of Penelope's grandchildren. She's been here many times, but I'd usually abscond to the attic whenever Penelope was having family over, so I never paid attention to who was who. I don't understand why my late friend left the home I built with my bare hands to the grandchild who hates it the most. It seems so wasteful.

The first day Lindsay arrived, she walked around with her hands on her hips and her face in a constant sneer as she surveyed the space. I heard, "Ugh," uttered many times. She also had the nerve to lay a towel down across the couch cushions before sitting, as if it were a piece of furniture she found on the side of the road, covered in the bodily fluids of woodland creatures. Perhaps I shouldn't have taken it personally, but I did, and still do.

"The heat works," Lindsay continues to her friend, "for when the temperatures start to drop."

"Wow," the friend says, dropping her many bags at her feet as they enter the living room. "Linds, you really undersold this place." She runs her fingers along the wooden archway that separates this room from the hall. Her wonder is abundant. There's even a smile tugging at the corners of her pink lips. "With a little tidying, this place could be gorgeous. Like a goth girl's wet dream. And that placard next to the doorbell that says 'Caraway Manor?' How cool is that?"

This newcomer...I don't want her here, but she's decidedly less irritating than Lindsay. Thus far, at least. I'm sure I'll find other reasons to loathe her presence soon enough.

"Oh, yeah. The original owners put that up. It's been there forever." Lindsay quickly changes the subject as she looks down at her phone. "I can't seem to get the stove or the dishwasher to work, so I bought a microwave and a dish rack until we can get new ones installed." She rubs her hand across her forehead in frustration.

I don't believe for a second that both appliances are broken. They're older models, purchased by Penelope decades ago, but my late friend and I were able to use them. When you want to use the stove, you have to wait a few minutes before you see a flicker of flame, and sure, it also makes a strange buzzing sound when it's on, but it works. The dishwasher needs to be turned off and then back on before you hear the water start to run. These quirks give the machines character, but clearly Her Royal Highness doesn't see it that way.

I reckon Lindsay is used to modern conveniences. If it doesn't work perfectly and immediately with the press of a few sleek-looking buttons, she deems it irreparable. What a sad lens through which to see the world. I'm tempted to say this aloud, but since she doesn't know I live here, it's better if I remain quiet. My goal is not to terrify these women, and if I let them see me, they'd likely start screaming.

"Oh, that's fine," the friend says in a soft voice. "I've been eating instant ramen and cereal, so my needs in the kitchen are very minimal."

She tucks a loose blonde curl behind her ear, and for some reason...I'm mesmerized by the movement. So subtle, so insignificant—yet it plays over in my head. Is her hair as soft as it looks? My fingers twitch at my side, eager to feel it for myself.

But why? I flinch in irritation at my body's reaction to her. I don't know this woman, this stranger, who's currently making herself comfortable in *my* house. In fact, the more I look at her, the less interested I become in learning anything about her. The clothes she wears are strange and impractical. A sleeveless bright red dress that hugs her chest and hips with a heart-shaped hole just above her bosom? Did she cut the hole herself? For what purpose? The hem brushes the tops of her knees, flowing out around her like an angry cloud, and it's sure to get caught on the many rough edges this house contains. And she wears strappy sandals with a sole no thicker than a slice of cheese. What kind of lunatic would wear these in the middle of a forest?

Lindsay pads over to the refrigerator and purses her lips as she surveys its contents. "There's still a ton of stuff here from my last trip to the grocery store. It's yours if you want it. Just keep an eye on that metal bowl on the top shelf. It fills with water. There's a leak somewhere. Make sure to empty it every few days." She straightens to her full height and opens the freezer. "Don't put too much up here. If it's full, not everything will freeze."

"No problem."

Lindsay flings the freezer door shut. The pots stacked atop the refrigerator shake from the force. "This thing is clearly on its last leg, too. I'm pretty sure it was here before I was born."

The refrigerator is about to die. She's correct about that. There's no saving it. I've tried.

The friend notices a piece of paper sitting on the kitchen island and grabs it. "What's this?"

"Directions to the grocery store. There's a coffee shop right next to it, and a bookstore. There's also a nail salon on the edge of town, but they don't work with acrylics, so beware."

"Oh, I haven't gotten my nails done in ages."

Lindsay looks horrified.

"Are you serious? Honey, I didn't know things were *that* bad." She grabs her friend's hands and examines the unpainted tips of her fingers. "Why didn't you come to me? I could've helped you out."

The friend carefully pulls her hands from Lindsay's grasp. "It's fine, really. I'm not interested in borrowing money. Not now, not ever. You're giving me a place to live. That's all I need."

This seems to calm Lindsay down. Her eyes dart over to the cabinets. "Take-out menus are in the top right drawer next to the silverware, but there are only, like, two restaurants in town and the food is mediocre at best, so don't get your hopes up."

A chuckle escapes the friend's plump lips.

Stop staring at her lips.

"I'm guessing your Bostonian palate is much more sophisticated than mine," the friend says. "Whatever the locals in Mapletown are serving up, I'm sure I'll love it."

After Lindsay shows her friend the second and third floors, and provides a quick tutorial on how the shower works, she tosses a few clothing items in a flashy duffel bag and tells the friend to call her if she has any problems. Then I hear her car speed out of the drive.

What now? This foolishly dressed woman is my new roommate?

I've had several since my death in 1901, and Penelope is the only one whose company I enjoyed. Most have been families. They move into my home, make it their own, and at some point, they leave. Penelope bought the house with her husband, Victor, in 1998, and within three months, Victor was dead. Heart attack in the driveway. She was devastated. I was certain she would leave soon after, since her children were grown—and having children of their own—and she was just one person in a house built for a large family. She didn't.

I made myself known the day after Victor's funeral. Up until that point, I floated around undetected, watching and listening, but mostly keeping to myself in the attic. The hidden room in the back of the attic is where my personal effects are stored. None of the residents of the home have ever discovered my secret room. None until Penelope, anyway, but that's only because I intentionally led her there on a snowy afternoon when she seemed particularly despondent after Victor's death.

She was never afraid of me, not even at first sight. I told her I was the person who built the house, the original owner, and she accepted my spectral presence without complaint. We became friends. She seemed grateful to no longer be alone, and I was grateful to finally have someone to talk to.

Penelope was a gift to this world. I had hoped her spirit would return after her death, just as mine did, but that hasn't happened. With each day that passes, I lose hope that it will.

Now the house belongs to Lindsay, and I have a feeling I'll be very displeased with whatever she plans to do with it. The odds are good that she'll knock it down and sell off the land.

What will become of me then? I've always assumed my spirit was tethered to the house, but if it's demolished, will I vaporize into thin air? Will my soul leave this realm and move onto...whatever comes next?

Until that happens, though, it seems I must share the place with this other woman. This friend of Lindsay's, with her baffling wardrobe and dark, thick eyebrows that seem far too severe for her small square-shaped face and yellow hair. If I were to make myself known to her, would she throw things at me? Call the police? I can't have the townspeople thinking the house is haunted. That would attract the wrong kind of attention, from people who wish to taunt me, exploit my past, or worst of all, camp out in my home in an attempt to catch me on camera for some silly ghost show.

I watch as my new roommate carries her bags upstairs to the second floor and begins unpacking her belongings in the bedroom Lindsay assigned her. She spends most of the evening dusting the shelves and organizing her personal items. At one point, her handbag falls off the dresser, and several cards scatter onto the floor. She groans as she kneels to pick them up, and I take the opportunity to hunt for a name. Though her small hands are quick as she gathers them into a neat stack, I spot a library card next to the dresser that she hasn't noticed yet. "Natalie Lambert," it says.

Her name is Natalie.

I'm eager to say it aloud. Turn the name over on my tongue to see what it feels like. See how it tastes. It's likely she would hear me, however, and I can't have that.

Eventually, she lets out a deep exhale and flops onto the bed. After a moment of staring at the ceiling, she turns onto her side and gazes at the navy-blue vase she placed on her night-stand not twenty minutes prior, then at the framed photograph next to it. In the photo, a much younger Natalie sits on the beach, sand covering her arms and legs, even her left cheek. Her wide smile exposes a few missing teeth, and her hand gently rests on the side of a sand sculpture she made. The sculpture is messy and concave, but you'd never know it by the pride emanating from her expression. A woman sits next to Natalie, wearing an equally proud grin. I assume this woman is her mother.

Natalie's eyes fill with tears, and she curls in on herself as she begins to weep. Her cries take on the erratic timbre of someone with a broken heart, and I would bet my hat that this loss is recent.

It's difficult to watch her in this state, though I'm not sure why. A moment of privacy is what she needs, but I can't seem to make myself leave the room. What do I care that she's grieving? I've certainly done my fair share of it. Loss is universal. No one is immune.

Perhaps this is her first experience with death. If that's the case, she should count herself lucky. Some of us have been grieving our loved ones since before we hit puberty. When that happens, the sky is never as bright as it once was. You learn that pain is inevitable, and those deep cuts will keep coming until it's your heart that stops beating.

When I finally float upstairs to the attic, I can still hear Natalie's faint cries, but they've softened. She'll be asleep soon.

It's then that I realize what a colossal problem I have on my hands. Living with Penelope was as easy as breathing. It was simple, devoid of complications. She stuck to her part of the house, I stuck to mine, and when we wanted company, we'd meet in the living room to play cards or watch the news. There was no pressure to be anything other than what we were: an elderly woman who wanted to gossip about her friends from Bingo club, and a thirty-seven-year-old man whose lonely spirit is trapped on the grounds of which he perished.

Natalie...she confuses me. She is mostly vexatious, much like Lindsay but in a different sense. She seems too sweet, in a way that can't be real. Something about her draws me in, though, and I don't know why. It's not as if she's some great beauty. Her features are rather plain. With dark circles beneath her eyes and hollows in her cheeks, it's clear she hasn't been taking care of herself, but even if she had been, would I find her attractive?

Yes.

Shit.

Yes, I would. Without a doubt. She's the opposite of plain. I can't take my eyes off her enchanting smile, her ample curves, or those sultry pink lips. Who am I kidding? She's easily the most captivating woman I've ever seen.

A house with five bedrooms, three floors, and two acres of land, and for the first time in over a hundred years, it feels cramped in here.

Chapter 3
Natalie

A breathtaking dark Victorian mansion all to myself, and I can't seem to enjoy it. The realization is embarrassing. The first few days here were okay. I kept myself busy by dusting the many surfaces, taking notes for Lindsay on the appliances that truly are broken, and the areas in need of repair, but then I ran out of things to do, and more so, the energy to do them.

Are there tasks I could be accomplishing? Of course.

I could look for a job in town or apply for remote work. I could go for a daily walk around the property. You know, enjoy the sunshine and get my heart rate up or whatever it is emotionally stable people do. I could take stock of the cleaning supplies, roll up my sleeves, and really get to work on making this place sparkle. Lindsay didn't ask me to do it, but I certainly could, especially as a way to pay her back for letting me live here.

I could also pull myself out of bed, shower, maybe shave my legs for the first time in weeks, and yet, here I lay, unable to perform the most basic daily functions. My hair feels greasy, and I know I stink, but I'm the only one here, so I allow the rot to continue. When my limbs get stiff, which usually happens around three in the morning, I get up and wander the creaky halls in my nightgown like the ghost of a sad pilgrim. That's been my only source of joy this week, and even that isn't enough for my lips to crack a smile.

It's like I'm too tired to smile. Too tired to do anything. I'm sleeping a lot, but only for half an hour at a time before I wake up and the memories of Mom hit me. It's not consistent, restorative sleep.

When I'm awake, I can't focus on anything. I'll remember I should do something, which gets me out of bed, but when I enter the room my feet took me to, I forget the reason I'm there.

Food has been an afterthought. I've been munching on a few of Lindsay's gourmet crackers at a time until my stomach stops growling. There are crumbs strewn about between the bedsheets and on the floor. It's not ideal.

I felt like I had a purpose, taking care of Mom for the last five years. Now that I'm not her caregiver, what am I? *Who am I?*

Is grief to blame for all of this? Is it perimenopause? Or am I losing my mind?

I know I just need to create a routine, stick to it, and eventually time will dull the pain. Fake it till you make it. It sounds so simple, but the thought of setting my alarm for a certain time tomorrow morning and hauling myself out of bed is enough to make me burrow deeper beneath the musty quilt that covers my legs and pinch my eyes closed.

Then I feel guilty, because I'm being lazy when I could be productive, and if I had even one box to check at the end of the day, wouldn't that make me feel better? Even a tiny, little sprinkle-of-cinnamon-sized feeling of accomplishment would make me less depressed, wouldn't it? Plus, Mom would've given anything to have more time on Earth, and here I am wasting mine. She wouldn't want that for me.

I grab my phone and head into the bathroom, pressing play on the last voicemail she left me. It was a week before she died. I was at the grocery store when she called. Her oncologist told her to eat like a teenage boy, packing as much fat and calories into each meal as possible, as long as she could keep it down. It sounded great at first. Ice cream for breakfast, fried food for lunch, and whatever the hell else she wanted for dinner and dessert. I was jealous as fuck. But each new food she tried was a gamble, and once it made her sick, she didn't even want to see it in the fridge. This meant I was going to the grocery store almost daily, trying to find anything that would taste good to her and wouldn't upset her stomach.

"Hi, honey," the voicemail begins. "Can you get some of that pineapple orange juice?" I can hear the exhaustion in her voice, and it breaks my heart all over again. "Maybe some sorbet? I'm craving fruit." She'd eat half of the sorbet before it made her sick. It was a good twenty-four hours, though. She was happy. Comfortable.

"Grab some russet potatoes, too. I can make you those hash browns you like." The potatoes never made it into my cart that day. I knew she was too sick to cook for me, and yet, she still offered. Two days before she died, when she was bedridden and sleeping constantly but still able to speak, she asked me if I was thirsty and offered to get me a glass of water from the kitchen. My needs were always more important to her than her own, even at the end. "Thanks, honey. Love you."

I read somewhere that when a person dies, their voice fades from your memories before anything else. Listening to her voicemails over and over again feels masochistic, but I can't let that part of her go. I refuse.

Eventually, I climb into the shower and let the hot stream

of water wash away my tears. It feels good to massage my scalp with shampoo, getting my hair all sudsy and smelling like fruit. I throw on a pale yellow short-sleeved midi dress made of cotton with a fitted but comfortable bodice and lace trim. It's my go-to outfit for when I want to look more put together than I actually am. Then I dry my hair and braid it into a loose side pony, pulling out a few pieces to frame my face as I summon the courage to do what I'm about to do.

It's a bad idea, texting Mark. I know it is. But I'm lonely and horny, and my last orgasm with a partner occurred over two months ago. While Mark isn't the best at making me come, he's a good distraction, a body that I can rub myself against for twenty minutes or so to get myself out of my head.

He's not the type of guy I'd ever be in a relationship with. Truth be told, I can barely hold a conversation with him, but he's always unattached and game to hook up. There's no pressure to put in a lot of effort, either. I don't have to bathe or shave or put on makeup. However, it felt rude to go to Bonetown with my previous level of unwashed stank, so I showered to be polite. As long as we keep the chitchat to a minimum, I can release some pent-up tension by riding his dick for a bit and then have him out of here by nine o'clock.

We text back and forth a bit as we make plans. He offers to pick up a pizza and drinks on the way, and I give him directions to the house. His current shift as a rideshare driver is ending, and he's only forty minutes away.

He shows up with a pizza in one hand and a two-liter bottle of soda in the other.

"Hi, Mark. Oh, you brought Pepsi," I say through a forced smile. It's fine. When he said he'd bring "drinks," I assumed it would be wine. That was my mistake, I guess. He's not the type to show up with wine, and it's not as if this is a date. It's not because he's sober, either. That, I'd be more than fine with. It's because he's cheap, and I matter to him as much as he matters to me.

"Yeah, it was only a dollar more with the pizza," he explains with pride as he shoves both into my hands. He takes one look around the foyer and tries to hide a judgmental expression. "New place? Or, I guess, not new."

I bring the pizza into the kitchen, and he follows me. "Um, yeah. It's just temporary."

Mark gets the glasses and pours the Pepsi, and I plate our slices before we carry them into the living room. The TV is on, and Judge Judy is yelling at someone for not getting a signed contract for something. It's the only channel that never cuts out, and it's a nonstop loop of court shows.

"Are you still on probation?" I ask without thinking. The defendant on TV starts talking about getting into a fistfight, and it reminded me that Mark got arrested for brawling at a bar last year.

He nods while chewing. "For another six months. My lawyer thinks he can get it cut down by three for good behavior."

I bite into a slice, and the cheese is so gooey and perfect that I have to tear the long string of it in two. "As long as nobody insults Tom Brady in your presence, right?"

Mark scoffs as he reaches for his drink. "I don't know who the fuck you think you are to come into Brady territory and openly talk shit about him."

I don't pay attention to football, but I'm pretty sure Brady left the team, and left the state, before retiring. Mark still seems to worship him, though.

"Right," I reply, realizing I don't know what else to say to him. It's then that I notice the dirt caked beneath his fingernails. He didn't wash his hands when he came in, did he? The stench of menthol cigarettes and sour sweat is wafting off his clothes. I suppress a shudder and shake the thoughts away before I abandon my plan to get laid.

He clears his throat. "By the way, the pizza was thirty-five bucks. Well," he pauses, "thirty-six with the Pepsi, and gas to get here was forty. Venmo me? Before I leave, preferably. Cash works too."

My mouth flops open. Am I really paying for this entire evening? I could see splitting it, but Mark also knows I'm not working right now, so I wasn't expecting him to ask me for any money at all. The only money I currently have, I made from selling pieces of furniture and decor from the apartment I shared with Mom on Facebook Marketplace. It's not much, but it should cover my groceries for the next few weeks, at least. Maybe only two weeks, after I pay Mark.

"How's your mom, by the way?" he asks. "Haven't seen her in a while. She good?"

On second thought, maybe he doesn't know I'm unemployed, because he clearly doesn't listen to anything I say. He knew Mom was sick, and I'm certain I told him about her passing when he sent a late-night "You up?" text the night after she died. Not that he cares. That much is obvious.

"She's great," I reply, my tone stiff as I shove my disappointment down deep into my belly.

Suddenly, a crunchy rattling sound from outside raises over the volume of the TV, and Mark is on his feet and charging toward the front door in a flash.

"What the fuck!" I hear him shout. Following on his heels, I watch as he chases his car down the sloped, gravel-covered driveway. He launches himself through the open window on the driver's side, and his legs flail about as the car continues to roll.

"Shit," I mutter, not knowing what to do to help. Part of me, I'm ashamed to admit, wants to pull out my phone and record the whole thing. Mark looks ridiculous with his feet jutting out the window, one untied steel-toed boot about to fall off as he lets out loud, panicky grunts. I have to grit my teeth to keep from laughing.

Before the car reaches the steeper part of the drive, nearing the end, he manages to get the car in park. Panting, he wriggles out the window and gets behind the wheel before driving it back up and ensuring the parking brake is in place.

He's cursing through heavy breaths as he climbs out. "That's never happened before. I could've sworn I set the parking brake when I got here."

"Well, at least you stopped it before it rolled into the road and hit somebody."

"Or into a fucking tree," he snaps. "If that car is totaled, I can't drive. If I can't drive, I can't pay my dealer the four hundred dollars I owe him this weekend. I need every driving shift I can get, Natalie."

"Right. Sorry."

I could point out that his tone is a bit too sharp for someone who's four hundred in the hole over what I assume is cocaine—his drug of choice—especially since his car didn't even get a scratch on it, but what would be the point? I don't need him to get more fired up. What I need is for him to chill out and stop talking so I can fuck him.

More pizza is eaten as another episode of *Judge Judy* plays in the background. I feel full after only two slices, probably because of how little I've eaten lately.

Mark empties his glass of Pepsi, and a loud burp rips from his throat.

I hear a loud crash in the hall and find a photo of Nonna Penny's wedding day face down on the floor.

That's odd.

Upon examination, the string on the back of the frame

seems taut and strong, and the screw in the wall is still in place. Luckily, the glass isn't damaged at all. I shrug it off and put the photo back where it was.

My fuckbuddy asks where the bathroom is, and I point him in that direction.

Please wash your hands, I silently pray.

When he returns, I discreetly try to check the dirt under his nails, but can't get a good enough look before he climbs on top of me and grabs hold of my hips. He gives me a wolfish grin, saying, "You look hot tonight," before bending down to kiss me.

My nose crinkles as he shoves his tongue in my mouth. I forgot how sloppy his kisses are. It's not out of eagerness, either, I don't think. The way his tongue traces the roof of my mouth and pokes the inside of my cheek makes me think this is probably how his first kiss went, and he never bothered to try another technique or seek feedback.

Though, I can't complain too much. He more than makes up for it when he goes down on me.

I tilt my head to the side and guide his mouth to my neck, so at least his wagging tongue will feel better on the sensitive skin beneath my ear. He takes my cue, and I let my palms roam over his thick arms and down his chest. Mark's a big guy, and his dark brown eyes are kind. It could be worse. He could think the earth is flat, or not believe dinosaurs existed.

His calloused fingers glide along my calf, bringing the hem of my dress with it.

My underwear is high-waisted, nude-colored, and extremely comfortable, but if Mark notices the lack of sexiness, he doesn't mention it. I feel him trace along my slit through the fabric as his hot breath fans my ear. "I've missed this tight little pussy," he groans.

A gasp escapes me as he pushes the fabric aside and enters

me with a single thick digit. He strokes my inner walls once, then freezes.

"What the hell was that?" Mark grumbles, looking over his shoulder.

"What?" I ask, dazed from his touch.

"That book just fell off the shelf," he says, panting. "Didn't you hear it?"

I'm too focused on getting off to care, so I place my hands on the sides of his face and guide his attention back to me. "It's an old house. Don't worry about it." Then I nip at his bottom lip to make him forget about it.

It works, and his mouth travels down to my chest. He sucks my nipple through my dress, and I arch into him. The smell of cigarettes no longer fills my nose. I'm not sure why. Now his scent has a pleasant, natural smokiness to it. Woodsy, even. Like a bonfire.

Mark's dark eyes meet mine, and out of the corner of my eye, I notice a large mass of orange that wasn't there before.

"Holy shit!" I shout, pushing Mark off me. One of the taper candles I lit to set the mood is on its side, and flames are spreading across the rug. I grab a glass of water from the side table and toss the contents onto the flames. Mark adds his Pepsi to the fire, and it fizzles out moments later, leaving minimal damage to the floor in its wake. The rug is ruined, but I doubt Lindsay will care. "That was almost a nightmare."

"Almost?" Mark replies, his eyes wild and filled with horror. He looks up at the ceiling and scans the walls. "This house is fucked. I don't like the vibes."

In an effort to calm him down, I go over to the two other candles I lit and blow them out. "Oh, come on, Mark. I shouldn't have lit those old candles. We're all good now." The car, the frame, the book, and the candle—yes, those are strange when you connect the dots, but they can be easily explained by either Mark's forgetfulness (the car), or that this house is old and sometimes the wood creaks enough to knock things over.

More importantly, I'm too worked up to care. I wrap my arms around Mark's neck and get up on my toes to kiss him. His hands settle on my ass, and he gives my right cheek a soft squeeze. I'm leading him back to the couch when the front door opens with a pitiful groan, then slams shut.

Mark jerks away from me. "Nope. I'm out."

I sigh as I watch him race out of the house, jump into his car, and speed down the driveway.

After locking the front door, I replay the last fifteen minutes in my head. Did he remember to shut the door after he put the parking brake in place? If he didn't, then a stiff breeze could explain the slam.

I don't know if he shut it or not. He was behind me when we came back inside.

I tidy up the living room, returning the fallen book to its place on the shelf, and grabbing our plates and glasses. I make a mental note to toss the burned rug in the garbage tomorrow, and once I'm done washing the dishes, I turn off the lights and head toward the steps.

Might as well pass out from the heady bliss only my vibrator can provide.

The ends of my hair lift as a breeze whips through the hall. My gut tightens, and I freeze in place. The downstairs windows are closed, as is the front door. I'm sure of it. Where would that breeze be coming from?

Nowhere good.

Goosebumps race over my skin as the air around me drops several degrees, holding me in a tight cocoon. Terror steals the breath from my lungs. I no longer feel alone in this house, and those little oddities that drove Mark out of here now seem like clear signs I should've gone with him.

Then a deep, gravelly voice that sounds like it's coming from everywhere says, "Don't ever invite him into my house again."

I choke out a scream. There's no time to wonder if I'm having an auditory hallucination. All I know is something is *very wrong* here, and I need to get the fuck out. I don't grab my purse or put on my shoes. I throw the front door open and race into the night.

Chapter 4
Winston

I couldn't take it anymore. That man, that *animal,* belching in Natalie's presence. Demanding money for the meal he brought her. Asking how her mother was. Did he really not know she died? He spoke to Natalie as if she were a child, and not only did she allow this behavior to continue, but she also actively sought his touch afterward. It's been a very long time since my days as a bachelor, but this is not how a gentleman behaves when he's trying to court a lady.

Have sexual relations changed that much in the last two centuries? Is this the way men act now? So arrogant in their ability to attract a woman that they abandon even the most basic manners and standards for personal hygiene? I'm appalled at that possibility.

Perhaps Mark is the exception, and society has not fallen so far from where it once was. Regardless, I know scaring him out of here was the right decision. It was obvious Natalie wasn't going to, and as frustrated as I've been with her messiness and melancholy, Mark was a thousand times worse.

Since the moment she arrived, I've watched her. Studied

her. Her needs are so simple, and it takes a second, maybe two, of looking into her sparkling brown eyes to know what they are. How could Mark be so oblivious? That revolting prick.

I didn't mean to frighten Natalie, though. Mark pushed me to the edge, and when I spoke to her, it was using a tone that should've been reserved for him. Now, my new roommate is running across the gravel driveway without anything on her feet.

I sigh as I follow her, knowing this is a disaster I created, and it will get worse before it gets better.

"Where do you think you're going?" I ask, allowing my mist-like form to come into view.

She spins on her heels to face me, stubbing her toe on a large rock and falling flat on her ass as she lets out a stream of curses.

"An aptly timed reminder that you're barefoot and won't get far."

"What in the——" she begins, then sees me, and starts crawling backward with fear tightening her features. "Oh my god. Wha——Who are you? What do you want from me?"

Her chest heaves, and she pauses, pressing the palms of her hands against her eyes.

"There's nothing there," she says quietly to herself. "This is grief. Just grief. It's consuming you, and now you're hallu-cinating."

"Not hallucinating," I point out, floating closer until I'm about a foot away. "My name is Winston."

"No, it isn't! Because you're not real!"

"I'm quite real, Natalie. Dead, but real."

She's whispering to herself now as she drops her hands in her lap, eyes still pinched closed. "Go in, get your shoes, your purse, and your keys, and get out of here."

"And go where? Will you chase after that Mark fellow? See

if you can stay with him for the night?" I ask, seething in disgust at the idea. "He might allow it, but I reckon he'd also ask you to pay a nightly rate for shelter, wouldn't he?"

I didn't notice the distance closing between us while it was happening, but now I'm hovering above her, so close that I could take my corporeal form and wipe the tear streaming down her cheek if I wanted to.

When she opens her eyes, they're glaring at me. Vitriol has her jaw clenching as she takes me in, not flinching or questioning my form.

"What the fuck do you know? You spy on him for an hour, and you think you know him? Or me?"

"I've watched you for many hours. Since the day you arrived and unpacked your things in *my* house."

"Actually, it's Lindsay's house. Does she know? Is she aware there's a pervy ghost floating through her halls?"

I scoff. "Please. I have no interest in peeping on you during private moments. I'm a gentleman and would never cross such a line. When you engage in sexual acts in the living room, however, and let the carpet catch fire, it's hard to ignore."

She throws her head back and lets out a mocking cackle as she gets to her feet. "Oh, like you had nothing to do with that candle falling over."

Why should I admit the role I played in getting Mark to leave? I don't owe this woman anything. In fact, she should be thanking me for helping her avoid a decision she was sure to regret in the light of day. Yet, here she stands, with her hands on her wide hips, scolding me like you would a child sneaking a slice of cake before dinner.

Then again, threatening to make Lindsay aware of the situation has me nervous. I decide to ignore the mention of Lindsay and try a softer approach, hoping she forgets she brought it up in the first place. "I was surprised you'd allow someone like *him* anywhere near you, and despite the execution, I swear that my intentions were good. I thought I was doing you a favor by getting him out of here. Clearly, I was wrong to get involved."

"Yes, you were," she shouts. "It's none of your business who I allow near me."

I hold up my hands. "You're right."

"Well," she begins with a huff, "thank you for apologizing."

"I didn't apologize," I correct her. The mere suggestion of that irritates me.

"Yes, you did."

"I said I was wrong," I tell her. "That's not an apology."

She rolls her eyes. "Are you serious? It's the same thing."

"An apology implies regret. I have no regrets about what I said. Mark is a loser. If your mother were still here, I doubt she'd approve of him." It's not what I meant to say, or the tone I meant to say it in, but the words are out, and I wish I could take them back.

This is what I should be apologizing for, but Natalie doesn't let me. She grabs a rock and hurls it toward me. It goes through me, and she lets out a frustrated growl as she stomps back into the house. I don't follow.

She returns to the driveway moments later with sandals on her feet, her car keys in hand, purse slung over her shoulder, and an old bottle of rum tucked beneath her arm that she must've taken from the liquor cabinet. Then she climbs into the backseat, stretching across it and opening the bottle.

"My car's almost out of gas," she shouts at me. "But you win, asshole. The house is yours. Tomorrow, I'll be out of your hair. Just please, let me sleep out here in peace tonight."

I nod before disappearing into the sticky night air, giving her the space she desires, but it's a farce. I'm still here, she simply can't see me. Would she drink and drive? I don't think she'd be that stupid, but I can't be sure, so I remain close by, ready to intervene if needed.

Natalie shuts the back passenger door, kicks off her sandals, and leans against the back seat as she takes a long pull of the rum. Fiddling with her phone, she puts on the same music she's been playing at an absurdly high volume, at all hours of the day and night since she arrived.

Goddamn Taylor Swift.

Chapter 5
Natalie

I wake up coughing, and my entire body radiates with pain. Even with the windows open, the inside of my car is swampy and gross. I need to get out of here, but I'm too miserable to move. A wave of nausea is what ultimately gets me moving, and I vomit as soon as I open the car door. I stumble outside into the blinding sun, and the loud hum of insects in the surrounding forest rattles my skull. My braid has come mostly undone, the freed strands damp with sweat against the back of my neck.

Rum was a bad idea. A *very* bad idea. I'm not a hard liquor girl, but I doubt I would've been able to sleep without it. Although, given how sore my neck is, the sleep I did get was shit.

I hesitate at the front door, wondering if I imagined the ghost criticizing my taste in men last night, or if that was just my subconscious. "Hello?" I ask once I step inside. "Ghost man?"

Silence.

The smell of butter and maple syrup pulls me toward the

kitchen, and I find a plate on the counter, with a steel plate cover over it, a single glass of orange juice, with a cloth napkin and utensils beside it.

Clearly, there's someone here, because I didn't make this. What confuses me is who this was made for. I creep closer, trying to determine what's under the plate cover, simply by scent. Pancakes?

Mm, pancakes.

Looking around and finding no one, I lift the cover, and my stomach growls at the sight of French toast, steam rising off the pile, and drenched in syrup.

"Have some," a deep voice says from behind me, making me jump and squeak in surprise. "I made it for you, Natalie."

Ghost Man is real. He floats into the room, a fog trailing him and slightly blurring his features. He must've been tall when he was alive—over six feet, I'd say—based on the height of his misty presence. Though he doesn't touch the ground, I can't even see his feet through the fog, he moves with the kind of grace and purpose I've only seen in predatory animals on nature documentaries.

"It's rude to stare, you know." His tone is cold, but the way his lips curve on one side tells me he's teasing.

I realize my mouth is hanging open, and I'm still holding the plate cover in my hand. I must look frozen in shock, and also, in my current state, like absolute trash. "Uh, sorry," I mutter, dropping onto the stool. "Thank you for breakfast. It looks delicious."

My mouth is watering, and I want so badly to take a bite, but his kind gesture doesn't make sense, given how terrifying he was last night. He doesn't want me here, so what's the motive? "Did you poison it?"

He chuckles, the gravelly sound lighting up parts inside me

that I assumed had gone permanently dark. "You've been here for eight days. If I wanted to kill you, you'd be dead."

A sigh of relief escapes me just before I shove a forkful of French toast in my mouth. I moan as the warmth and sugar and buttery goodness makes me forget about my splitting headache, and Ghost Man's eyes darken as he watches me. "S'good," I mumble. Then, after a sip of orange juice, "What was your name again?"

The darkness fades as amused composure takes its place. "Winston," he says. "I told you last night, but I knew you weren't listening."

"Yeah, I guess I was a little distracted by you slut-shaming me in the driveway." My tone is cutting, and I have to suppress the urge to apologize. This isn't how I speak to people, especially if I find them intimidating, and I definitely find Winston intimidating. But he acted like a dick last night, and my hangover and sore neck are entirely his fault.

He rolls his eyes. "I wasn't slut-shaming you. My comments had nothing to do with you. It was more about your choice of sex partner."

I chuckle at the furrow in his brow, and the way he says 'sex partner' as if the words are laced with acid.

He tilts his head to the side as his body floats closer, his gaze narrowing as it sweeps over my face. Blood rushes to my cheeks. He's inches from me now, two, maybe three. "You're not afraid of me anymore, are you? Do you have experience communicating with the dead?"

"I'm not *not* afraid," I say, my mouth suddenly dry. "You're dead, and somehow, you're right in front of me. It's weird. Definitely weird. It freaks me out that I can see through you, but no, I've never met another ghost. Though, I figured your kind existed. I hoped so, anyway." Mom's smile pops into my head, and I wonder why I'm stuck being haunted by this rando and not her. I clear my throat, bringing my mind back to the present. "Why are you being nice to me? I thought you wanted me to leave. Is this a pity breakfast?"

Winston shakes his head. "I don't pity you. Do you think you're the only one who's lost someone they love? I watched my wife and son die within hours of each other. My father, mother, my brother, and sister—I outlived all of them. Loss is part of life. You," he pauses, sighing heavily, "you get used to it."

My stomach sinks like a stone at his words. I want to be mad at him for comparing our levels of grief, but I can't. He lost his wife and child on the same day? That kind of trauma is unfathomable.

"I'm sorry. That's awful." The words are utterly inadequate, given what he's gone through, but it's all I have to give.

Is his spirit lingering here so he can process it? I have so many questions about how long he's been dead, what killed him, and what his wife was like, but they all feel too personal.

Besides, I need to get my first question answered before we start getting to know each other. "Um, so you made me breakfast because..."

"Right," he says with a jerky nod of his head, as if trying to shove his pain into the back of his mind. I imagine that's where he's kept it buried for far too long. "I was hoping you could help me."

"Help you? With what?"

"I did some thinking last night, and while I may not approve of the men you choose to date–"

"Mark? We're not dating," I interject. "Just sex."

He floats around the kitchen as he continues. "Or the trail of crumbs you leave with your obscene cracker consumption, or the way you leave every cabinet door open without closing them, or how you play the same songs over and over..."

I hold up a hand to stop him. This is the worst possible time to hear a list of my flaws. Maybe if I weren't so hungover, I could handle a roast, but not now. Not when my tongue feels like it's wearing a turtleneck. "Is this you asking me for a favor?"

He smiles, and there's a twinkle in his eye that makes me long to know the color. The spectral fog that's attached to him steals the color from his eyes, skin, hair, and makes him a tall grayish wall of smoke. I want to see him. The real him. Was he handsome when he was alive? I'm pretty sure he was. Even without color, I can't tear my eyes away from him.

"Not quite. I think we will be helping each other. You see," he explains, "if you move out, Lindsay might find someone else to stay here while she decides the fate of my home. That person could be even messier than you are. With even more," he pauses as he tries to find the right word, "baffling musical tastes."

I jerk back. "What's wrong with Taylor Swift? When I'm depressed, she's my go-to. As you've noticed, my mental state has been baseline terrible for a while now."

The muscle in his jaw leaps. "She's fine. Perfectly mediocre. But why not try a little variety?"

Perfectly mediocre? *The* Taylor Alison Swift? Forget how hot he must've been when he was alive. This guy's a moron. "It's not like I knew anyone else was here. I was blasting *my* music the way *I* like to listen to it because I assumed I was alone."

"Now that you know you're not..." he trails off, a clear plea for me to give him what he wants.

"Fine," I huff, taking a spiteful bite of my breakfast. That's when I realize this is a negotiation. If he wants me to stay, then I can toss out some demands of my own. "But you need to stop spying on me. I don't want you listening in on my phone calls, or peeping on me in the shower–"

"I'm a married man," he interrupts, with a hand over his

heart. The silver wedding band is still on his finger, after all these years. "I would never do that."

"Your desire to spy on women without consent shouldn't have anything to do with your marital status, just FYI." He rolls his eyes as I continue. "Swear on your wife and child that you won't be a total creep and I'll take your word for it." It might be a cruel thread to pull, but it's the only leverage I have. Based on the way his voice cracked when he first mentioned them and the tortured look he's giving me now, it'll work.

"Done. Can you clarify your terms? I don't want to make assumptions and unintentionally cross a line."

Now we're getting somewhere.

"No more judgmental comments about Mark. I was weak and horny, and that's why I invited him, but I don't care about him enough to defend him. When you mock him, it feels like you're mocking me. So drop it, okay?"

He dips his chin in agreement. "What else?"

"This is the important one. If I'm behind a closed door, you need to knock before entering. I don't want to worry about being watched while I'm sleeping or doing anything else. No floating in and scaring the shit out of me or coming in without me seeing you," I tell him. "I assume that's how you've stayed hidden until last night?"

He nods. "Yes, I can make myself invisible. In your presence, I no longer will. I swear it. On Susanna and Daniel." His eyes look wet as he says his son's name, and I wonder if ghosts can cry. If they can, do the tears actually fall? Or just disappear? "But in the presence of anyone else, I will not show myself."

"Right, and this whole deal is in an effort to keep your presence a secret from Lindsay, correct?"

"Mm. As long as she doesn't know I exist, she will continue to think of this as a dusty old house she wants nothing to do with. She'll let you stay here, and nothing will change for me. That's what I want."

I don't feel comfortable lying to Lindsay, especially since she's trusting me to keep the house in order until she decides what to do with it. However, until I get a job and start making money, this is the only rent-free housing I'll be able to get, so it benefits me to keep Winston's existence hidden.

"Anything else?" he asks.

"When the door is open, you can come in, as long as you're visible. Obviously, we'll share the common areas." A thought occurs to me. "Where do you sleep? *Do* you sleep?"

"The attic is my room, and it's off-limits. That's where my personal items are kept. I don't require sleep, so most nights I will read in the study, or I will roam the property, checking to see if repairs are needed anywhere."

"Got it. I'll stay out of the attic."

"Then, we have a deal?" he asks, his lips curving with hope and showing off a large dimple in his right cheek. A dimple I want to curl up and take a nap in, and will no doubt keep picturing for the rest of the day.

I hold out my hand, then pull it back. "Oh, right. You can't shake." The scene from *Casper* plays in my head, when Kat and Casper's hands float through each other. Is that how it would be with Winston? "Or can you?"

He chuckles softly. "Hold out your hand."

When I do, he outstretches his much larger hand, and it crosses right through my skin and blood and bones, and the only thing I feel is a cold, tingly sensation. Like sticking your hand into a snow pile and getting pins and needles.

"I can do *this*," he says as I start to giggle, "or *this*."

His translucent hand retreats, and when it inches back toward me, I notice a difference. Color. His rough fingers wrap around mine and grip as he shakes. An earthy scent fills my nose, and as I breathe it in, I realize it's his. Pine and woodsmoke. A comforting, alluring smell that reminds me of autumn.

The rest of him is still that misty gray from before, but from his elbow down to his fingertips, there's a real hand. It's cold, but it's firm. His skin is a light tan, his fingers are thick with trimmed and clean fingernails, and soft brown hair covers the corded muscles of his forearm.

"Wow," is all I can say. We've stopped shaking, and now we're just holding hands. "This is crazy, but it's real, right? I'm not imagining it? Or you?"

Winston lets go and guffaws loudly at my question. "I'd hope your imagination could do a lot better than a stubborn asshole like me, Natalie."

Normally, I'd be quick to protest such a comment. I'd say, "Oh, you're not so bad," even without knowing much about him. I'd still want to make him feel better. But something about Winston makes me want to push back.

I tilt my head to the side, letting my gaze slowly drift up and down the length of his form as I straighten my spine. "Good point. The ghost of Pedro Pascal would be a much sweeter roommate."

"I don't know who that is," Winston replies, his brows pinched together, as if he assumes I made him up.

"Shame. You could learn a lot from him."

I go back to eating my breakfast with a smirk tugging at my lips, knowing I rattled my grumpy roommate. That's never been a skill of mine. I'm the woman who agonizes over what she *should've* said days, even weeks later.

Winston floats out of the room, and I let out a deep breath of relief once I'm alone. What is it about him that puts me on edge? And is he truly an asshole? Or just annoying as hell?

He's rude, and nosy, and he definitely needs a hobby, but I

get this feeling he's, I don't know...misunderstood? Like there's a deeper layer to him that's self-effacing and affable.

My feelings are famously flawed, though, especially when it comes to men. The ones who seem broken by trauma and just waiting for The Right Woman to come along and put them back together seem to flock to me, and I can never resist.

It's a problem.

I've wasted too many years on men like that—one man in particular—and I don't want to keep making the same mistakes. I'd like to settle down someday. Maybe get married. Kids probably aren't in the cards for me anymore since I'm in my forties, and that's okay. As long as I have someone to come home to, someone who loves me as much as I love them, does what he says he's going to do, and doesn't take advantage of how much I'm willing to give, that's all I need.

I wonder what Winston was like as a husband. Was he attentive and— *No. Stop thinking about him as anything other than your dead roommate.*

Catching feelings for the ghost in the attic would be a colossal mistake, and one I can't afford to make.

Chapter 6
Winston

All is peaceful at the manor for the next twenty-four hours. The boundaries Natalie and I have put in place seem to work, for the most part.

It's a quarter past eleven when I look for the broom to sweep the front steps. Acorns have begun falling in buckets, and the pinecones won't be far behind. I sweep the steps every few days, and I know when I last did it I put the broom back in the pantry next to the kitchen, where it's always been kept. So why is it missing?

At first, I think Natalie has decided to sweep the floors, and the thought gives me hope that we could divide some of the household chores. I look everywhere for the broom. Each room of the house has been checked, and nothing. I'm taking a second lap through the kitchen when music starts pulsating through the floor above, and heavy-gaited steps move back and forth at a frenzied pace.

I find the door to Natalie's room closed when I reach the second floor, but the music is so loud, I can understand the lyrics. Natalie doesn't hear me knock the first time, or the second, so I begin pounding with my fist. After knocking the tenth time, I lose my patience and open the door.

My roommate is pacing across the abstract rug, her feet bare, as she hums along with the song playing. She's wearing a sleeveless teal dress that lands just above her knees, her golden waves whirling around her shoulders as she spins on her heel to go in the other direction. The scent of her hair wafts toward me—strawberries—and I breathe it in, holding my breath to keep it in my lungs. Her right arm, from shoulder to elbow, is covered in a large black tattoo of an elephant surrounded by wildflowers. It's incredibly detailed, and I want to know more about it. Why an elephant, of all things?

She still hasn't noticed me leaning against the door frame, and I don't announce myself. Instead, I watch her. Her brows are knitted together as she chews the inside of her cheek, her hands fisted and punching down at her sides. It's clear that this is nervous energy she's trying to work off, and I laugh quietly at how ridiculous she looks. However, I can't deny how adorable she is in this frazzled state.

I start to feel guilty about spying, and even more guilty about my level of fascination in this woman, when I'm still a married man. What is wrong with me? Why am I so captivated by her? Watching her without her consent is a direct violation of our deal, so I yell, "Why wasn't I invited to the party?"

She makes the same squeak that she did yesterday when I entered the kitchen. The one that sounds like the tail end of a sneeze. "Hey!" she replies, gritting her teeth at the sight of me. She looks enraged, but the redness of her cheeks implies she's mostly embarrassed. "You said you'd knock first."

"I did. Ten times."

She grabs her phone off the dresser and turns down the volume.

"Why aren't you wearing your ear sticks?" I ask. "They

could probably hear your music across town. I wouldn't be surprised if the police arrived with a noise complaint."

"My ear*buds* are charging. This isn't Taylor Swift. It's Cardi B, to hype me up, because I'm about to go into town to look for a job, and I'm freaking out because I'm not emotionally prepared to get rejected again."

I have no idea who that is, but it doesn't matter. "What makes you think you'll be rejected?"

She huffs a breath and starts pacing again. "Before I moved here, I went job hunting all over town, and no one wanted to hire me. I didn't even get a call or email back about an interview." The skirt of her dress swishes around her. "Not that I blame them. My resume makes me look like a flake. Over the last six years, I've had a handful of jobs, none I was at for more than a year, and they're all low-end jobs a teenager could do. Then there are the gaps in employment. They always give me a side-eye on that one. Even though it was to care for my mom, it's like they don't believe it, or it wasn't a good enough reason to stop working."

Her pacing quickens, the skin on her knuckles going white. "But what was I supposed to do? We couldn't afford to have a live-in nurse, so I did everything. I gave her her meds." She stops to look at me. "Do you know how many pills a person with cancer has to take per day? It's easily two dozen."

"That is a lot of pills," I reply, nodding. I want to say more, but the words would be hollow compared to what she endured, so I remain quiet.

"I drove her to all her chemo appointments, I helped her to the bathroom, helped her bathe, tried to find the magic combination of foods that wouldn't make her sick, and when she was, I made sure I was right there with a vomit bag. Was I really supposed to sacrifice the three hours of sleep I got each night to work on a side hustle?"

Letting her talk through her nerves doesn't seem to be helping. I was sure it would, and when she was finished speaking, she would be calmer, and I could offer some reassurance that someone in town will hire her, but it must be too raw for her to relive being her mother's caretaker.

What she needs now is a distraction. Something to take her mind off the pain, even if her frustration shifts from the people she's about to meet in town to me. It has to help at least a little. "You'll get a job. More importantly, however, I can't find the broom. Do you know where it is?"

"Uh, I," she stammers, her brown eyes swirling with confusion. She looks as if she'd prefer to yell at me about the quick dismissal of her misery, but is stuck on the answer to my question. "I...Yeah, I used it to sweep the floor in here last night. The dust was making me sneeze. I put it in the closet with the vacuum."

It's an honest mistake. I can't fault her for it. "Splendid. Just so you're aware, the broom is kept in the pantry in the kitchen." I go to leave when I hear Natalie scoff.

"Why would you keep it in the kitchen?" she asks.

"Because it's closer to the front door, which is where I'm going now. To sweep."

The pacing has stopped, and now she's looking at me as if I've grown two heads. I suppose my distraction worked.

"You're going to sweep the stuff that lives outside, to another part of the outside, and then you're going to bring that broom back inside and put it away in the pantry? Where all the food is?"

She doesn't understand. "The front steps are covered in acorns. It looks sloppy. I won't tolerate it."

"Why don't you just wait for the wind to take care of it? Or the squirrels?"

"Or why don't I just wait for winter to come and let the

snow cover it? Let the elements destroy the wood and the earth wrap its vines and roots over it completely?" I reply, trying to show her how drastically she's missing the point.

"So wait," she begins, a smirk tugging at her lips. "You're obsessed with the neatness of the exterior of the house, but not the decades of dust covering the entire interior?"

"I wouldn't say *obsessed*." When she says it like that, she makes me sound like a buffoon. It's not that I like having dust on every surface, but it doesn't bother me as much as the acorns do. Plus, dusting is my least favorite chore. If it's not bothering me or getting in my way, I see no need to fixate on it. I refuse to engage with her question. "Just put it back in the pantry from now on."

"That doesn't make sense," she replies. "The broom belongs in the closet with the vacuum and the other cleaning supplies. Besides, I don't want to encourage ants or other pests that might cling to the bristles of your ratty old broom to start eating the food in there. Not unless you plan on cleaning it after you sweep outside."

"The broom is a cleaning tool. Why would I clean the cleaning tool? Would you also like me to wash the outside of the washing machine?"

She rolls her eyes. "I'll just buy another broom, and we can designate that one as the indoor broom. Leave the other one outside or in the shed."

"That's a complete waste of money," I protest. "No house needs to have more than one broom. I could make one myself by the time you get back from your job search."

"A broom is probably ten dollars. It's fine. And if it ends this conversation, it'll have been worth the cost." She pulls a pair of white socks from the dresser and sits on the edge of her bed as she puts them on.

"I didn't realize you were rolling in cash," I say, crossing my arms over my chest. "See, I thought you were here because you had no money and no place to go."

"Oh my god. You know what?" She throws up her hands. "I wasn't planning on leaving for another half hour, but I might as well start my job search early."

Grabbing her purse off the dresser, she stomps past me down the stairs toward the front door.

This woman is maddening.

"Bye, weirdo. Hope you're happy."

Am I happy? Yes, because Natalie is now marching toward the very task that had her pacing in fear just five minutes ago. Once I hear her car head down the steep drive, I realize how quiet it is without her.

That, I'm not happy about.

Chapter 7
Natalie

No one in Mapletown is hiring. Not the florist, not the coffee shop, the pizzeria, the bookstore, the occult shop, the grocery store, or the bakery. The owners seemed nice enough, but I got the feeling that even if they were hiring, I wasn't going to be considered a candidate. I don't know why. It didn't seem like it had to do with my resume. Most barely glanced at it before telling me they didn't have any open positions. Maybe it's all in my head, and this tiny town is fully staffed. I'm probably imagining the unwelcome vibe I was sensing, and if there's one thing I've clocked ten-thousand hours doing, it's overthinking. I've reached expert-level.

After I swing by the home goods store on the edge of town for a broom, I take the long way home. Winston is going to be relentless with his mockery when he finds out my job search was a bust.

How did Nonna Penny put up with his obnoxious ass? Maybe she was less particular than I am and let him make whatever house rules he wanted and followed them to a T because she was too exhausted to care. I can't imagine any other way to live with him without wanting to smother him with a pillow.

At least he doesn't clip his toenails in my bathroom sink or sing Limp Bizkit at the top of his lungs, or fart loudly and make me guess what he had just eaten—a truly disgusting game a guy I dated in college insisted on playing.

I take a right onto Mountain View Road, which is the long, winding road that'll lead me home. The windows are down, and the wind is whipping through my hair. The stone-colored clouds have that clumpy, marshmallowy look to them that says a storm is coming, and the smell of rain confirms it. Even though it's September, it's still pretty balmy during the day, but I'm hoping that'll fade in a few weeks, along with the summery shades of green, to the warm oranges of fall.

I'm about half a mile from the house when I notice a wide wooden sign on the side of the road peeking out between two paper birch trees with the words "Fast Glass Tavern" carved into it with a neon-lit arrow pointing ahead.

This must be the closest neighbor we have, and it's a bar. I've never gone this way home before; otherwise, I would've noticed this, and I would've gone in to check the place out. They might even be hiring.

I pull onto the dirt driveway, and it takes me past the circular keg shaped building. There are two other keg-shaped parts of the building that are shorter, one on each side of the central barrel, and attached. Outside, there's an area with picnic tables beneath rows of twinkling string lights, and a stone path from the outdoor seating to a manicured lawn with several games including cornhole, oversized Jenga and Connect Four, and a giant chessboard.

Since it's three p.m. on a Wednesday, the place is relatively empty. My car is one of four in the lot.

Inside, there's a booth to the left against the circular wall with a few men who look to be in their fifties, drinking tall glasses of beer and playing cards. In the center of the room is the glistening mahogany bar. It takes up most of the space in this main part of the building, with the bar wrapping in a wide sphere, with a round shelving unit above it made of glass, holding the various bottles of liquor and clean glasses. An elderly man occupies one of the stools at the bar, his glass empty and his neck craned back as he watches the baseball game on the TV above the bartender. The bartender lifts his head at the sound of the door closing behind me.

He smiles, and my jaw falls open. This man is so unbelievably gorgeous, it's difficult to look directly at him. It feels like I'm looking at the sun. A sun that also rides a motorcycle and would break the nose of a guy who cat-called you.

His inky black hair is shaved and faded on the sides, but the top is long and tousled. There's a clump of hair in the front that's gone gray, a tidy burst of silver that looks intentional, adding to his naturally cool aura. He has a trim, mostly gray beard that surrounds a set of pouty lips. My gaze drifts over his cheekbones—sharp enough to cut my hand on—and I notice that his skin has a greenish tint to it. That's weird. It must be the lighting in here.

"Hi there, ma'am," he says, with a slight Southern drawl. I've never minded being called *ma'am*. It doesn't make me feel old, just awestruck that there are still men in this country with manners. "Sit anywhere you'd like, and I'll come to you."

Goosebumps race across my skin, and I can't decide if it's because of the air conditioner they seem to be blasting in here, or if it's the power of his velvety voice. "Uhh, hi. Yup, okay," I mumble, willing my feet to move. I grab the bar stool closest to me, and when I put my purse on the stool to my right, I notice my folder full of resumes and remember why I'm here.

Stop drooling. You need a job. Money. Stability.

Mr. Dreamy Drinkman strolls over, his shoulders and biceps straining against the fabric of his heather-black t-shirt. He tosses a towel over his shoulder with such ease and charisma, you'd think he got lessons from Ted Danson himself. "What can I get for you?"

I'm going to have to learn how to string together a sentence if I have any hopes of working with him.

"I, um... Well, I just moved here, and I wondered if you were hiring?" My voice comes out shaky and small, and I worry I've already blown it.

He takes my resume and scratches his beard as he looks it over. "Actually, yeah, I could use some help behind the bar. One of my full-time bartenders just left for college. It looks like you have a few years of experience as a waitress. Ever mix a drink before?"

"Yes, at my last job, I'd help out if the bartenders were short-staffed." My right hand is pinching part of my skirt into a little wrinkled ball—an anxious tick—but it's doing nothing to calm me down. "There are a lot of drinks I don't know how to make, but I've made dozens of martinis, negronis, and whiskey sours."

"Well, hey," he says with an easy smile. "That's a great start. We can teach you the rest. Name's Dominic, by the way."

He offers his hand, and when I shake it, I can't help but compare it to Winston's. The way his hand felt when it was just cold fog passing through mine, and immediately after, when his hand took on a corporeal form and I could actually shake it. Butterflies fill my stomach at the way his rough palm rubbed against my own, and the soft, rumbling chuckle he let out at my reactions to both. Dominic's hand is equally large, but I don't feel the same crackle of electricity that I felt when I held Winston's.

"What do you think of Mapletown so far?" Dominic asks,

bringing me back to the present. He steps away to pour me a glass of ice water.

"Truthfully, I haven't gotten to explore much of it yet. Today was the first time I walked around town," I explain. "It's cute, but I was mostly looking for job postings in windows, so I didn't try any of the delicious food I saw or spend hours in the bookstore like I would've wanted."

"Where are you staying? Pebblebrook Inn?"

"Uh, no. I'm right next door, actually. An old house called Caraway Manor. Know it?"

His light blue eyes widen at first, then his expression morphs into something else. Like he's impressed. "Really? You bought the haunted house on the hill?"

"Ha! No. There's no way I could afford a place like that. My best friend inherited it from her grandmother, and she's letting me stay there."

Dominic nods, coming back to my place at the bar and leaning down on his elbows. "Right, I was sorry to hear about Penelope. Nice lady."

The old man on the other side of the bar lifts his glass and groans to get Dominic's attention.

"Coming right up, Vlad." He turns to me and holds up a finger. "To be continued."

When he places the full glass in front of Vlad, it's red. It also looks...thick. Is he having a Bloody Mary in the afternoon? Where's the celery stick?

Dominic wipes his hands on the towel still strewn over his shoulder as he returns to me.

"Now, where were we?" he asks, picking up my resume again. He goes back to staring at it, and my palms get clammy.

He's looking at the gaps. Judging the time between jobs. Thinking I'm an unreliable fuck-up.

As the self-loathing thoughts get louder, I panic and blurt,

"I know it looks like I jump around, never settling at one job long enough to figure out what the hell I'm doing, but I promise it's not like that. My mom got sick, then she got better, but then the cancer came back, so I was her caregiver until she passed last month. I'm here now, and I want to stay here."

His gaze softens as he puts my résumé flat on the bar. "I'm sorry for your loss, Natalie. Truthfully, I wasn't thinking that. I was thinking how incredible your timing is."

"My timing?"

He nods. "I lost a bartender, and then you show up lookin' for a job. Plus, you're staying at Caraway Manor, so obviously you're cool with...you know."

I...don't.

"The strange and unusual."

Is he talking about Winston? Does he know him somehow? If I'm supposed to keep my dead roommate's existence a secret from Lindsay, there's no way I'm exposing him to Dominic aka Mr. Dreamy Drinkman aka my potential new boss.

Rather than answer him, I quote one of my all-time favorite movies. "Well, of course. I, myself, am strange and unusual."

Dominic laughs, throwing his head back and exposing his thick, muscular neck. "Nicely done. I have a feeling you'll fit right in." Then his mood shifts to something serious. Darker. He interlaces his fingers in front of him, his mouth forming a flat line. "There's one rule here that the staff follows, and really, everyone in town follows. I need you to promise me you'll do the same if I hire you."

"Of course."

"We don't judge anyone who walks through that door. We serve them drinks, feed them, listen to them, and protect them from causing harm to themselves or others. But no matter what they look like, where they came from, how they sound, or how they live their lives, we *do not* judge. This is a no-tolerance policy here at Fast Glass for judgement. Understand?"

Does Dominic think I'm racist? That I'll refuse to serve a customer based on their skin color or who they love? I try not to take it personally. Maybe he's had a few bad apples roll through here in the past.

"We serve. We don't judge. Not a problem," I vow. "Totally on board with that."

His lips quirk up on both sides before revealing his supremely white teeth in a wide smile. They also appear to be slightly pointed at the ends, but maybe the lighting is to blame for this too. "Then welcome to the team." He puts a menu in front of me. "Dinner's on the house. Let me know what you want, and I'll tell you about some of our more peculiar regulars."

Chapter 8
Winston

Natalie doesn't get home until dark. Luckily, the meal I made for her doesn't spoil quickly. It's not a grand feast. Just peanut butter and jelly spread on the multigrain bread Lindsay left here, with a handful of potato chips and sliced apples on the side, but after several hours of searching for a job, I imagine Natalie will be hungry.

It's not as if I've been waiting around for her, wondering what she'd like to eat. I spent some time in the study reading and drawing in my sketchbook, then I went outside to trim the hedges along the driveway.

Since then...

Okay, fine.

I've been floating aimlessly through the house, debating whether to use the marinated steak tips in the freezer and make her kebabs on the grill out back with corn on the cob. It seemed like a good idea at first, but I haven't seen Natalie eat much meat since she arrived. It's possible she's a vegetarian, and if that's the case, the steak kebabs would be a waste.

She doesn't cook much, which could explain the lack of

meat in her diet. Natalie opts for the easiest, quickest meals to prepare, and that typically consists of salads, crackers and cheese, or vegetables and hummus. Ultimately, peanut butter and jelly seemed like a safe choice, mostly because I've seen her make that before and I know she enjoys it.

Caring for her has quickly become a priority for me, and I'm puzzled as to why. Beyond her striking beauty, what is it about her that holds so much of my attention?

I hear her humming "Shake it Off" by Taylor Swift as she enters the house. The smell of strawberries hits my nose and calms me instantly. She's removing her white sneakers as I come around the corner, and she suppresses a squeal at the sight of me.

"Oh hi," she says with a bright smile. Flecks of gold sparkle amid the deep brown of her irises.

"You seem happy. Does that mean you're employed?"

She nods eagerly as she hangs up her purse. "I'm officially a bartender at Fast Glass Tavern." Natalie heads toward the kitchen, doing a triumphant dance as she goes. I follow on her heels, becoming entranced by the way her backside jiggles with each movement. She is soft all over, but this particular part of her deeply entices me, especially when the dimpled skin of her ass and thighs is visible through the fabric of her dress. My dick strains painfully against my pants at the sight.

Fuck. I need to put a stop to these thoughts, but the harder I try, the harder they are to ignore. Maybe resisting them is part of the problem. Natalie is soft and tempting, and there's nothing I can do about it. I need to accept my attraction to her, and just...not act on it. I will *not* let my feelings be known.

I pull my gaze up toward the top shelves of the kitchen, reminding myself that I'm still Susanna's husband. It doesn't matter that her heart no longer beats. My eyes shouldn't be wandering over another woman's body. I know better.

She spots the plate of food on the counter, and her brow furrows, confused. "Is this for me?"

I nod. "Thought you might be hungry after your job search. I'm glad it was a success. I knew you'd find something."

"Oh," she replies, her features tightening in pity. "I already ate. Um, Dominic, the owner of the bar, gave me a free dinner tonight as a way to welcome me to the team."

"Dominic. This is the man who hired you?" His name is bitter on my lips. He hires her and immediately treats her to a meal? Is this a workplace or a hunting ground for him to prey on vulnerable women?

"Yes, and oh my god. He's so gorgeous, I could barely speak when I first walked in. We're talking, underwear model hot."

Of course, he is.

"Wow," I reply sarcastically, unable to hide my ire. "Yet he remains in humble Mapletown, serving booze to the average folk. I'm sure he'll be granted Sainthood any day now."

Natalie nods, ignoring my barb. "Such a nice guy. I was nervous at first. Wondering how I was going to concentrate, working closely with someone that good-looking..."

"That would be quite the struggle, I'd imagine." I stop listening after that as my fists clench at my sides. Her voice becomes a distant murmur. At one point, I hear the words "so sweet," but that only makes it worse. Whatever game this Dominic is playing, Natalie seems to have fallen for it. I don't trust him, and I hate that she does.

My gaze lands on the uneaten sandwich I made for her. Tidying settles me, so I reach for the plate with my hand in corporeal form and bring it to the trash can.

"Wait," Natalie says, holding up a hand. "You're throwing that away? Why?"

"Because you already ate." *Dominic fed you,* I want to say, but it would make me sound jealous and petty, which I'm not. I'm concerned about her safety in the workplace. That's all.

"Well, don't waste it." Her voice has softened, and I look up to find her smiling warmly at me. "You were so kind to make me dinner. I'll wrap it up and have it for lunch tomorrow."

Words leave my head as she approaches, the scent of strawberries making my head fuzzy.

Natalie takes the plate from my hand, and her slender, delicate fingers brush against mine, sending sparks down my spine. She tilts her head to the side. "Thank you, Winston."

I forget what I was doing, what I was thinking. Was I upset about something? For the life of me, I can't remember what it was. My hand shoots out, grabbing hers and pulling her close. She gasps but doesn't pull away. Her breath is hot as it fans my chest, and it smells sweet. Not like the fruity smell of her hair. More like a decadent cupcake. I can't stop staring at her lips, slightly parted and so unbelievably soft.

"What are–" she begins, but when I swipe my thumb across her bottom lip, she stills.

"Chapped."

Her forehead scrunches up. "What?"

I reach for the glass on the edge of the counter and put it to her lips without looking away. "You're dehydrated. Drink."

She shakes her head defiantly. "No, I'm not. How would you even know that?"

I can tell by the way she sticks her chin out that she's being difficult on purpose. Trying to goad me. *Brat.* But she has no idea how closely I've paid attention. I know when she hasn't had enough water. I know far more about her than she realizes. "How much water have you had today, Natalie?"

As she chews on the inside of her cheek, I see defeat in her eyes. "Fine," she says, taking a large gulp.

I feel victorious and can't hide my smile. Then a spot on Natalie's dress catches my attention. "What is that?"

She looks down and chuckles, taking a few steps back, seeming grateful for a reason to put space between us. "Oh, ketchup from my burger. Guess I should be more careful, huh?" I watch as she grabs a plastic bag from one of the drawers and puts the peanut butter and jelly sandwich into it.

When the drawer remains open, I step in front of it, clearing my throat. "See this here? When you open a drawer or a cabinet, it's customary to close it once you're done."

A pretty pink color climbs up her throat and colors her cheeks as she makes an *oops* expression. "My bad. I thought I did."

"If you had, you would've heard the sound it makes when it shuts." Irritation sends a growl through my chest, and it becomes harder to suppress when she's looking at me like that. Like she sincerely meant to close it, and in no way sought to bug the daylights out of me. It's hard to believe, considering how often she leaves things wide open, but instead of pushing the subject, I let it go. The sight of her twirling a loose blonde curl around her finger is too distracting anyway.

"By the way, I learned some crazy shit about Mapletown while I was there," she says, unbothered by my criticism. "Dominic seems to know every*thing* and every*one*. He knows about you too."

I feel the blood drain from my face. "What? What do you mean?" I'd never heard of this Dominic person before today. How can he know about me?

"When I told him where I was staying, he implied that this place was haunted. He didn't mention your name specifically, but it didn't seem like it was news, either. That this house is filled with old ghosts."

Ghosts, plural? That's not good.

"It's just you here, right?" Natalie asks with a teasing grin. "Don't tell me there are more of you."

I laugh, trying to mask how uncomfortable I am. "Just me in here," emphasizing the *in* and telling myself it wasn't a total lie. She doesn't need to know the truth yet. It would overwhelm her.

She puts the sandwich in the fridge and the chips back in the cupboard. "Well, that was probably the least batshit thing Dominic told me today. Did you know this town is filled with monsters?"

"Monsters? You mean those modern Nazis? Penelope never mentioned encountering them when she went into town."

"Ugh, no," she says with a look of sheer disgust. "Can you imagine? No, I'm talking about vampires, gargoyles, zombies— monsters of the mythical variety."

"Natalie," I say in a gentle tone, "those creatures do not exist." I don't mean to sound patronizing, but she can't seriously believe this nonsense, can she? I'm sure drop-dead gorgeous Dominic can be convincing when he wants, but I'd hope she could see through such preposterousness.

"Winston." Her tone matches mine, but it's clearly mocking. "You're a ghost, babe. You shouldn't exist, either. Yet here you are."

I ignore the heat that races to the top of my ears, and other places, upon hearing the pet name, and consider her main point. Before I became a ghost, I certainly didn't believe they existed. "Did you see these mythical creatures with your own eyes?"

My roommate nods, her eyes wide. "One of the regulars is a vampire. He looks like your average old man, but Dominic was serving him glasses of type A blood. He even flashed me a fang at one point."

A vampire? A blood-sucking vampire lives in Mapletown? How is this possible?

"Dominic is a zombie," she adds. "He doesn't eat human brains. He was adamant about that. Apparently, raw meat is his sustenance of choice, and not human meat. He also doesn't have any rotting parts that I could see, and there aren't any issues with his speech."

Pity. I was hoping his body would be rife with decay, but then, Natalie probably wouldn't deem him "underwear model hot" if that were the case.

"But how?" I ask, still baffled by this information. "Penelope never said anything about this."

She holds up her hands. "No idea if Penelope knew or why she chose not to tell you, but it's true. Dominic said Mapletown is protected territory, meaning it doesn't show up on any maps. I guess some witch from a hundred-some-odd years ago put a spell on the town, protecting it from outsiders, making it a haven for those who don't feel like they belong in the human world. You can only enter if you're invited or if you have an ancestral link to one of the many breeds of monster that live here. I don't know what that says about Penelope or Lindsay, but I was invited in, so that answers that."

A witch from a hundred years ago? "Did you get the name of this witch?"

She scrunches her nose, deep in thought. "Uh, Martha Crane, I think he said."

"Martha Crane?" I bark out a surprised laugh. She lived two doors down from the shoemaker's shop, where I worked before I married Susanna. She was an odd, gangly thing. A timid girl who only ever spoke to birds and stray cats. I suppose it makes sense that she had mystical abilities. "Huh."

Natalie opens the fridge and pours herself another glass of water. "You knew her?"

"I did. She was younger than me by about fifteen years, but I remember her. The town wasn't heavily populated when I was alive. There were maybe three hundred people here." I sigh heavily. "A lot has changed since then."

"You never float down to Main Street just to see the sights? People watch?"

Suddenly I feel heavy, as if there are cement blocks chained to my feet. "I can't." My voice is barely a whisper. "I can't leave the grounds. My spirit is...stuck here."

"Oh."

There's that look of pity again. It makes my skin crawl and my blood heat with rage. The last thing I want from Natalie is pity. It makes me feel like I'm an inch tall. "Well," I say, clearing my throat, "congrats on the job. I have things I must attend to. Goodnight, Natalie."

I don't look at her. I can't. Her gaze follows me out of the room. I can feel it. Pity is thick in her voice when she replies, "Goodnight, Winston."

I was given a chance to leave this plane of existence not long after my death. To go wherever one goes after they die. Not once have I longed for another opportunity. Until now.

Chapter 9
Natalie

I didn't cry myself to sleep last night, which means I didn't wake up with crusty goo sealing my eyelids shut this morning. That alone feels like a victory. It's a new day. I have a job, finally. Early-twenties Natalie would've sighed, disappointed, and thought, *it's just a bartending job. Aim higher. Remember those career goals you had? Revive them. It's not too late.*

But the forty-one-year-old Natalie feels nothing but relief.

Sure, I could start looking up the closest nursing schools and seeing if the credits I got a million years ago before I dropped out would still transfer. I could apply for education grants and loans and see how many hours I could work at the bar while also going to school. That was the original plan, after all.

I'm not twenty-six anymore, though, and I'm not sure it's still the life I want. Loss ages you, mentally and physically, and it puts everything into perspective. For the first time in a year, I feel emotionally stable enough to leave the house and have a full-time job, and I'm excited to start my first shift tonight. That's the only plan I currently have, and that's okay.

I no longer feel the pressure to achieve as much as possible in the shortest amount of time. Quiet, simple, and fulfilling—this is how I want my days to feel, and if I can achieve all three on a bartender's wage, then that's enough.

After I shower and brush my teeth, I eat the PB and J Winston made me at the counter in the kitchen, then decide to go for a leisurely stroll around the property. There are acres of land I have yet to explore, mostly because I'm not a huge fan of nature in general, but the weather is starting to cool down. Not by much, but today is a high of eighty-three, which is five degrees cooler than yesterday, so I'm taking it as a good sign. The sky is a mix of fluffy, cheerful clouds and sun, and there's enough of a breeze that my hairline isn't instantly damp with sweat when I step outside.

From the front steps, I take a right and follow a narrow dirt path into the woods for about twenty minutes. It's the kind of path that was never intentionally cleared but rather tamped down by decades of feet. There are occasional roots that pop out of the ground and tree branches I need to duck beneath, but otherwise it's a curving, flat path that allows me to move at a slow pace and listen to the wide array of birds chirping in the trees above.

I notice a wooden fence to my left several feet away that encases the Caraway land, and I let it lead me once the dense trees open to reveal patches of wildflowers. Here is where I stop to watch the tall flowers dance in the wind.

Out of the corner of my eye, I see movement, and I suck in a breath before realizing it's a deer. It scampers deeper into the woods the second I meet its gaze.

Seeing wildlife out here reminds me of everything Dominic said, about monsters living in this town, and despite seeing

Vlad's fangs as he drank actual blood from a glass, and Dominic showing me just how green his skin is beneath the bright lights of the kitchen, part of me still can't believe it. I mean, shouldn't I be terrified?

Pulling out my phone, I send a text to Lindsay, letting her know about the job at the bar. She must be between conference calls, because she replies within seconds with "CONGRATS" in all caps and about a thousand applause emojis.

I'm not sure what to tell her about the monsters in town, and until she comes up here and asks me to go barhopping with her, I don't see much of a need. They aren't my secrets to reveal, and I want Winston to be able to trust me. I want the rest of the town to trust me, too. It feels like this is a place where I could settle, at least for a while. I don't want petty gossip to mess that up.

The path continues around the edge of the wildflowers and ducks back into the woods, but I spot a bench swing next to the garden in the backyard that looks extremely cozy, so I make my way over there instead.

"Holy shit," I mutter quietly as I walk through the rows of strawberries, tomato and pepper plants, entire bushes of cilantro, mint, and basil, and a dozen or so cucumber plants wrapped through tall trellises. There are a few rows of what look to be root plants, and an entire section separated by a wide, landscaped path for flowers.

Is this Winston's doing? The garden is not only massive, but also extremely well cared for. There are hardly any weeds. I don't even see a yellowed leaf that needs to be plucked or rotting vegetables that need to be removed. He must prefer to do his gardening at night, since he doesn't sleep, because I've never seen him out here during the day. Granted, I'm not out here much, either, but since learning about his existence, it seems like he's always inside when I am. Always nearby. Always hovering.

Why does the thought of him floating near me cause my stomach to flip upside down?

I sweep the hair off my neck as a soft breeze comes through, sighing contentedly at how quickly it dries the beads of sweat running down my back. The bench swing creaks as the wind rattles through the chains, and I plop down, pushing back and pumping my legs to get it moving. The act takes me right back to childhood, when I'd stay on the swings at the park for hours, seeing how high I could climb before the swing did a full loop over the bar.

I lean my head back and close my eyes, and memories of Mom fill my mind. This is the kind of peaceful place she'd want her ashes to be spread, I think. Maybe when the leaves start to change.

At some point, the gentle movement of the swing paired with the calm breeze has me dozing off, and what awakens me is the angry screech of a woman whose voice sounds dangerously close.

Leaping off the swing, I turn toward the voice and see a woman marching toward me from the direction of the shed, with dirty gardening shears in her hands, the blades pointed out. It would terrify me if the rest of her outfit didn't seem so out of place. The straw hat and gardening gloves clearly indicate her purpose here, but she's also wearing a cream-colored sleeveless silk blouse, high-waisted navy-blue pants that zip up the sides and taper at the ankle, and matching navy-blue ballet flats. Her brown-black hair is also swept off her face in an old-fashioned style that looks like it was set by big rollers. Her red lipstick is perfectly applied, without a speck on her teeth. Did she just come from a vintage fashion photoshoot and forget to change?

Why does this gorgeous stranger look like she wants to chop me into a hundred pieces?

"You shouldn't be here!" she shouts, snapping the shears closed before opening them again. "How dare you come to our home looking for him!"

"What? L-Looking for whom?" I stammer as I hold up my hands in surrender. "Winston?" Is this Winston's late wife? Is she a ghost too? I think he would've told me that. And I'm certain Lindsay would've told me if she'd hired a gardener, especially if that gardener was a total babe.

The gardener's blue eyes are filled with rage, and her hands are shaking as she gets closer. "Don't play coy with me, you trollop!"

I stumble backwards, unable to see where I'm going, but hoping to god, I don't accidentally stomp on one of her plants. All I know is that the house is somewhere behind me, and I need to get there as soon as possible. "I'm sorry, I have no idea what you're talking about," I explain, hoping she'll realize she's got the wrong girl. "My name is Natalie. I'm a temporary guest."

"My Thomas will be home any day now, and once he's back, he's *mine*. All mine. I won't let you get in the way of our love, do you hear me?"

"Thomas?"

What the hell is she talking about? Who is Thomas?

She's getting closer now, and those shears look sharp enough to cut through bone. Who does she think I am?

There's noise coming from behind me, but I can't tell what it is, and I refuse to take my eyes off the threat in front of me.

"I swear to you, I don't know anyone named Thomas."

"You lie!" she shouts, snapping the blades closed mere inches from the tip of my nose. I stumble backwards and fall flat on my ass.

A flash of light gray fills my vision, blocking my view of the shear-wielding pageant queen.

"Ethel, enough!" Winston bellows.

The gray has receded entirely from his features and limbs, and he's fully corporeal. It's not just his hand this time. It's all of him. I've never seen him like this before.

He's...holy shit. The man is stunning.

Like I suspected, he's tall. Definitely over six feet. His shoulders are broad, and his arms are thick with layers of muscle. My gaze follows the ripple of his back muscles to his trim waist, and down to his adorably tiny but tight ass. It looks like I could fit the whole thing in one hand. Like two firm plums, just begging to be squeezed.

He's wearing a billowy white shirt tucked into light brown tweed pants. The pants are tucked into black lace-up leather boots that look worn-in enough to be buttery soft. But the best part of his outfit, by far, are the suspenders.

I've only ever seen suspenders worn in a jokey, obnoxious kind of way, so I never found them attractive. However, the more I look at them crossing in the middle of his back and hugging his shoulders, the more I want to straddle him and hold on to those suspenders for dear life as I ride his dick.

Shit, what is wrong with me? Maybe I can chalk it up to the adrenaline of being almost attacked by the hot gardener.

"She's not here for Thomas, okay?" Winston explains to this Ethel person. "She's with me. This is Natalie. She's..." I hear him swallow, "my wife."

He turns to face me and offers a hand. I take it and whisper, "Your what now?" The scent of pine and woodsmoke wafts toward me as I stand, and it's so comforting, it feels like he's just wrapped me in a blanket.

"Go with it," he replies under his breath.

"Wife? Why have I never seen her here before?" Ethel demands, still holding the shears blades out.

"She just moved in. It's new," Winston says, not sounding convincing at all.

"We're very much in love," I add, popping my head out behind Winston's arm. Unfortunately, I don't sound convincing either. The adrenaline is making my voice shaky. "It's a p-pleasure to meet you, Ethel." I'm still frazzled from the proximity of the blades to my face before Winston arrived, but I take a breath and plaster on a bright smile, hoping it shows Ethel that I'm not a threat.

Winston slowly reaches out to her, softening his tone. "I assure you, I wouldn't let another woman looking for Thomas onto our property. You know that, right? Put the shears down, Ethel. Please."

She drops them next to a cluster of ripe jalapeños, the blades sinking into the dirt. "My heavens," Ethel says, fanning herself with her hand. "I'm sorry, Winston. I feel so foolish." Her eyes grow wide with confusion as she surveys the garden, and then the rest of the property. Is she looking for Thomas? Is Thomas even a real person? "You'll forgive me, won't you?"

"Of course. There's nothing to forgive. Just a mix-up," Winston assures her. "My wife and I are going for a stroll around the lake. Have a good day, Ethel."

Winston takes my hand and tugs me toward the woods behind the garden. I make a weak attempt to yank my hand back, but Winston's grip is too strong, plus, what am I going to do? Walk back to the house and pass by Ethel alone? No, thanks.

Once we make it inside the tree line and are hidden from Ethel's line of sight, I turn on Winston, ready to ream him for keeping Ethel a secret, but before I can, he pulls me into his arms and presses my head against his chest. "I'm sorry, Natalie," he says against my hair. His hand is cradling the back of my head, while the other is rubbing slow circles over my back. "Are you okay? Did she hurt you?" He pulls back to look me over, worry knitting his brows together.

I've never seen him so *afraid*. I wasn't sure it was an emotion he was capable of feeling, to be honest, but the way he's looking at me now wipes the anger from my mind, and makes my bones feel like they're starting to melt.

With such focused attention from him in his corporeal form, I can admire the boyish beauty of his face, without the gray mist blurring his features. The swirl of his green eyes stills me. Like I'm in a trance. The shade of green is closest to tourmaline, probably. A natural, plant-like green with hints of gold and dark gray, but with an unnatural heaviness that makes me wonder about his past. How I can help him overcome the pain that follows his every step.

His medium brown hair is swept neatly off his face, apart from one thick piece that falls in the middle of his forehead. His brows are thick and straight, making him look slightly annoyed all the time, which is a stark contrast to the softness of his eyes. He has a surprisingly straight nose, given the large bump on the bridge of it.

His lips are the real star here, though, with a plumpness that would inspire collagen injectors everywhere. In the center of those soft lips is a pointy Cupid's bow, the V so dramatic that I want to trace it with my finger.

I watch his jaw muscles leap as he continues to assess me, and I realize the reason he's starting to look even more concerned is because I've been eye-fucking him for who knows how long while he's been waiting for an answer.

"I'm fine," I tell him.

He's not buying it, though. He grips my arms, rubbing them up and down. "You're shaking. Come here."

I suck in a breath, surprised as he pulls me back into his strong embrace. I sink into him, letting him hold me as his lips press against my hair.

Tears prick at the corners of my eyes as I wonder how long it's been since I've been held like this. Too long. I'm greedy for this kind of intimacy. His arms feel so safe, like nothing harmful could reach me here. Like he's a mile-thick stone wall that not even grief could sneak past. A shiver rips through me at the feel of his breath on my ear, and he must think it's still the shock of the encounter with Ethel wearing off, because he pushes a lock of hair behind my ear and whispers, "Shh. It's okay. I've got you."

He's *got* me. Fuck, it feels good to hear someone say that.

As much as I want to stay here with him, my curiosity wins out. "I have questions," I say, pushing back enough to look up at him. "Who the hell is Ethel? Is she dead too? And this Thomas person, why does she think I'm sleeping with him?"

He sighs as he lets go and starts walking deeper into the woods. I follow along, eager to hear the tale he's about to tell. "Ethel lived here for about four years in the fifties. She and her husband, Thomas. They were newlyweds."

Winston shoves his hands into his pockets, his head hanging low as he continues. "I heard them talk about the kids they wanted to have, and what their names would be. They seemed incredibly happy, until he went off to war. That was about a year after they moved in, and suddenly, Ethel was all alone. No one ever came to visit. No family, or friends. I don't know. Maybe they were new to the area and didn't have anyone close by.

"Loneliness took hold of her and didn't let go. She started to drink. I'm pretty sure she had a sickness of the mind. A doctor would've written it off as female hysteria at the time, I'm sure. She didn't have the care or support she needed. Thomas would write her letters, but they were few and far between. Since she didn't have anyone else to talk to, there wasn't much keeping her away from the bottle. Gardening was the only thing that brought her joy."

I nod, understanding. "So she died here?"

"Yeah," he replies in a solemn tone. "One night, she mixed alcohol with pain medication her doctor prescribed her for migraines. She came outside to check on her garden. It was cold that night. Almost winter, if I recall. She laid down next to her marigolds and never woke up."

I don't know what to say. "That's awful."

"I could've intervened," he starts, his voice cracking with emotion. "I was nervous, about how she would react to my presence. I could've done...something, though."

Maybe that's true, but he'll never actually know if it would've helped, and given the haunted look in his eyes, he's still beating himself up about it, seventy-five years later. No one should hold on to guilt for that long. "You're doing something now," I tell him. "She may not have Thomas here, but she has you."

Something flashes across his gaze. Something that looks like yearning, but it's gone just as quickly. He runs a hand through his hair, mussing it up in a way that has me biting my lip.

"The worst part is, she died before Thomas returned." Winston stops and has a distant look in his eyes as he shakes his head. "I have no idea what happened to him. Because Ethel was gone, she was no longer his next of kin, so if he died in battle, they would've contacted his parents, or maybe his siblings to let them know. No one ever came here, and the house was sold less than a year after she died."

"Is that why she's so confused?" I ask.

Winston starts walking again, and I can hear the faint

babble of water flowing over rocks in the distance. We must be getting close to the lake.

"That's a bit more complicated," he says, rubbing a hand over his jaw. "When you die, it's important to have a link to who you were when you were alive. Not only do I have this house, but I have some of my belongings in the attic. I can look at them and remember."

"Ethel has her garden," I point out. "Is that not enough?"

"Not always. See, Ethel's memories from right before she died are clouded with booze and whatever it was that was plaguing her thoughts. She became paranoid near the end and had multiple theories as to why Thomas hadn't come home. There were days she was certain Thomas fell in love with someone else, or that he was being kept prisoner and couldn't write to her to let her know. There was even a brief time when she thought he wasn't really drafted and used the war as a cover to travel the world and accrue a string of mistresses.

"Most of the time, the garden is her sanctuary, and as long as she can tend it, she's happy and calm, but on the days she forgets she's even dead, or gets confused and locks onto one of those paranoid memories, there's nothing you can say to reason with her.

"I kept her photographs for her. Tucked them away in the attic before her belongings were cleaned out. I've tried showing them to her, you know, to strengthen that link between her life and death. She never wants to see them. It upsets her, I think, even considering that she and Thomas will never be reunited."

"That's so sad." I try to see this whole thing from Winston's point of view. It would be difficult to explain Ethel's situation to someone you don't know who's just moved in. That, I understand, but given how angry she was today, if he hadn't shown up when he did, what would've happened to me? Or Lindsay, if she were staying here instead? As much as my heart breaks for Ethel's story, I'm frustrated Winston didn't prepare me for what she's going through. "Why didn't you tell me?"

He scrubs a hand down his face, shame tightening his features. "I should've told you, and I'm sorry I didn't." He chuckles, startling me, as he says, "Truthfully, I didn't think it would be an issue, given how rarely you go outside."

My immediate instinct is to smack his arm, which I do. "That's not true!"

He gives me wicked side-eye. "Exclude the times you're walking from the house to the car."

Shit. I can't argue with him. "In my defense..." I begin, trying to come up with something reasonable. I land on, "the heat has been brutal, and you know, bugs."

He barks out a laugh, throwing his head back. The creases in his smile are so long they almost reach the crinkles of his eyes. And there's that dimple again. That heart-stopping dimple. "Excellent point. Bugs."

I laugh with him, even if just to release some of the tension from earlier.

"Ah, here we are," Winston says, speeding up toward the clearing. When we reach it, he turns to face me. "Now that that's behind us. Care for a swim? I need a reset."

"A reset?"

"Yeah, you don't feel like a new person after a bath or shower?"

"I do, it's just...I'm not wearing a bathing suit," I say, waving my hands in a polite decline.

"Neither am I. Who cares?"

I continue to protest, self-consciousness twisting my insides at the idea of swimming in my underwear, showing that much skin. Winston has stopped listening to me, though. He's too busy ripping off his clothes while striding purposefully toward the water.

Chapter 10
Winston

Natalie shoots me a puzzled frown when I step into the cool water of the lake with my underwear still on. Was she expecting me to swim in the nude? Is that what she wants? My cock twitches at the thought of her wanting to see me, wanting to touch me.

I can't be sure that's how she feels, and it's not a risk I'm willing to take. What if I try to kiss her and she pushes me away? I don't know how I'd be able to face her after that.

We shouldn't be coming anywhere close to kissing, anyway. We are roommates, not lovers. Her stay here is temporary, and mine is eternal.

I've given up on using Susanna as an excuse as to why I should keep my hands to myself. In truth, she hated me when she was alive and probably wouldn't have cared if I'd taken a lover during our marriage. She would've been relieved, in fact, to see my attention fall on someone other than her.

Something has shifted between us, though. I can feel it, and the way Natalie's cheeks redden when I smile at her, she must feel it too. Whatever *this* is, I must be patient until I know for sure that she returns my interest.

It was foolish of me to keep Ethel a secret from her. I convinced myself to wait for the perfect opportunity to reveal the truth, and that asking her to keep my existence and Ethel's a secret from Lindsay on the same day would be asking too much. *Wait a few days,* I told myself. Then a few days turned into a week, and it got easier and easier to keep the lie hidden.

Today, when I heard Ethel's violent shouts from the garden, I felt my world tilt on its axis. Natalie was in trouble, and if she were harmed, it would've been my fault. Just as Ethel's death was. Seeing that she hadn't been hurt, after calming Ethel down, I was so elated that I couldn't keep myself from touching her. Holding her.

I never expected Natalie to feel the way she did in my arms: *Perfect. Right.* As if her voluptuous curves were sculpted to fit against me and me alone. It made me wonder if I'd ever truly felt desire before I met her. I had sexual partners before marrying Susanna, but those encounters were quick and clumsy, until I learned the proper way to pleasure a woman.

By the time I met Susanna, I was more confident. I knew what I was doing. I longed to learn her body like only a good husband could, but she kept me at a distance. She didn't let me hold her often, but even in those moments, it felt different.

There was an innate wrongness with the way our bodies came together. Lovemaking was awkward, which can be expected in the beginning of a courtship, when you're still discovering the way your partner moves and what they like, but we never emerged from that initial phase. Rhythm and harmony evaded us in every way they could. Our sex was for procreation alone, and there wasn't a moment of rightness to it.

Natalie is the first woman I've held since Susanna, and I wasn't expecting the power her touch has over me. Even just being near Natalie's body, with her dimpled thighs and beautifully cushioned stomach, I feel like an inexperienced teenage boy. My dick is constantly hard. I had to make a concentrated effort to angle my hips away from her while I held her to keep from coming in my pants.

Is this...how it's supposed to feel? The way I hoped to feel with Susanna but never did?

I'm grateful for the cover of water the lake provides. I don't go in deeper than the top of my stomach, and even that feels too shallow once Natalie starts removing her black leggings. The smirk she gives me is shy, as she says, "Turn around. I'm not used to people seeing me in my underwear."

Jesus.

I turn around to give her privacy, but I have to tuck my cock into the waistband of my underwear to alleviate the throbbing ache that feels like it's never going to fade. Why did I suggest going for a swim? This is going to be torture, regardless of the amount of Natalie's bare skin I get to see. Whatever is hidden from my eyes, I'll be fantasizing about for days to come. If I make it out of the lake without spilling in my underwear, it'll be a fucking miracle.

"Ah, feels nice," she says, her melodic voice now right behind me. "I haven't gone swimming in ages."

"Uh, may I turn around now?" I ask, scrubbing a hand down my face.

She chuckles. "You may."

Natalie's body is mere inches from mine. The water kisses her square chin as she stands in the lake, her hands outstretched on both sides, waving through the gentle ripples we've created. Her brassiere is white, and the fabric is threadbare. It doesn't seem to offer much support, and the water has made it translucent.

Don't look at her nipples.

Don't think about her nipples.

"Such a spontaneous activity, Mr. Caraway," she says, casting me a look of suspicion. "And you're in such a pleasant mood. Where has this version of you been?"

I suppose that's fair. I haven't been the easiest or most pleasant to live with, nor was I trying to be. It felt safer to despise Natalie, to find reasons she's impossible to share oxygen with. This isn't a path I want to continue following, however. It's getting harder to resist the voice in my head that tells me to seek her out, to close the distance between us, and to acknowledge what a lucky bastard I am to merely be in her orbit. Getting to know each other should be the first step in improving our relationship as roommates.

"My last name isn't Caraway," I tell her.

Her eyebrow lifts. "No? But the sign on the house–"

"My wife, Susanna, it's her maiden name. Her father put that sign up. He was proud of their ancestral line, or rather, their obscene wealth, and he once told me that 'Duffy' is a common laborer's name that shouldn't be displayed anywhere."

She scoffs. "Didn't you build the house?"

"I did, but with his money," I admit, shame reddening my cheeks as I continue. "I was a shoeshine for the cobbler's shop on Main Street. Came from nothing. My family was dirt poor. I would've died that way, too, but I happened to be in the right place at the right time."

Natalie's eyes look like pools of melted chocolate as the midday sun shines down on her face. It makes her rapt attention feel like a gift. "What do you mean?"

Susanna's father grew tired of her lack of ambition. Often called her a lazy sack of hormones in front of me. Such a vile excuse for a man. "He wanted Susanna to get married and start having children. Really, he wanted an heir to the Caraway fortune, so he threatened to cut her off financially if she didn't get married and have a child by the end of that year," I tell her. "The next day, I was having a drink at the pub next to the cobbler's shop when she walked in." I shrug, still shocked by my dumb luck, and bitter from the knowledge that it was more of a curse. "She picked me out of the crowd, and we were married a week later."

"Wow. Fast courtship."

It's hard for me to look at Natalie now, knowing what I'm about to say next. So I don't. I focus on the blurry reflection of my face in the water instead. "I was dumb enough to think it was love at first sight, and lonely enough to ignore all the signs that told me I was merely a sperm donor."

"Yikes," she says, then scrunches her nose into a knowing expression. "You mocked her taste in music too, didn't you?"

The comment shocks me, and she must see it in my gaze as she splashes me with water, chuckling loudly.

"I'm kidding," she insists, coming closer as I wipe the lake water from my eyes. I notice her playful smirk and easy posture, and it makes me crave more of this side of her.

"That sucks, Winston. I'm sorry you were treated like that."

The way she says my name, with that gentle throatiness of hers, makes me wonder what she would sound like screaming it.

"It's in the past," I tell her, becoming increasingly aware of how much of my personal life I've revealed to her with very little prompting. How did she do that? How did she pull that information out of me? I didn't even speak of Susanna with Penelope. "Now, you go."

Her dark brows pull together in confusion.

I want to feel less alone in this. "You must know heartbreak. Not just familial loss, but romantic as well? Tell me your tales of woe. Make me feel like less of an ass."

"Oh yeah. Me and heartbreak are like this," she replies,

crossing her middle finger over her pointer. "There's no way you're a bigger fool than I am, okay? You were a married man trying to make your wife happy. I, on the other hand," she continues, clearing her throat, "sacrificed everything for a guy who didn't want me, and even when he was breaking up with me, telling me all the reasons he didn't love me anymore, I begged, *actually begged*, for him to stay."

Natalie huffs a breath as she shakes her head in disgust. "I don't carry many regrets from the past, but that one sticks—the begging. Feeling him totally shut down, outright rejecting me, and trying to hold on to him anyway. We weren't even married."

I wish I could say it's hard to believe that Natalie could love someone more than they love her, but I do believe it. I see how her face lights up when I do something mildly generous. When I made her a peanut butter and jelly sandwich, the way she looked at me... it was as if I had emerged from a burning building with her kitten in my arms.

It's obvious how little she thinks she deserves. How little she's used to getting. When she invited that diaper load of a human to the house for casual sex, it was as clear as day. She may have been lonely, but if she could see herself through my eyes, she never would've given that man a second glance, let alone allowed him to touch her.

Even thinking about that night fills me with simmering rage. The assumption that the person she's speaking of now is someone different isn't helping, either. I picture a man of similar stature to the one with the dirty fingernails, with the same lack of manners and unearned confidence. I wish I knew who he was, or could see a photo of him, so when I fantasize about the loud crack his spine would make when I snapped his neck, it would be a more accurate depiction. "What's his name?

The jackass who didn't love you the way you deserved. Tell me."

Natalie must sense my fury, because she places her hand in the middle of my chest and offers me a teasing grin. "You going to kick his ass for me, Ghost Man? How, when you can't even step past the property line?"

It's enough to pierce through my anger and pull a matching grin from me. "A lot of psychological damage can be done from afar, sweetheart. Isn't that the primary achievement of the internet?"

She nods, chuckling. "I suppose that's true, but you don't have to worry about that. Kyle can't hurt me anymore."

"What happened?" It's none of my business, and the deeper we go into this subject, the quicker my anger will return, but I opened up to her about Susanna, and I'm eager to know more about her life before she showed up at my door. "You don't have to talk about it if it's too painful."

Natalie heaves a sigh as she floats on her back. This angle provides me a perfect view of her dark pink nipples as they poke out of the water. The hardened tips look like they're begging for my mouth. I swallow hard and look away, but not before I notice her hand cup her lower belly in a way that tells me there's much more to this story.

"Yeah, let's not," she finally says. "I'm having a good time, which hasn't been the norm for me lately."

I understand, and the last thing I want to do is push her back into sadness when she's finally able to smile. In fact, I think I have a way to make that smile grow even bigger. "Come here."

Her gaze narrows, sizing me up. "Why?"

She doesn't trust me. Why would she?

"I want to show you something."

Natalie takes a hesitant step in my direction.

I open my arms, and gesture for her to come closer.

"What are you going to do?"

I let out a groan, pretending to be annoyed. "Do you think I'm going to hurt you? Give me a little credit, Natalie."

Her front teeth sink into her bottom lip as she considers whether I'm friend or foe. I can't help but smile the moment she decides to trust me. Her small hands are warm as she places them on my shoulders, yet a shiver rips through me, going straight to my balls.

"I'm going to lift you, okay? Wrap your legs around my waist."

"Oh, no. You don't have to. I don't want you to hurt yourself."

Is she serious? "Natalie, I'm dead. I can lift a car and toss it across the driveway. There's no way picking you up would hurt me. Got it?"

She nods, a hesitancy in her gaze that disappears when I haul her out of the water. She wraps her arms around my neck, and I breathe in her strawberry shampoo as I grip the back of her thighs. As she crosses her ankles at the small of my back, I forget what the point of this was.

I had a plan of some kind, didn't I? Now that she's in my arms, and I feel her nipples scrape against my bare chest, feel the heat of her pussy against my lower stomach, I can't think about anything other than pressing my lips to hers. Tasting her. Learning her. Branding her skin with my mouth.

"Now what?" she asks, shaking me from the fog of lust.

"Right. Okay, in three...two..."

"Wait, what?"

Before I reach one, I let my corporeal body fade into the misty shadow I became the moment my heart stopped beating, disappearing beneath her grasp.

Her arms flail as she plops into the water, and a second

later, she snaps back up, spluttering with laughter as she wipes water from her eyes. "Christ!" she shouts, looking a little angry, but mostly amused. "That was so strange." She pushes the wet hair off her face as she continues to look at me in awe. "It wasn't like diving into a pool, where, for half a second, you feel like you're flying. This was..." she trails off. "I mean, you were holding me, then I just dropped straight down, and even though it wasn't from high up, it felt like my stomach was going to shoot up through my throat."

I laugh as she looks from the water to me, back to the water. Her grin turns gleeful as she places her hand on my forearm.

"Do it again."

Knowing how easily she intoxicates me, I move quicker the second time, not allowing the heat of her core to settle against my stomach, but rather slipping into mist as soon as her heels touch my back. We continue this game twice more, with her giggle increasing in volume each time. My chest puffs a bit at the sight of her so carefree, knowing I gave her this. This brief respite from pain.

Our chests heave as we stand there, still chuckling about our silly game. Perhaps that's why we don't notice our bodies moving closer together of their own accord. Soon, I can feel her soft stomach pressing against mine. We're out of breath and smiling like idiots as her arms wrap around my neck.

I don't know if she leans up, or if I lean down, but the distance closes between us, the forest fades away, and our lips find their way to each other at last.

Chapter 11
Natalie

The kiss is slow at first, sensual, but there's clear hesitancy coming from both of us. Did I kiss him? Or did he kiss me? I can't remember how it happened, but I'm screaming on the inside that it did. Every part of him steals my breath, and for once, he's not actively trying to piss me off. He's been sweet and protective.

I wasn't expecting that.

Winston's tongue swipes along the seam of my lips, and I let him in. He tastes like bourbon, with a hint of vanilla. I wonder if that was the last drink he had before he died.

Then the kiss shifts from sweet to scorching. His hands are rough as the left grips my hair and the right splays against the middle of my back. I moan against his mouth, and he jerks back, giving me a look I can't decipher.

"What's wrong?" I ask, worried he regrets this and is about to end it.

He smiles, his eyes heavy-lidded with lust as he says, "Absolutely nothing, sweetheart. That sound you made. It's the most beautiful fucking thing I've ever heard."

I can feel the blood rushing to my cheeks, but before I can get embarrassed, Winston crushes his lips to mine once more, his mouth rough and hungry as he hauls me against him and into the air. I promise myself that I'll punch him in the dick if he chooses this moment to disappear and drop me again, but that never happens.

At one point, he strides deeper into the water until it reaches my shoulders, then he removes one arm from around my waist and cups my cheek so tenderly I feel tears prick behind my eyelids. I don't think I've ever been kissed like this before. I've never felt so desired and cherished at the same time.

He nips at my bottom lip, and I suck in a breath, my chest arching into his. My hands find their way to his hair, and I revel in the silkiness of each strand as my fingers run through it. "You have no idea how many times I've wanted to do this," he rasps.

"I thought you hated me," I whisper against his lips.

Winston pulls back to look at me. Shame fills his gaze as his mouth forms a frown. "I've never hated you, Natalie. Not for one second."

Our bodies melt together as his lips make their way along my jaw, then my neck, then my collarbone.

"Winston," I whimper, my hands still traveling freely over his body. His biceps, the dusting of soft light brown hair on his chest, tracing the V of his stomach, the muscles tightening beneath my fingers. I'm kissing someone with a six-pack. With a beautiful face and mouth-watering body. How did that happen? I could grow addicted to this. To *him*. The feel of him. The taste of him. The smell of him. The combination makes me feel drunk.

Is that how I should feel about my roommate, though? My centuries-old ghost roommate, that is. Are we entering messy territory here?

His hand brushes against my breast, then down to my side, where he lets his fingers stroke across my belly.

Fear makes my blood run cold. Instinctively, I wince and yank out of his arms, swimming backward as I put distance between us.

Why did he do that? I've never had a partner touch me there. Not lovingly, anyway. During the best sexual encounters I've had, my stomach was ignored. That's what I'm used to.

The cruel voice in my head wants me to think he was mocking me, like my classmates did throughout middle and high school.

Winston's lips are swollen from our kiss as he gives me a confused glare. "What is it?"

"Nothing," I quickly reply. What am I supposed to say? Tell him that he touched my stomach, and it sent me plummeting into a dark hole of self-loathing? I've spent years trying to deprogram the negative thoughts and forget the hurtful comments made about my body, and for the most part, I like my shape. Since this is the only body I'll ever have, I know I need to be kind to it. The negative thoughts are especially hard to ward off when there's an unexpected trigger, like a hot ghost touching my belly while his tongue flicks my earlobe, for instance.

His jaw tics as he steps toward me. "No, it's not nothing. Did I do something wrong? Something you didn't like?" His face falls, and knowing I put that agonized expression there makes me feel like a pile of shit.

"No," I begin, trying to figure out how to explain something that fills me with such shame, "it's not that, I just—"

His large hand wraps around my arm, his strong grip loosening to a gentle hold. "Tell me, Natalie." Winston's voice is pleading, and it shatters my resolve.

"Okay, so I have a hard tim——" A high-pitched jingle cuts

through the silence of the forest, interrupting me. It's the alarm on my phone, blaring from the beach, and saving me from having to put these complicated feelings into words.

"I need to get ready. That alarm means I have an hour before work starts."

He sighs heavily, running a hand through his wet hair. "Fine. Let's head back."

We get dressed, and Winston doesn't say another word on our walk back to the house. Neither do I. Luckily, Ethel is long gone by the time we pass the garden shed, so at least there won't be any more murder attempts today.

He follows me up the stairs and stops at the door to my bedroom. We stand there, looking at our feet, like two teenagers at the end of a first date, not knowing what to say, and I hate myself for crossing this line with him. Things between us were improving. He still bugged the hell out of me, but he was a tolerable roommate. Why did he have to kiss me and make it weird? Or wait, did I kiss him?

"Well, I'm going to shower," I say. "Thanks for, uh, saving my life today, with Ethel."

"Oh, yeah," he says, as if he'd forgotten all about it. Then he puts his hands in his pockets and gives me a lopsided grin. "Anytime."

My hand is on the doorknob when he grabs me by the elbow, spinning me around, and I stop short of slamming into the wide expanse of his chest. "Natalie," he rasps.

I shouldn't look up. Up is where those captivating green eyes are, and that soft, perfect mouth of his. But I can't resist. "Yes?" I reply, breathless.

He opens his mouth to say something, then looks away with a wince. It feels like an hour passes before his gaze meets mine again. "Good luck tonight."

"Right. Thanks."

Then he turns on his heel and heads up the stairs to the third floor, turning into that gray mist before he reaches the top step.

I blow out a breath once I'm inside my room, giving myself a beat to process what just happened. Then, I immediately try to forget, because that was easily the hottest kiss I've ever had, and if I want to get through my first day of work at the bar, I need to get Winston and his perfect lips out of my head.

* * *

My first shift is relatively slow at first. I don't mind that one bit, since it takes me a few tries before I learn how to use the tablet register thingy to input orders. Vyla, the orc bartender on staff tonight with me and Dominic, shows me how to mix a Ghastly Megan, a Fuzzy Doug, and a Slurpy Steve on the Rocks, which are their three most popular signature cocktails.

"Who came up with these drink names?" I ask Vyla. Her silky black hair is tied back into several neat Viking-esque braids that reach the middle of her back, and the overhead lights make the intricate purple tattoo on her face look like it's shimmering. The tusks that jut out of her mouth are just as intimidating as her massive biceps, and I couldn't be happier about sharing a shift with her. No one is going to fuck with me as long Vyla is by my side.

She snickers as she pours a Mapletown Mule into the copper mug in front of her, before adding a lime wedge to the rim. "That would be Riz," she says, referring to Rizlan, the dragon-shifter bartender I have yet to meet. "He finds human names amusing, so when he was building the drink menu, he included the most basic names he could think of."

"That's adorable," I reply, jotting down the recipe to the Mapletown Mule in my notebook so I can refer to it later. "So that was one shot apple cider and one tablespoon of maple syrup? Or was it two tablespoons?"

"One shot, two tablespoons." She delivers the drink to the shy gargoyle at the end of the bar. He's been here for two hours and has barely spoken. Vyla told me he owns the bookstore, Tome Time, in the center of town.

Vyla must catch me eyeing him because she whispers, "Interested in Clark? He's *very* good in bed. Want me to put a good word in for you? We used to be neighbors."

Panic dries up my throat as I say, "Oh, no. That's not necessary."

Her eyebrows lift at my quick dismissal. "Are you seeing someone?"

"No, no, it's not that." It's not...right? Even if I didn't pull away from Winston's kiss earlier, it's not like we're dating. Technically, we can't even go on a date, since he can't leave the grounds. We're nothing. Just roommates who kissed.

I'd be lying if I said I didn't have a crush on him, though. Can forty-somethings still have crushes? It feels like a term I'm much too old for, but what else would I call it?

Even before the kiss, I was thinking about him a lot—his lips, those strong hands, that deep rumbling voice. And fucking hell, that body of his. He doesn't look like a bulky gym rat. His muscles look like they were built from manual labor, rescuing damsels in distress, that kind of thing. Lean, but expertly efficient. A boyish face with the body of a *man*.

"Oh, are you queer?" Vyla asks, pulling me out of Winston-filled haze. "I am too! Most of the town is pan, actually."

"That's so cool," I tell her. "But no, I'm straight."

"Aw," she says with a sympathetic frown as she pats my shoulder, "sorry, babe."

I laugh. "Yeah, thanks."

She starts listing everyone in Mapletown that she's had sex with, and whether she recommends them as sexual partners. At one point, Dominic takes a break from beer inventory to gently scold her for gossiping. Vyla brushes him off, and I half expect her to reveal she's slept with him too once he's out of earshot. She must read my expression because she shakes her head without me asking.

"I wish," she says. "Him and his ex have been off and on for years. They're off right now, but I haven't seen him show an interest in anyone else."

"Who's his ex? Has he or she been in here yet?"

"No, she's a succubus. You'll probably meet her tonight, though. Whenever there's a softball game, the winners come grab a drink here after."

That doesn't end up happening. Apparently, Dominic's infamous ex plays for the team that lost tonight, and they don't make an appearance. The winning team, however, piles into the bar covered in dirt and eager to celebrate their victory at quarter-to-six. The Big Bloomers are sponsored by the town florist, and according to Xavier, the burly werewolf who plays first base, they "crushed the Sweet Tsunami's into motherfucking oblivion."

"Wow, was it a shutout?" I ask him as I pour a dozen tequila shots for him and the rest of the team.

"Nah, they got a few runs in, but we blew them out of the pahk. A grand slam and three homahs."

His Boston accent is thicker than my waist, and it instantly calms my nerves. It reminds me of family gatherings with my mom's side of the family on Cape Cod.

"You're new here, aren't you?" he asks.

Xavier's hazel eyes are kind as he watches me from behind his glasses. He's got wavy reddish-brown hair that falls over his forehead, and a smattering of freckles on his nose and cheeks. The man is built like a tank, big and wide all over, with a softness to his middle that makes me think he's an excellent hugger.

"Is it that obvious?"

He chuckles. "Very. Mostly because you're human. We don't get too many of you in Mapletown."

I would guess he's around my age, but werewolves might age slower. Vyla gave me a detailed rundown of the different monsters I might meet tonight, but there's still a lot I don't know about each species.

Scanning the bar, I see a wide range of them milling about, including vampires, satyrs, a Minotaur couple, a harpy, several gorgons, zombies, a gargoyle, and the rest appear to be human, which makes me think only a couple are actually human, and the rest are either witches or shifters.

No part of me is afraid, which might be because none of them seem to notice me. They're minding their business, enjoying a drink after winning a softball game. Not one of them appears to want to eat me, so that's good. Just regular folks looking to blow off some steam.

Xavier thanks me for the shots with a wink and carries the shot glasses in his giant hands as he walks gingerly to the booth near the front doors.

I notice the garnish tray is low, so I start cutting lime wedges before the next rush begins. Dominic calls me to the end of the bar a few minutes later, where a short woman in a crisp baby-blue pantsuit is sitting. Instead of heels, she's opted for white sneakers, giving her an approachable, sensible vibe. She's sipping a Guinness from a frosty pint glass as she wraps one of her long, black ringlet curls around her finger.

"Natalie Lambert, meet Mayor Emma Crane," Dominic says with his winning smile. "Mayor Crane, this is our new bartender, Natalie."

"Ah, yes. The famous Natalie," Mayor Crane says as she holds out her hand. "I've heard a lot about you." She watches me carefully as I shake it, as if she's trying to decide something.

I chuckle nervously. "You've heard about me? Nothing bad, I hope."

"I promise, I've been singin' your praises," Dominic vows as he reaches for a wet glass to dry with the towel on his shoulder.

"I know the name of every person who enters Mapletown," Mayor Crane adds. "I also know the exact date and time when they arrived."

Okay, that's not ominous or anything. "How?"

She nods to the phone sitting beside her glass. "Your phone. It's some kind of high-tech GPS tracker my chief of staff, Ezra, created. I don't know much about it. Anyone who crosses town limits, we can access the data on their phone."

"That seems like a breach of privacy." Has the mayor seen the nudes I sent Mark last year? Or the litany of dick pics he's sent back? My cheeks grow hot as I try to recall the other potentially embarrassing stuff on my phone. Like that time I searched for a Thor-shaped pillow with arms that I could wrap around myself. Or when I googled "Can you tickle yourself?" on a night I was feeling particularly sleep-deprived and depressed.

Mayor Crane shoots me a proud grin. "Oh, it definitely is."

I swallow the lump in my throat as my palms begin to sweat. "So, you can see *everything* on our phones?"

"Technically, yes, but we're not searching through your private messages and stealing photos if that's what you're worried about. It's a program that scans the contents of your phone and looks for things aligned with typical human behavior."

That makes me feel a little better, I guess. "Like what?"

"Oh, you know," she says, drumming her freshly painted red nails on the bar as she ponders this, "period trackers, food and exercise trackers, and most of the games in the app store that claim to be free." She leans in, lowering her voice, "No offense, but humans tend to be more gullible than most monsters. Especially when agreeing to give away personal information in exchange for a game that just overheats your phone."

I'm relieved that none of those are on my current phone. Or...wait. I deleted that old period tracker, didn't I?

"Unfortunately, we've been burned too many times in the past to trust humans. Too many have tried to harm us or expose us. It's easier this way. And it *would* go against the federal privacy laws, except that Mapletown doesn't adhere to federal laws. It's considered protected enchanted land, so the town is governed by a committee of monsters."

"Shit. Really?"

It's like they live outside of space and time. In their own little world—a world I'm eager to remain part of.

She nods. "The rule used to be that humans can enter Mapletown with an invite from a resident, and since it doesn't show up on digital maps, that invitation would be your only way in. That's the mandate my great-grandmother created anyway."

"Right," I reply. "Martha Crane."

Mayor Crane smiles as her gaze drops to the bar top. "She was a brilliant witch. When she cast the spell to protect Mapletown, however, she didn't anticipate how much the town would grow over time. I think there were only a couple hundred people here back then. Now, the population is almost fifteen hundred. We've had to adapt accordingly."

I have so many questions, and the one that pops out is by far the dumbest. "Does that mean you're a witch too?" Of course, she is. Why did I even ask? "I mean, do you still practice?"

She nods. "Indeed. I wouldn't be an effective mayor if I didn't. The town is run by magic, and the committee wouldn't give me access to the portals if I were no longer practicing."

"I'm sorry, did you say portals?"

Chapter 12
Natalie

Mayor Crane did indeed say portals. She spent the next hour of my shift telling me all about the portals that connect the monster towns across the U.S. There are seven including Mapletown: Redwood Cove in California, Pine Hollow in Colorado, Elmwood Falls in North Dakota, Magnolia Village in Louisiana, Hemlock Hollow in Michigan, and Cedar Grove in South Carolina. Our portal is located beneath the bookstore on Main Street, and the mayor is the only one who has access to it. It allows her to travel to the other towns within seconds for council meetings or trade deals with other mayors. She also oversees resident transfers via the portal, which allows safe and speedy travel for monsters looking to relocate.

My mind is still reeling over this as I pull into the driveway at the end of the night. The moment Mayor Crane paid her tab and left, I couldn't wait to get home and tell Winston. I know we left things on kind of an awkward note earlier, but this is going to blow his damn mind, and I'm hoping it's enough for us to brush past the weirdness and go back to being roommates who playfully bicker over random shit.

I grab my purse from the backseat and notice the gift I forgot to give Winston the other day. He's either going to think it's lame or cute, and I'm okay with either, given how little I spent on it.

He tends to hover in the living room or the kitchen whenever I return home, but tonight, I find the first floor of the house eerily silent. Kicking off my shoes, I hang my purse on the hook by the front door and head upstairs. My room is completely dark, as is Nonna Penny's old room, but there's a dim light coming from the study. I follow it and find Winston seated in the high-back velvet chair, the emerald-green cushions slightly faded from where the sun streams into the room. The desk lamp is on, and a few of the candle sconces are lit, casting shadows across his jaw that make him look even more handsome than usual. His forehead is scrunched as he focuses on the book in his lap.

A floorboard creaks under my feet as I enter the room, and our eyes meet. For the briefest of moments, his face lights up, and in his gaze, I see reverence and hunger—the same intoxicating combo from when he kissed me. But he must remember how we left things before I went to work, because his lips quickly flatten into a line, and his gaze drops to the page he's on. "Welcome home," he mutters. His tone is cold, standoffish.

"H-Hi," I say, not knowing what to do with the excitement I still feel at coming home to him, paired with the look of obvious displeasure.

"How was your first shift?"

"Um, great," I tell him. "I met a lot of the monsters in town. They were all very friendly and patient with me. Nothing like the day I went out job hunting. I'm guessing now that I have a job in town, I won't be seen as a sketchy outsider."

Winston turns the page of his book, as if I'm not even here. I could take this as a hint to leave, but I'm eager to fix things between us, so I keep blabbing about my night. "I met the mayor. She's Martha Crane's great-granddaughter, Emma Crane. Did you know that?"

He doesn't answer.

"She seemed nice, told me all about the secret portals that connect the monster towns across the country. Can you believe that shit? Actual portals. Like, you step inside and poof! You've arrived."

Still nothing as he turns another page.

"She invited me to the town meeting in a few days. I guess they have one every month at the Pebblebrook Inn."

He scratches his chin as he continues to ignore me, and my patience evaporates. I decide to fuck with him a bit, to see if he's listening. "And apparently after the town meeting ends, they put on some Sugar Ray, and it turns into a wild orgy."

His gaze doesn't meet mine, but instead of on the page, now it's on the floor. I see his jaw tic and his knuckles are turning white as he clutches the book in his hands.

Finally, a reaction. He's still not talking, but I can see it affecting him.

"I wonder what I should wear. What does one wear to an orgy? Should I just walk in naked?"

His knee begins to bounce up and down. Time to land this plane.

"I'm in charge of bringing the chili mac and cheese, since it's an orgy slash potluck."

Winston scoffs. "Since when do you cook?"

I toss the broom at his feet. "That's the part you question? Seriously?"

He grabs the broom off the floor, examining the blue handle

and matching bow I tied around the top, and the handwritten label that says, "Winston's Special Outdoor Broom."

Letting out a heavy sigh, he leans the broom against the side of the chair as he gets to his feet. "Natalie, I want to tell you something." He looks down at the book in his hand, then at the chair behind him before patting his pockets with confusion twisting his features. "I just need to find my bookmark. Hold on." The more he searches, the more visibly upset he becomes. "Where did I put it?"

"It's not a big deal, Winston. Just fold the corner of the page down."

He stops, leveling me with a venomous glare. "What? Why on earth would I do that?"

I shrug. "You can just unfold it when you're done using it to mark the page."

Winston jerks back as if I slapped him. "What kind of miscreant would defile a book by damaging the delicate pages instead of using a bookmark?"

I can't help but chuckle at his theatrics. "Okay, this is an absurd overreaction. You know that, right?"

"Is it, though?" he asks, sarcasm dripping from his tone. His gaze drifts over my shoulder, out into the hall and toward my room. "Do you... Have you done this to any of the books from this room?"

Ugh, I hate that I actually feel ashamed to say yes. Folding down pages instead of using a bookmark is a preference. Just like pizza toppings. The fact that I'd rather fold doesn't make me as inherently evil as Winston is making me seem. Yet, I can feel the blood rushing to my cheeks as he glares at me. I'm so busted.

"Unbelievable!" he shouts as he turns into mist and whips around me toward my bedroom.

"Hey!" I call out after him, trying not to slip on the smooth hardwood floors in my sock feet as I follow. "What the hell?" Winston is back in his corporeal form as he scans every surface in my room.

"A-ha!" He grabs the two paperbacks off my nightstand and holds them above his head, well out of my reach. "You'll get these back once you've learned how to properly respect a book."

"Are you fucking twelve years old?" I jump and scramble to grab them out of his hand, but he's too damn tall.

He wags a finger in my face. "Nuh-uh-uh. This is for your own good. And for the good of all literature."

I sink down into a squat before leaping as high as I can, and while it does get me a little higher, it's still not close enough to reach the books, and I stumble into Winston as I land on my feet. I'm not sure what's happening as we struggle to regain our footing. The books thump on the floor somewhere behind me as Winston wraps his arms around me and whirls us around until my back slams against the wall, his hand cradling the back of my head to protect me from the impact.

We're slightly out of breath, our faces just inches apart. The books forgotten, the only thing I can focus on now is the distance between Winston's lips and mine. He brings both hands to either side of my head and presses them against the wall, caging me in. "Um," is what I manage to squeak out, but I have no idea what I was about to say, or even what I want to say.

"Natalie," he says, a low rasp. His expression is serious but tender. "I wanted to..."

"I'm sorry about earlier," I blurt, cutting him off. I haven't been able to stop thinking about how I pulled away and didn't explain why. Being at the bar was a nice distraction, but Winston needs to understand that it had nothing to do with him. "When I pulled away...at the lake." I clear my throat. "It was because you touched my stomach. It caught me off guard, and it, I don't know, put me in a weird headspace."

I become entranced by the sight of his tongue darting out as he licks his lips. His gaze is intense as he says, "Please explain."

"I-I've struggled to accept that part of my body, so when you tou—"

"I touched your stomach because I love it," he says, cutting me off. "Your stomach, your eyes, your ass, those lips—every single part of you is fucking perfect, Natalie. I haven't been able to think about anything else since the day you moved in. All I want to do is touch you."

"I..." I don't know what to say to that. I thought I bugged the shit out of him.

He takes a step back to look me up and down. "I don't know who made you feel like there's something wrong with your body, but I find you quite dazzling."

The anxious part of my brain wants to dismiss it as a line to get me to sleep with him, or just a lovely sounding lie to make me feel better. But I can't deny the hunger in his eyes. Winston makes me feel desired, and that's an entirely new feeling.

Even when Kyle and I were at our happiest, it felt like he was overlooking parts of me he didn't like to maintain the status quo in our relationship. The lights were always turned off during sex, doggy-style and reverse cowgirl were his favorite positions, and when I shopped for bathing suits, he'd always push me toward the one-pieces. I'd never connected those dots before, and maybe I'm overthinking it, but Winston wanting to touch my stomach because he actually likes that part of me paints these memories in a new light.

"So, I was okay?" Winston asks, shaking me from my memories of Kyle. His expression is shy as he waits for my answer. He rubs the back of his neck nervously. Winston is a tree of a man, but right now he looks like a lost little boy. Shy

Winston is probably the most charming version I've seen thus far.

"You mean the kiss? It was better than okay. It was," —I sigh heavily as I remember how hot it was, how wet it made me—"incredible."

He smiles as his gaze dips to the floor. "I thought I did it wrong. Or not the way people do it nowadays. It's been over a century since I've kissed anyone."

I chuckle at his admission, relieved that I wasn't the only who spent the evening obsessing over it. "I can assure you that your kissing game is still very strong."

I reach out to pat his arm, but he grabs my wrist and pulls me against him.

"Natalie," Winston rumbles, and fuuuuck me, that voice alone makes my pussy clench. He pulls my hand up to his face and presses my fingertips against his lips. "I want to do it again. Will you let me?"

I practically melt where I stand. Who knew seeking consent could sound so hot?

"Yes," I mutter. My voice oozes with desperation, but I don't even have time to feel embarrassed before Winston's mouth crashes into mine, hot with need. Our teeth gnash against each other at first, but then we find a rhythm, our tongues dancing, twisting as he walks us over to my bed. I push the suspenders off his shoulders and pull his shirt free from the rigid tuck it's always in. "Take this off."

His laugh is husky as he follows my command, tossing the shirt behind him.

"Mm," I moan as I run my hands along his chest, then his abs, tracing every dip and curve of his muscled upper body, eager to learn it. "You are also quite dazzling, you know."

He kisses me long and deep, then presses his forehead against mine as he whispers, "Glad you think so."

A shiver rips through me as his hands cup my breasts, lifting them, testing the weight, then rubbing both nipples into hardened peaks through my shirt. "What's this?" he asks, eyeing a stain in the center of my t-shirt.

"I spilled a shot of rum."

He shakes his head, an amused expression softening his features. "How can one person be so messy?"

"I came out of the womb knocking shit over. What about you? How can one person be so stubborn?"

Winston's face falls. "I wasn't always like this. Neatness was the only way I could show I belonged. Like I was one of *them*. That, and speaking eloquently with an authoritative tone. I was told that these behaviors would fool enough people in their social circles into thinking I came from wealth."

Them? "Your wife and her family?"

He nods. "I didn't have money, or class, but if I kept things tidy, and lost my cool when they weren't, they'd treat me like I almost fit in. Stomping around looking for someone to yell at seemed to be my ticket in with the wealthy white men in the area."

"The path many mediocre white men take to the top," I add.

I wrap my arms around his neck and pull him close, rubbing the tip of my nose against his. "You can be as messy as you want around me."

He looks skeptical. "I might be too far gone. Old habits die hard, or so I've heard."

"That's okay, too. Just be who you are. Be you. That's who I want."

"And what if who I am," he pauses, tracing a finger along my jaw. The green of his eyes darkens as he stares at my mouth, "is a man aching to taste you?"

The mattress hits the back of my legs, and I fall onto it, lying back. He drops to his knees in front of me.

"Take off your clothes, Natalie."

His gaze remains locked on my body as I remove my shirt, then my pants. Any self-conscious thoughts that pop into my head are easy to ignore under his heavy-lidded gaze. It feels like a caress. He doesn't skip over my tummy, either, like Kyle used to. Winston's attention is focused on every jiggle and roll as I remove my bra.

"Fuck," he groans as he takes me in. "You are *marvelous*."

He crawls over me, and I suck in a breath as his lips close around my nipple. My back arches and my fingers get tangled in his hair as I hold him against my chest. I feel his tongue flick against it, sending a jolt of electricity down to my toes. His hand works my other breast, squeezing it and plucking my nipple until it aches in the most delicious way.

"Yes," I whimper, my nails digging into his scalp. I'd worry about hurting him, but he's dead already. Plus, with his grip tightening and the way he's growling against my chest, I think he likes it.

His mouth moves to the other breast, giving it equal attention, and my clit throbs. God, I want all of him right now, but I don't want to rush this. I want to let him worship me with his mouth. I deserve to be worshiped. Every woman does, and I can't even remember the last time I was, so it's my turn, and I'm taking it.

Winston releases my nipple with a soft pop, and moves down between my breasts, leaving soft, tender kisses along my skin. He pauses before reaching my stomach. "I want to kiss you here, Natalie. May I? Please?"

"How could I deny a begging man?" I say with a teasing grin.

He shoots me that winning smile, that incredible dimple

emerges and I feel like I've been given a gift. Perhaps it's this moment, or maybe it's just him. Sure, he may act like a cranky old man most of the time, but there are so many other layers to Winston. I'm eager to peel each one away to see what I'll discover next.

His hands stroke over my belly, his lips following suit, and I prop myself up on my elbows so I don't miss a moment. He's taking his time as he kisses up and down and around my belly button, telling me without words how much he adores this part of me. Seeing it, the way he's caring for me, I start to believe him. Tears sting my eyes, but I blink them away before they can ruin the moment.

His fingers trace the edge of my underwear, and he dips between my legs, running his nose along my seam as he takes a deep inhale. "You smell so fucking good." Quickly, he pulls my underwear down my legs and tosses it aside. "Open wider for me," he commands, his palms pressing against the insides of my knees. "Let me see all of you."

For someone who was worried he forgot how to kiss, he clearly remembers how to do everything else. He's so confident. Determined.

His pupils expand as he spreads the lips of my pussy. "You're so wet, Natalie. Is this all for me?"

He doesn't let me respond before he runs his tongue from the bottom of my seam to my clit, making my body buck. He chuckles, the sound reverberating through my clit as he laps at my center. I cry out, my body already shaking. We've only just begun. It usually takes me forever to orgasm.

There's always that part at the beginning where I need to tell myself to relax and get out of my head so I can actually enjoy it. Then the part where I wonder how I look from that angle, and if my lower half has been properly groomed. After that passes, I start to get into it.

But Winston has me skipping those stages, and I can feel my climax starting to build at the base of my spine. If I had known a ghost could get me off this fast, I would've been summoning spirits with a Ouija board every night instead of swiping through dating apps.

"You taste amazing," he whispers between licks. "I knew you'd taste divine, but this... *Fuck*."

When his head dips back down between my thighs, he devours me like a ravenous beast.

Chapter 13
Winston

I never knew it could be like this. Natalie is glorious, her pussy glistening with her come, her lips swollen and pink from my mouth—the sight is breathtaking. I can't stop licking her, sucking her. Her skin is so hot and smooth, except for the short curls covering her mound, but those carry her incredible scent, so I can't resist shoving my nose into them and breathing her in. The flavor of her arousal is a heady mix of sweet and tangy, and I want to drink her down. Every last drop.

My pants grow uncomfortably tight as my dick turns into a steel rod. Natalie lets out a whimper, and I swear it goes straight to my balls. The sounds she makes, dear god. Each time those luscious lips part, I feel like I'm shoved to the edge of a cliff, dangerously close to falling over the side.

Her juicy thighs quiver against my cheeks as I thrust my tongue into her channel, using my fingers to play with her clit. She gasps, her perfect teardrop tits bouncing as her back arches for me. I love watching her, lost to the pleasure I'm giving her. Part of me—a large part of me—wants to make her addicted to me, to my hands, my tongue, and my dick, ruining her for other men.

If I'm honest with myself, I don't want her to even look at other men. It's the caveman in me, and I know Natalie wouldn't be pleased to hear how possessive I'm becoming of her I'm. She's a modern woman, and based on the stickers covering her folding computer, she's also a feminist.

But I don't care. She's mine. Every part of her belongs to me, and I want to be the one responsible for satisfying her every need.

"*Ohh, yes,*" she pants, her small hands fisting the comforter beneath her as she cants her hips.

I thrust my tongue harder, showing her the intensity and cadence I wish to provide once it's my cock inside her wet heat instead of my tongue.

"More," she cries.

Using my thumb, I draw circles around her clit, pressing harder on the left side, which I've noticed is the side that makes her moan a little louder, makes her knuckles turn a little whiter as she fists the blanket.

I decide to swap my tongue and my fingers, knowing how much better I can make her feel this way. My cheeks are soaked with her nectar. She's dripping for me. It's perfect. She's perfect.

I don't bother testing her body with one finger at this point. She can take two. Slowly, I insert my pointer and middle fingers, and she proves me right, the walls of her pussy squeezing and pulling me in, slick enough to take my fingers easily. My good girl. I can't wait to be inside her fully, hip to hip.

My tongue flicks against the hood of her clit, tracing along the edges of her labia. I curl my fingers inside her pussy as I suck on her clit, seeking that place deep inside that will make her lose control. Swirling my tongue around and around, I can tell she's close.

"D-don't stop, oh fuck. Oh fuck!" she screams, her hips rocking faster against my face as her walls flutter around my fingers erratically.

I thrust against the side of the bed; I can't help it. The feel of her. The sight of her. She's too exquisite. I pinch my eyes shut and try to envision mundane, unsexy things to keep from coming in my pants. Cleaning damp leaves out of the gutter. Ethel attempting to carry a tune while gardening, and the awful screech when she gets to a high note. The mice infestation I discovered in the attic two years ago.

Natalie's breath gets caught in her throat, and my eyes fly open. Her movements are becoming erratic, which fans the flames of my desire.

"Yes, sweetheart," I pant against her clit, "come for me."

As if waiting for my command, she unravels at my words. The walls of her pussy grip my fingers like they're never going to let me go. The pressure of her cunt is so delicious I struggle to breathe. I hope I stay stuck like this forever. Her legs kick out, and her entire body jerks as her breath lodges in her throat. A thin coat of sweat makes her body shimmer, like her skin was made from stardust.

I follow her into the abyss, moaning against her cunt as hot come fills my underwear. Giving her pleasure is as close to heaven as I've gotten in the hundred and some odd years since I died. It might be all I ever get, and that would be enough.

"Wow," she says, breathless, letting out a soft chuckle. "That was amazing."

I suck the rest of her sweet come off my fingers before I crawl up her body and settle in at her side, pushing damp curls off her forehead and tucking them behind her ear. She gazes up at me in awe, her features soft and sleepy.

Her hand goes to the button of my pants. "Your turn," she says, tugging at the loose waistband.

I grab her wrists, stopping her. "That's okay, really. Tonight wasn't about me."

Her brow furrows. "What? But I want to."

"Well," I clear my throat, gesturing down to my crotch.

She notices the large wet spot, and her big brown eyes widen. "Oh."

"I came right after you." Perhaps I should be embarrassed, coming in my pants like a pubescent boy seeing his first naked breast, but I feel the opposite. There was no way I could watch Natalie come undone and not follow her. My body feels languid and settled, my mind matching it. The only regret I carry is that my come is soaking through my pants, and not covering her beautiful tits and stomach. Or, even better, filling that tight pussy until it leaks back out onto her thighs.

Next time.

I wrap my arms around her, pressing her cheek to my chest. "You're so cold."

"Ah," I say, starting to extricate myself from her. "That would be the whole *dead* thing. I'm sorry if it's unpleasant."

She looks up at me, her big brown eyes pleading. "No, don't you move. I like it. It's cooling me off." Natalie lets out a contented sigh.

I lay back down, relieved she isn't frightened or put off by the otherness of my body.

"Did you want to change clothes?"

"No," I say. "Once I shift out of my corporeal form, the stain will be gone. But that would mean I'd have to let you go, and I would return to this form fully clothed."

She grunts, her gaze heated as it moves from my bare chest down to my stomach. "We can't have that. Fuck it. Bring that wet spot over here."

I laugh. "I'm already here, sweetheart."

Natalie grabs the side of my hip and tugs me closer, tossing her leg over mine and tucking her head into the crook of my neck. "Better."

I press a kiss to her forehead as I run my fingers down her spine. She smells so good like this, the strawberries present but muted against the sweet scent of sex. It's intoxicating.

Her breaths quickly even out, and I wonder if she truly fell asleep that fast. Carefully, I lean back to turn off the light on her nightstand, trying not to jostle her body too much.

"Stay until I fall asleep?" she asks, her tone surprisingly timid, given that my face was just buried in her pussy. "Unless you need to go. I'd understand."

My sweet Natalie. Hoping for the bare minimum of decency and expecting half of that. She has no idea how tightly I'm already wrapped around her finger. I plan to raise the bar of what she deserves myself, spoiling her with every comfort she's ever desired. If she'll let me. "I'll stay as long as you want me to."

She lets out a little sigh of relief, her warm breath fanning my chest. "Thank you."

In my arms, I feel her muscles relax, one by one, as she falls asleep, and her soft snores fill the room.

I stay for another hour, maybe more, just holding her, loving the way she fits against me. There are moments when her brows pinch together and her hand grips my side, and I wonder if she's caught in a bad dream. I lightly kiss her nose, and her grip loosens, as if she needed to know that I'm still here before returning to restful slumber.

Eventually, I slip out from under her, pausing at the foot of the bed when I spot her panties on the floor. I want to take them, smell them, keep them in my pocket as a reminder of how I made her come. But that would surely be a breach of her privacy, yes? And a clear violation of the rules we've set as roommates?

Those rules are likely obsolete at this point, however. We're no longer just roommates. So...what are we?

While I currently don't have an answer to that, the lines we previously drew have been blurred. Lowering into a crouch, I snatch the panties off the floor and quietly close the door behind me as I leave. In the hallway, I press the panties against my nose. My room in the attic is another two floors away. I can't wait any longer. My knees buckle as I inhale her ambrosial scent. So fucking perfect.

I stay (mostly) quiet as I jerk off right outside her bedroom door, on my knees with my pants and underwear down around my thighs, my groans muffled by the soft cotton of her purple panties blocking my airways. I come in a handful of strokes, unsurprisingly.

She might not be happy I stole her underwear, but I already have plans for how I'll make it up to her in the morning.

* * *

"I hope you like sausage," I say as Natalie enters the kitchen. My heart leaps at the sight of her. Her blonde curls are mussed from sleep, and there are creases on her cheek from her pillow. An oversized t-shirt hangs loosely off her body, the hem hitting the middle of her thick thighs. Her nipples poke through the threadbare fabric, making my mouth water. I swear I can still taste her on my tongue.

She is radiant.

"Um," I stammer, almost forgetting the plate I'm holding in my hand. "D-Do you like sausage? I've never seen you eat meat, but there was some in the freezer, so I thought–"

"Mm, I love sausage," she replies, grabbing a napkin and taking the nearest stool at the counter. "Both kinds." She winks.

I lean on the counter next to her, crowding her space. "Are you flirting with me, sweetheart?"

She giggles, the sound delicate and lilting. "Hey, will you come for a walk with me in a little bit? I want to show Ethel this book on gardening my coworker lent me."

Ethel? After she almost cut Natalie's throat with her shears? "Why would you want to talk to Ethel after what happened?"

She takes a few bites of the French toast I made for her and moans, the sound making my dick throb with need. "She was scared and confused. This time, if you're with me, I can properly introduce myself without her freaking out."

I don't understand why this is so important to her. "Why do you care what Ethel thinks of you? Do you think you'll even see her that much while you're here?"

Her expression turns somber. "I don't want my presence to upset anyone—dead or alive. We both live here. It'd be nice for us to get along."

Natalie might have the softest heart of anyone I've met, and that's what concerns me. I don't think Ethel would've killed her if I hadn't shown up, though maybe that's wishful thinking. Would she have hurt her? That, I don't know. Ethel is unpredictable. And even though she doesn't deserve it, Natalie is eager to not only forgive her but become her friend. It's this emotional generosity that leads Natalie to tolerating poor treatment from others and ending up with partners who aren't worthy of her attention. That's my theory, anyway.

My stomach twists when a chilling thought enters my mind.

Am I one of those partners?

Just another sloppy simpleton like Mark? An insufferable asshole like Kyle?

I wasn't good enough for Susanna. She was eager to remind me of that on a daily basis.

What makes me good enough for a woman as gorgeous and kind as Natalie?

"Please?" she asks, making me realize she's still waiting for my answer.

"Uh, yes. Of course, I'll go with you."

Natalie eats the rest of her breakfast, moaning several more times, which leaves me no choice but to jerk my cock while she's in the shower just to relieve the discomfort. I replay the previous night as I stroke myself, with my tongue deep in her pussy and her come soaking my chin. Once I'm sated, chest heaving, I shift into my mist-like form, and then shift back, to ensure my underwear and pants are dry and clean before I meet Natalie by the front door.

We find Ethel on her knees in the garden, filling a basket with various long-stemmed flowers. She smiles when she hears us approach and offers a bright smile. It's a gorgeous day, cloudless and sixty-eight degrees. I wonder if it's too cold for Natalie, but she seems pleased by the cooler air.

Ethel remembers Natalie and offers her sincerest apologies for the misunderstanding. The two of them agree to forget all about it and begin chatting among themselves about which fruits and vegetables Ethel is preparing to harvest before the first frost. Natalie hands over the book she borrowed, and Ethel clutches it to her chest, thanking her over and over. They start discussing the book, I think.

I don't pay much attention to what they're saying. I can't. Natalie's wearing a light rose-colored sleeveless dress with cherries on it that nips in at her waist and flares out down to her knees. Her pale shoulders are sun-kissed, a pretty pink that reminds me of the post-climax glow of her skin last night. I watch as her wide hips sway in front of me as she follows Ethel around the garden. I'm entranced by her body. Addicted to it, even, and I have yet to fully take her.

I close the distance between us and push her soft blonde curls off the left side of her neck, baring the delicate skin before I lean down and press my lips to it. The little hairs on her skin stand to attention, and goose bumps race down her arms. She turns to me with flushed cheeks, and a scandalized expression as she nods toward Ethel.

I shrug. *Who cares?* I mouth to her. "She's not looking."

Her teeth sink into her bottom lip as she gazes at Ethel's back.

At that moment, Ethel turns around and says, "Don't you agree?"

"Oh! Oh, yes. Definitely," Natalie hastily replies.

"I think so too," Ethel says, before continuing her chatter.

We remain close behind Ethel as she walks, but far enough away to let the wind cover the sound of our whispers.

"I need to touch you," I say to Natalie, wrapping my arm around her waist and burying my nose against her neck. "I can't help myself."

She turns toward me, her hand cupping my jaw as she leans in for a quick peck on my lips. It's not nearly enough. I need more of her.

"I don't want Ethel to catch us. We're becoming friends."

I tickle her ribcage. "Don't worry. She's not paying attention."

My dick is painfully erect as Natalie steps in front of me and places her hands on my stomach. I don't need to beg her to drop her hands to the front of my pants. She does it on her own. I gasp as I throw my head back, eyes pinched closed in ecstasy as she strokes me through the tweed fabric.

"Mm, I can't wait to get this in my mouth," she whispers, before flicking her tongue across my collarbone.

"Fuck," I groan, my fingers biting into her hips as I press her against me. "You have no idea what you do to me."

Her touch is electric as it continues to rub my cock, the friction of the fabric making it impossible not to thrust into her hand.

"If you don't stop," I warn her, panting, "I'm going to come right here. Right now."

She smirks against my lips. "You started this. Don't you want me to finish it?"

I love this side of Natalie. She's a shy, passive creature, but sexually, she's a masterful seductress. While she may not feel confident in her body at times, she's vocal about her needs. I appreciate that about her.

I growl as I take her lips hungrily, sucking and biting her bottom lip. Encircling her wrist, I pull it away from my crotch and press her palm against my chest. With my other hand, I grab her chin and tilt it up, deepening the kiss. "Not like this, sweetheart," I whisper into her mouth. "Ethel is straight as far as I can tell, but I'm a greedy man, and I'm not sharing you with anyone."

Natalie chuckles quietly. "*You're* the one on the verge of coming."

I cup her face with both hands, stroking along her smooth cheek, then down the slope of her nose. Her gaze is lustful, her pupils blown out, as she stares up at me. "So, if I were to pull up your dress and stroke along the seam of your pussy, I'd find your panties dry? Or are they soaked for me?"

Her lips part as she sucks in a breath, enjoying my vulgar words.

"Tell me the truth, gorgeous. They're drenched, aren't they?"

"Y-Yes," she moans, her hands gripping my lower back. "So wet."

God, she's perfect. I wish I could back her up against the shed and fuck her right now. But Ethel's here, still yammering on as far as I can tell, completely unaware of us groping each other mere feet away from her. Besides, I don't want my first time with Natalie to be rough and quick. I want to take my time, licking and sucking every inch of her body until she comes, and comes, and comes until her body is limp and sated. Only then would I make sure my needs were met.

For now, I'm content just kissing her. To hold her generous curves against my body and drink from her lips. She sucks on my tongue, surprising me, and I moan into her mouth, unable to keep my hips from bucking against her belly.

"Hello!" Ethel shouts.

Natalie and I pull apart, dazed and drunk on each other. Her lips are swollen, and her lip gloss is smeared on her chin.

Ethel laughs as she uses her hand to block the sun from her eyes. "You two are just darling." She sighs, the sound wistful. "Typical newlyweds."

She shoos us toward the house, insisting we can visit another day, before thanking Natalie once more for the book.

We stroll back toward the house, fingers entwined, shooting each other wicked smirks filled with promises of what we intend to do once inside. But the moment we make it to her bedroom, her phone rings. She sees that it's Lindsay, and frowns as she tells me she has to take the call.

I give her privacy as I head downstairs to wait for her. An hour later, she emerges from her room, wearing a fitted graphic t-shirt and dark chinos—her standard work outfit.

"Vyla texted me while I was talking to Lindsay. Dominic's not coming in tonight. I guess he had a personal emergency. Vyla asked me to cover."

"And?"

I'm annoyed. Not at her. At Lindsay. At Dominic. At everyone even distantly involved in preventing me from spending the evening with my stunning roommate.

She sighs. "I can't turn down any shifts right now. Not with all the bills I'm still behind on."

"I understand," I tell her truthfully. Pulling her into my arms, I kiss her hair, breathing in her strawberry scent. "Be careful, Natalie."

I keep my gaze on her delightfully plump ass as she walks out the door. The silence of the house near deafening.

Shifting into mist, I float toward the attic where I've left my sketchbook. Suddenly, I feel inspired to draw. As I reach the third floor, Lindsay's sharp, angular features pop into my mind, stopping me short.

This is *Lindsay's* house. Natalie has no legal claim to it. How could I have let that slip my mind? Here I am, becoming obsessed with Natalie's scent, her taste, the mere presence of her, and soon she'll have to leave. How soon must I face that reality?

The thought feels like a knife through my chest.

Chapter 14
Natalie

I'm exhausted. Three days in a row of working double shifts at Fast Glass has been great for my bank account, but terrible for my sleep schedule and sex life. I've been dying to get Winston alone since we teased each other in the garden, but I've been working so much that by the time I get home, I barely have the energy to make it up the stairs before I pass out.

That hasn't stopped Winston from crawling into my bed each night and snuggling with me. It's surprisingly sweet. I didn't think he'd be interested in sexless cuddles, but it's been nice having someone to hold me at night. Even when I wake up and start pawing at him, he presses a kiss to my forehead and gently scolds me about needing more sleep.

"My body no longer requires rest," he reminded me last night as I tried to unbutton his pants. "Yours still does. I'm not selfish enough to rob you of that in favor of my sexual pleasure."

My ghost is so noble. It's incredibly annoying.

Though, it's possible he's more worried I'll fall asleep in the middle of it, which would be an obvious blow to his ego. I can't blame him. It'd be hard not to take it personally if the roles were reversed.

I should hate it when he gets bossy with me, but I find it kind of hot. Especially when he's reminding me to drink more water or other basic things that grown-ass adults should do that somehow always slip my mind.

After I finish wiping down the bar and putting the clean glasses on the shelf, Dominic drives Vyla and I over to the Pebblebrook Inn for the town meeting. They have a massive white tent behind the inn that can be enclosed and heated for winter weather or opened up for warmer days. The tent seats two hundred people, and I'm shocked to see that almost every seat is taken when we arrive. This is one dedicated community.

It doesn't hurt that there's a giant pitcher of apple cider at the front table. I fill two little cups just for myself before taking my seat.

Mayor Crane welcomes everyone to the meeting and begins by addressing the list of concerns residents had at the previous meeting, as well as the steps she has taken over the last month to address those issues. Her chief of staff, Ezra, records the minutes on a tablet, and looks extremely serious while doing so.

"You should see that one on karaoke night," Vyla whispers to me, chuckling. "No one gets more drunk than Ezra."

With how buttoned up and rigid they look with their perfect posture, pinstripe vest, and matching pinstripe slacks, I can't even picture them having a beer at the end of a long day, but hopefully I'll get to witness Ezra sloppily belt out a few pop hits at the next karaoke night.

Mayor Crane goes through a few announcements, mostly regarding the upcoming 5K race that's routed through town. There will be street closures, swag bags for the participants, a prize ceremony for the top finishers, and a pizza party at Crust Lust Pizzeria for the participants and volunteers afterward.

"We are in dire need of volunteers," Mayor Crane says. "We need people at the registration table, handing out water, and stationed along the route to make sure we don't have anyone getting lost."

She gestures to the uniformed man standing to the right of Ezra. "Sheriff Diaz and his team will be re-directing traffic, but since there are only four officers serving Mapletown, we'll need about ten volunteers spread out along the race route to assist them. Please see me at the end of the meeting if you'd like to volunteer."

The next part of the meeting is a public forum for residents to air their grievances. The gorgons who live next to the vampires complain about too much noise late at night. The elder werewolves want to see newer puzzles added to the rec center. A family of crow shifters wants the zoning codes changed so they can turn their old colonial into separate elevated nests.

More than one person complains about someone named Ziggy coming onto their property and stealing their shoes. This is apparently Mayor Crane's familiar, a black cat who likes to take one shoe from each house. Mayor Crane laughs it off and instructs them to check at the base of the W-shaped trees in Mapletown Forest, since that's where he likes to keep his stash.

"Just not on the eleventh of the month," a resident adds.

The mayor's face hardens. "Yes, that's right. For anyone new to town, do not enter the forest on the eleventh of the month. This is true for every month."

"What happens in the forest on the eleventh?" I whisper to Vyla.

She visibly shudders. "The tree god overseeing it forbids

any mortal creature from entering. Those who've tried didn't make it back."

"Are you serious?" I ask, louder than intended.

Dominic shushes me.

Chase Palmer, aka the Cider King, wants to serve what he calls his "famous" apple cider potato stew at the finish line of the race, to which Mayor Crane says, "Once again, Mr. Palmer, you can park your food truck at the end of the race route, but we will not be handing out cups of hot stew to runners in need of hydration."

Just like in most small towns, resident requests need to be submitted via the applicable form at town hall—typical red tape—but most of the people here seem relatively pleased with Mayor Crane's leadership. They're engaged and eager to help improve their community. It's adorable, and it makes me want to stay here even more.

On my way out, I add my name and phone number to the volunteer form for the upcoming 5K.

Mayor Crane approaches as I'm about to leave, a pleased grin on her face. "Volunteering for us at the race, I see. Does that mean you're sticking around?"

Oh, right. At the bar, I told her I was staying at a friend's house and wasn't sure how long I'd be in town. But seeing how warm the people of this town are, and how quickly I'm getting attached to Winston, I can't imagine leaving. "That's the plan," I tell her. "I love it here."

She crosses her arms over her chest and nods. "Very good. You're welcome here for as long as you'd like."

The mayor seems like a tough woman to please, so getting her seal of approval means a lot. I doubt that's something she gives out often, especially to a human without any supernatural abilities.

* * *

I wake up the next morning with a headache, but despite the throbbing between my eyes, I'm determined to organize the kitchen cabinet with the mismatched piles of dishes. Lindsay doesn't want any of them, she said as much the last time we texted about things she wanted to donate, so I figured I'd go through them and set aside the ones I like for myself. For my future home, which, hopefully, is somewhere in Mapletown. And hopefully, Lindsay will keep this house in some capacity so I can visit Winston.

No matter how this shakes out between me and him, hopefully we can be friends. Friends who make out and have lots and lots of sex, preferably.

The kitchen cabinet reaches the ceiling and holds six shelves, all of which are completely full. After I pull down the bowls and plates from the lower two shelves, going through them and washing the ones I'd like to keep, I find I'm too short to reach the higher ones. There isn't a stepladder in the broom closet, so with the grace of a gorilla attempting a pirouette, I haul myself onto the countertop and roll onto my knees. There isn't much surface area on this part of the counter, so I carefully push up to standing while holding on to the cabinet door.

Completing this task in fuzzy socks was a terrible idea, but I'm only realizing that now, as my foot slides a few inches toward the edge. I catch myself, take a deep breath, and huddle as close to the shelf as I can while I look through the mugs.

There are so many in here, I wonder if every resident of Caraway Manor left their mugs behind when they moved. How else could one acquire a collection this big? There must be close to fifty in here. Some look to be clear souvenirs from vacations, a bunch of them chipped or cracked, but the rest are ceramic with dainty handles, soft pastel colors, and matching saucers. Those, I'm excited to examine more closely.

My gaze lands on a yellow and gold teacup with matching saucer. The design on the side is a baby elephant walking toward its mother, its trunk outstretched, reaching for her. I've always had an interest in elephants, and the scene of the mother and baby makes me think of Mom. This one is definitely going in the keeper pile. As I'm reaching for the cup and saucer, several brown legs emerge from behind it, and before I can see the rest of it, I start screaming.

A spider.

No, that doesn't quite cover it.

A massive fucking spider with a bloated brown body and eight thick brown legs that look as sharp as needles is not only crawling out from behind my new favorite mug, but is quickly moving toward me.

I don't think before hurling myself backward, away from the creepy crawler. Sadly, I should have, since now my arms are flailing, my feet kicking in the air, and the sharp corner of the kitchen island likely seconds away from connecting with my spine.

Pinching my eyes closed, I brace for death, or paralysis, or some kind of catastrophic and highly preventable injury, but... my body never hits the ground. Instead, a strong hand cradles my neck as another supports my lower back. Winston is holding me like he's just dipped me in the middle of a dance floor.

"Natalie." Winston utters my name like it's a prayer, and maybe that's exactly what it was. He must have heard me screaming and entered the room just as I started to fall. His gaze is filled with terror as he looks me over from head to toe. "What happened?"

Mortified, I cover my face with my hands. "I'm sorry. I

was going through the mugs and this spider, this fucking huge spider the size of a muffin, just comes out of nowhere and–"

He helps me to my feet and cups my cheeks. The movement is so fast and tender I stop talking. "Why do you apologize so often, sweetheart? And why do you do it now?"

"Because I probably freaked you out by screaming, and then you had to rush in here and catch me before I cracked my damn head open..."

His lips curve into a lopsided grin that makes him look boyish, and I wonder for a moment what would've happened if we had grown up at the same time. I certainly would've noticed him. Cheekbones like his are hard to miss. Would we have found each other? Been attracted to each other, like we are now?

"Ah, yes. It was certainly a hardship to open my arms and have a radiant goddess fall into them," he says, then crosses his arms and tries to look stern. "The trauma will probably haunt me for many lifetimes."

I playfully shove at his chest. "Okay, fine. I take back my apology."

"As you should. You screamed because you were frightened. There's no need to apologize for such things."

He's right. I toss out apologies far too often, just like every other woman I know. Then, something occurs to me. "How did you know where I was? Were you in the hallway?"

Blood rushes to his cheeks as he pretends to fidget with his suspenders. I notice the subtle tan line around his ring finger where his wedding ring used to be. When did he take it off? "I..."

"You...?"

His voice lowers to a whisper. "I always know where you are."

A pleasant heat unfurls in my chest, spreading down to my belly. "How?"

His mouth twitches as he tries to find the right words. "I have no idea. At any time of day, if you're home, I can feel where you are. My body just *knows*."

I want to focus on how convenient that is, for moments like this when I fall off a high surface and come close to death, but I can't. Not when he's looking at me like that. Not when the words, *my body just knows* are so loaded and full of longing that I worry I've soaked my underwear to the point I'll start to drip. I'm tempted to demand Winston bend me over the kitchen stool and fuck me into oblivion, but there's a matter much more pressing that needs to be dealt with first.

I square my shoulders and take a deep breath. "Can you kill the spider for me, please? If we lose track of that thing, I'm going to have to burn the house down."

Winston chortles as he removes his boot. "How would Lindsay feel about that?"

"She'd fully support my decision. We don't fuck with spiders."

"As you wish." He turns to mist and floats up to the cabinet. "Allow me to vanquish this beast."

Once he reaches the mugs, he lifts the boot in his hand and says, "There you are," just before he slams the heel down onto the shelf. The shelf snaps in half, the rest of mugs and saucers sliding down into the crack. Winston launches himself away from the cabinets, landing at my side. As the mugs tumble onto the shelf below, it, too, breaks, and the rest of the shelves follow suit. The shelves hit the counter, then fall to the floor in a raucous clatter, the ceramic shattering into tiny pieces. One of the cabinet doors falls on top of the pile, the other dangling by a single weak hinge.

"Jesus, Winston!" I shout, horrified by the destruction. "I

asked you to kill a spider, not make it look like we dropped a grenade in here."

He shifts into his corporeal form, his face frozen in a *yikes* expression. "I didn't hit it hard enough to wreck the cabinet."

I sigh. "Did you kill the spider, at least?"

He looks down at his boots, then lifts each one to examine the soles. "Shit. I don't know."

"Fantastic. What the fuck am I supposed to tell Lindsay?" My head is pounding so hard I assume Winston can hear it. "This is a disaster."

"There it is," Winston hollers, leaping over the pile of wood and glass and coming down hard. He lifts his left boot and smiles. "Got it." When he shoots me a proud grin, I'm only slightly relieved.

After he wipes the spider guts off his boot, he picks up the broken shelves, looking closely at each one. "See this here?" he brings a board toward me, pointing at the edge, where the paint has been stripped, several layers of wood gone, and there are little holes going almost completely through to the other side. "Looks like termite damage."

"Oh god, termite damage?" My gaze roams around the room, and bile rises in my throat at the thought of termites feasting on every piece of wood in this gigantic mansion. "If they're in here, they're probably everywhere, right?"

He nods, his brows pinched together. "Yes, that's likely." Bringing his hand in front of his face, he flexes his fingers before curling them into a fist. "That explains how the shelves broke so easily."

When his lips form a slight frown, I can't help but chuckle. "Did you think you suddenly gained the strength of an Avenger? Are you hiding a magic hammer somewhere under that billowy shirt?"

He jerks back, looking wounded. "Well, I certainly have

more strength than the average man. Have I not proven that to you yet?"

He did mention throwing a car across the lawn at some point, didn't he? I doubt he was lying about that. Teasing him is just too amusing to resist, though. I pat him on the shoulder. "Of course. You're a big, tough guy, okay? The biggest and toughest I've ever seen."

"You're mocking me," he seethes. For a moment, it looks like he's about to lose his shit. Then his gaze softens, and his grin turns wicked. "Fine, then." He bends toward me and buries his shoulder into my stomach as his hands grip the backs of my thighs. Suddenly, I'm upside down, staring at his adorably tiny but firm ass.

Bastard tossed me over his shoulder like a sack of flour. "What the fuck?"

"Come along," he says, smacking me on the butt. "Time to show you what I'm capable of."

He carries me up the stairs, his stride never slowing. It's not exactly a comfortable ride, though. With every step, my ribcage collides with his hard shoulder, more blood rushes to my head, and dizziness threatens to overtake me.

When he sets me down next to my bed, my legs feel like noodles. He has to grip my shoulders to keep me steady, but it's not enough. My vision is blurred, my headache feels like it's radiating throughout my body, and I worry my breakfast is about to make a very unpleasant return.

"Natalie, what is it?" Winston's hand cups my cheek, the coldness of his palm instantly settling my insides. "Tell me."

"I-I'm fine," I say. I'm just feeling woozy from the way he carried me. This headache certainly isn't helping, though.

"You shouldn't go into work today. Call Dominic and tell him you aren't feeling well."

"No, no, no. I'm not sick. We need to deal with that mess downstairs."

A gentle push is all it takes for him to get me seated on the edge of the bed. He grabs my ankles and straightens me out, taking the folded blanket off the end of the bed and covering me with it.

"You will rest," he instructs. "When you awaken, if you still feel like this, you'll call Dominic and take the night off. Understood?"

Absolutely not. Unless I'm puking my guts out, I'm not giving up a shift. But Winston won't budge. I know that already. It's not worth the energy to argue, especially since I'm feeling so drained at the moment. A little fib won't hurt anyone. "Fine, but either way, I need to clean up that pile of wood in the kitchen."

He leans down, pressing a kiss to my forehead, then lowers his mouth to my ear. "I'll take care of it. You sleep. You'll need energy for what I'm planning to do to you later."

Heat pools in my belly at his words, at the throaty rumble of his deep voice. Even when the world is spinning and my head feels like it's going to implode, this man can get me wet with a single sentence.

Winston's gaze is locked on me as he walks backwards out of the room, smirking confidently, like he knows exactly what he's doing to me. It makes me want to smack him a little, but mostly tug his pants down and run my tongue along his hard length. I fall asleep wondering what he tastes like.

I wake up a few hours later, slightly sweaty. My headache remains, but it doesn't feel worse, so I take that as a good sign. A full night of sleep will get rid of it. I just need to get through my shift first.

The destruction in the kitchen is completely gone when I head downstairs. Winston has disposed of the wood and broken glass, and all that remains is the large rectangular shell that used to contain the shelves. He's stacked the dishes I've decided to keep neatly on the island, and the rest are wrapped and boxed for donation. I'm surprised he was able to do all of this without waking me. I guess my body needed the rest.

He meets me by the front door and frowns when he sees me putting my shoes on.

"I feel perfectly fine," I tell him. A headache isn't enough of a reason to leave my coworkers stranded on a Friday night. It's not like I have Covid symptoms. Besides, can monsters even get Covid? Or other human diseases, for that matter?

He purses his lips but doesn't say anything. I appreciate his restraint because this is a battle he won't win.

I get up on my toes to press a quick kiss to his lips. "I'll see you tonight, okay?"

That disarms him enough to turn his frown into a smirk. He grabs me by the waist, pulling me against his hard chest. I briefly get lost in his green eyes. They seem warmer, the color lighter, somehow, when he's like this. When he's not so closed off and cranky. "Come home to me as soon as you can."

Well, now my stomach is fluttering, and I'm regretting my decision to go into work. It needs to be done, though. The quicker I finish my shift, the quicker I can get home to my ghost, and finally get him inside me like I've been dreaming about.

Chapter 15
Winston

My Natalie has been gone for three hours. I've hated every minute we've been apart. Even looking at the grandfather clock in the study heightens my anger. I'm beginning to despise it. The big hand taunts me with each tick. I've spent the time with my sketchbook and charcoal pencil, filling up the pages that have remained blank for months. When I pause, adding a new line to my drawing, my gaze travels to that big hand on the clock, hoping it's made much more progress than it actually has.

I understand she needs to work, but knowing I'm stuck here while she's able to roam the world freely leaves me feeling unsettled. What if something happens to her out there? I can catch her when she falls off the counter here, but I'm powerless if something like that happens at the bar. Will *Dominic* be there to catch her? Or what if something worse occurs, like a car accident, or she gets caught in the middle of a monster brawl? I won't be there to get her to safety. My pencil snaps between my fingers at the thought.

Gray smudges cover my palm and fingertips, and I grab a

tissue to wipe them off with a frustrated grunt. Dominic better keep his hands to himself. If he touches her...well, what can I do? Not much, unless he comes here. Perhaps there's a way to lure him here under false pretenses. All he needs to do is cross the property line and I can... *No.* I can't waste my time thinking about hypotheticals.

Tossing my sketchbook onto the desk with a huff, I start thinking about what to make Natalie for dinner. She prefers to eat here, despite getting a free meal at the bar each shift, since most of the food there comes out of the deep fryer.

A mushroom risotto, perhaps? Or is it too hot out for something like that? Maybe a Greek salad with grilled chicken and garlic breadsticks on the side. I know that's one of her favorites, and she has yet to taste mine. I'm certain she'll find mine to be the best she's ever had. No other Greek salad will ever compare.

A car horn blares from the driveway, pulling me from my thoughts. It beeps once, then several quick beeps follow it. The familiar screech of the brake pads tells me it's Natalie's car, and something must be terribly wrong. I become mist and shoot through the floors down to the front door, flying through it.

The headlights are blinding as I reach the driveway, but once my eyes adjust, I see a hulking man with green skin emerging from the driver's seat of Natalie's car.

"Hey man, Natalie's sick," he says, racing around to the passenger side as Natalie throws the door open and retches on the gravel.

I race to her side, shoving Dominic out of the way. Her forehead is burning and clammy against the back of my hand, and her skin is pallid, lacking its usual pretty pink flush. I knew she shouldn't have gone to work. Whipping around, I face Dominic with a clenched fist, grabbing the collar of his shirt with my free hand. A growl rumbles up my throat, and I start to see red. "What have you done to her? If your repulsive germs are to blame for this, I will fucking destroy you."

"Out of the way!" Natalie shouts, covering her mouth and racing inside the house.

Dominic slips from my grasp, holding his hands up in surrender. "Easy, bud. I didn't do a damn thing. I'm just bringing her home."

There's a subtle twang to his speech, indicating that he grew up somewhere in the South. Some may find it charming. I find it obnoxious. He's as muscular as Natalie described, his biceps stretching the sleeves of his t-shirt in such a blatant way I want to laugh. Can he not find shirts in a bigger size? I'd offer the suggestion if I weren't so worried about Natalie.

"I think it's the flu," he notes calmly. "I told her to take tomorrow off, and however long she needs."

I step toward him, crowding his space, my teeth gritted. How can he know that? What if it's food poisoning, or something more serious? Is this "underwear model" and bartender also a doctor all of a sudden? "How does a human pick up a virus in a bar filled with monsters?"

I expect him to match my fury, slam his fist into my cheek, even, but he doesn't. Dominic seems concerned for Natalie, but unbothered by my interrogation. Why are his shoulders so loose?

He takes a step back and scratches the stubble on his chin as he considers the source of Natalie's sickness. "We have other humans in town, and even though they wield magic, the witches can also contract human viruses. She probably caught it from someone who came into the bar. It happens, especially with the witches who have kids in school." He chuckles. "Those youngsters are always sick with something."

We both turn toward the house when we hear Natalie getting sick in the bathroom down the hall, the front door still open. Dominic takes a step in her direction, but I block his path. "She's not yours to care for, *bud*. Leave. Now."

Dominic smirks. "Winston, my man, I'm not tryin' to steal your girl. Pinky swear." He extends his green pinky finger, looking at me expectantly. When I don't return the gesture, he drops his hand to his side. "Look, I'm sorry we're meeting this way, but I'm well aware that Natalie is yours. She talks about you all the time. Besides, she's my employee. I'm not looking to cross that line." He hands me the keys to her car. "Here. I can walk back."

"Winston!" Natalie shouts from the doorway. "Stop harassing my boss!" Her hand clamps over her mouth just as she spins and runs back to the bathroom.

My Natalie needs me. I can't waste any more time out here with this fool.

Dominic starts walking down the gravel driveway. He waves a hand over his shoulder. "Till we meet again, neighbor. Hope it's on friendlier terms next time." He begins whistling a tune I can't name as he strolls into the darkness.

Part of me is disappointed I didn't get a chance to sock him in the mouth—arrogant jackass with his tiny shirt—but he makes that a difficult task to complete with his unwavering tranquil mood. At least he brought Natalie home. I'll give her everything she needs.

I become mist and fly the short distance from the driveway to the downstairs bathroom, where Natalie is resting her head on the toilet bowl, groaning in agony. Shifting back to my corporeal form, I take the spare elastic off her wrist and use it to tie her blonde curls into a knot against her nape. Then, I grab a washcloth off the shelf above the toilet and run it under the faucet until the water turns cold. Squeezing the excess water from it, I sink down onto my knees behind Natalie, lifting her head and pressing the cloth to her forehead.

"Mm, thas good," she mumbles, her voice scratchy from sickness, or yelling at me, perhaps. "Please don't say, *I told you so.*"

I chuckle as I rub circles over her back. "I won't. It's only fun teasing you when you can fight back."

"Thank god."

"We can have this discussion in a few days when you're feeling better."

"You're the worst."

"You adore me. Don't deny it."

She retches again, and I'm not sure how to take that. I continue to rub her back until she's done. Her stomach must be empty at this point. She lays her head on the toilet seat and lets out a long whimper.

Pretty soon, her joints will start cramping up, and exhaustion will take over. I don't want her to pass out in here. "Let's get you off the floor and into bed."

"Mm okay."

I carefully pull her into my arms and carry her up the stairs as if she were my bride, and we're crossing the threshold. Her eyes remain pinched shut as I gently lay her down on the bed, pulling the sheet over her. I leave the blanket folded back, since her hair is damp with sweat. I don't want her overheating. The AC is on high, but it doesn't seem to be cooling her down.

"I'll be back in a flash," I whisper before pressing a kiss to her forehead.

She grunts and turns on her side, curling into the fetal position.

I race around the house, gathering a clean bucket, tissues, a glass of water, and a thermometer.

"Everything okay in here? I heard yelling from the driveway," Ethel hollers from the foyer. Her dirty gloved hands are clutching a basket full of cucumbers and tomatoes to her chest.

"We're fine, Ethel," I reply. "Don't worry. I've got it handled."

I appreciate her offer to help, but I want to…no, *need* to care for Natalie alone, if only to prove to myself that I can.

"Very well," she says. I hear the front door shut behind her. Relieved, I rush back to Natalie's side.

"Open up," I tell her, lightly poking her lips with the end of the thermometer. She frowns but eventually opens for me. Her temperature is 102.9 degrees, and I know that 103 or higher would be cause for concern. She should be admitted to the hospital if it gets any higher than it is. I can't let that happen. If she's taken to the hospital, I won't be able to go with her, won't be able to make sure they're taking proper care of her. I need to nurse her back to health myself. If I can't manage that, do I have any right to want to claim her as my own?

I notice a stain on her shirt, likely from her retching, and droplets of it linger on her chin. Taking her hand, I help her into a seated position, using the washcloth to clean her face. She leans into my touch, moaning quietly at the feel of my palm on her cheek. I'm reluctant to release her, but this isn't about me. I go through her dresser and find one of the oversized t-shirts she prefers to wear to bed. "Arms up, gorgeous."

With a sleepy look on her face, she follows my command. I toss her shirt aside, along with the washcloth, making a mental note to rinse them in the sink before I bring them downstairs to the laundry room. I remove her bra while averting my eyes. Despite having seen them, it seems wrong to peek at her perfect tits in this situation.

I pull the t-shirt over her head and kneel in front of her. "How do you feel? Do you think you'll get sick again, or would you like to lay down?"

Natalie scowls and unbuttons her pants. "Why is it so fucking hot in here?" With her eyes half-open, she pouts as she shoves her pants down her legs, kicking them to the side and toeing off her socks. It reminds me of a child's tantrum, and I would find it annoying it weren't so fucking cute.

"Because you have a fever," I remind her, amused.

She plops back down on the bed, yanking the sheet over her with a huff. I don't feel right about leaving her alone like this, but would she be upset to find me in her bed without being invited?

Since she's not entirely aware of her surroundings, I think it's okay for me to get comfortable. I don't intend on leaving her side until the sickness has passed. As quietly as I can, I remove my boots and get in next to her, covering myself with the sheet.

She turns onto her side, and her eyes flutter open. Her face is twisted in pain, and I wish more than anything that I could take it from her. "I feel like I'm dying."

"You're not dying, sweetheart. Not on my watch."

A pregnant pause fills the air between us, then she asks, "What does it feel like?"

The question catches me off guard. "What?"

"Dying. What does it feel like?" Blood rushes to her cheeks, as if she's embarrassed. "I'm sorry. We don't have to talk about it."

"No, it's okay," I promise her. "Do you want to know about before, or after?"

"Tell me everything."

Knowing how heavy this is about to get, I move closer and pull her into my arms. She nuzzles against me, resting her head on my chest. "I died from tuberculosis—it was quite common back then—and because of the nature of the disease, my memories from the end are hazy at best, but I do recall struggling to breathe, coughing up blood, and having trouble sleeping because the crackling sound in my lungs was so loud. It was complete and utter misery.

"But toward the very end, the last hours or minutes of my life, it was a blur. I'm not sure how long it took me to die; I just know that one moment I was in agony, and then...the pain was gone."

"Was there a light at the end of a long tunnel?" she asks.

I laugh at the common misconception. "No, nothing like that. There was nothing at first. I was just...here. Standing at the foot of my bed, looking at the vessel that once housed my soul. Eventually, the milkman found me; he came inside on one of his deliveries. He and a neighbor down the street buried my body in the forest behind the house. There wasn't a funeral or anything, because by that point, everyone I cared about had already died.

"One day, I think it may have been a week after my death, there was a door. It just showed up in front of me. I was in the study, trying to move a book without shifting to my corporeal form, and poof! A door. Clearly out of place. It seemed like an invitation of some kind. I had no idea what was on the other side, heaven, maybe, or hell. Or whatever comes next for spirits like me. Maybe just eternal nothingness."

"A door? Was there anything special about it? Was it white, with a glowing light behind it and a harp playing from the other side?"

I shake my head. "No. It was a nondescript brown door. Red oak, I believe, but there wasn't anything particularly special about it."

Her eyes widen. "So you didn't open it?"

"Nope."

"You mean to tell me, you had the opportunity to get The Answer to life's ultimate question, and you chose not to?"

I can understand her reaction. Who wouldn't want to know what happens when we die? It's a mystery that not even those with the most money can solve. The great equalizer. But she's missing the point. "I was still in the house that I built, my belongings were here, and I had peace and quiet. There's nothing else I wanted."

She chuckles, the sound making my skin prickle with need. "Okay, fair. But what about—"

"My wife?"

She nods, biting her lip as if she regrets asking.

"I haven't told you how she died, have I?"

"No, and I didn't want to ask."

I take her hand, lacing my fingers through hers. "It's okay. She, um,"—I swallow the lump in my throat—"she died during childbirth. It was a long, difficult pregnancy. Susanna hated every minute of it. She needed a child to keep her inheritance, but she never actually wanted to be a mother. Most of the time while she was pregnant, she would scream at me for being the cause of her discomfort. For getting her pregnant, even though that's the only reason she married me...why she chose me at all. I would cook for her, offer to rub her feet, massage her shoulders, and no matter what I did, she pushed me away.

"I felt helpless. I couldn't take her pain from her, and she wouldn't allow me to be the husband I wanted to be. Then, when my son emerged from her body, I saw her smile for the first time in months. The joy she radiated stole my breath. It was brief. So brief that I thought I was dreaming. But it was there, and it was real. She was delighted to meet her son. Proud of what we made."

My palms begin to sweat as I relive that day. The worst day of my existence. "She wanted to hold Daniel, but the doctor wouldn't let her. There was so much blood. Too much. He couldn't stop it." I don't notice the tear running down my cheek until Natalie gently wipes it away. "She never," I pause, needing to catch my breath, "got to hold him. I think she would've been a good mother, if she had gotten the chance. It's not what she wanted at first, but she would've found her footing if she had lived. Susanna hated me, but she loved our baby boy. I know she did. I could see it in the way she looked at him." Maybe it's wishful thinking, but I do believe that.

Natalie sniffles, and squeezes my hand, letting me know she's got me.

"Daniel died two hours later. He had trouble breathing right when he entered the world, and it never ceased. The doctor did what he could. There were times during that excruciating two-hour period, when I was a newly widowed single father, praying to god and the rest of the deities to keep my son alive, that it sounded like Daniel had taken a normal breath. A shallow, quiet little breath. It was a sliver of hope. My heart felt like it was going to thump its way out of my body with how much hope I had, but then the doctor would hear a wheeze with his stethoscope or Daniel's skin would get this blue tint to it, and I would shatter all over again. Eventually, the breathing stopped altogether, and he was gone."

"Winston, I'm so sorry," Natalie says, swiping at her wet cheeks. "I don't know what to say."

I press a kiss to her hair. "You don't have to say anything. I've been living with this for a long time."

"No, that's not what I mean." She grabs my chin, forcing me to look into her rich brown eyes. I feel lost in them, but at the same time, safe. Like I'm falling into their depths, knowing my landing will be soft and warm. "That's why you didn't open the door, isn't it?"

I almost forgot why I started telling her this story. "Yeah," I reply, my voice hoarse and shaky. "Even if they are on the other side of it, they don't want me there."

"How can you say that?" Natalie's tone is harsh, as if she's offended I would even consider such a thing.

"She hated me, Natalie."

She flinches at the boom of my voice, and I feel sick for yelling at her. Here she is trying to comfort me, and I'm fucking it all up. My chest heaving, I say quietly, "I was nothing to her, okay? And Daniel," I pause, my voice cracking with emotion, "I couldn't keep him alive for a single day. If they're out there, wherever *there* is, they should be together...without me."

We sit there for a while, staring at each other, tears streaming down our cheeks, saying nothing. I'm too afraid of what might come out of her mouth next, so I revel in the silence. Does she agree with me? Is she starting to look at me the way Susanna did? Am I nothing more than a pile of inadequacies in the shape of a man?

I don't know how much time passes, but eventually, I press my hand to her forehead and tell her I want to recheck her temperature.

"It's 102.1," I tell her when it beeps. "Going down. That's good."

I busy myself with refilling her glass of water, getting her a fresh, cold washcloth for her head, and giving her a dose of the extra-strength flu medication I found in Penelope's medicine cabinet. When I return to her side, her eyes are puffy from crying, and her lids are heavy with exhaustion.

"You need to sleep, Natalie."

As I rise to my feet, her hand latches onto my wrist. "Lay with me." I've never seen such a serious look on her face.

"I wasn't planning on leaving."

"Good." She lifts the sheet on my side of the bed, patting the open spot. "Take off those clothes first."

"Uh." Is she serious? She can't possibly want to do *that* right now, can she? "As much as I'd like to ravish you right now, you need rest."

"What? No. You're like a giant ice pack. I need you against me. I'm still burning up over here."

That makes more sense. Deeply disappointing, but certainly the more rational explanation for the request. I do as I'm told, stripping down to my underwear before sliding in next to her. She wraps herself around me, her leg thrown over mine, her cheek pressed against my bare chest, and her hand featherlight on my stomach. She fits perfectly against me, her softness pressed against my hard edges.

"You feel so good." Her voice is throaty and smooth as silk. It makes me wonder if this is how she'd sound while taking my cock. Being painfully hard while Natalie's sick seems inappropriate, but when the tip of her tongue darts out to wet her lips, I have to suppress a moan.

"T-Thank you." I clear my throat, shifting my body slightly to avoid my dick poking her hand.

She lifts her chin, and I meet her gaze. "Just so you know, Winston, you deserve to be on the other side of that door. I hope one day you'll see that."

Her words break something inside of me. A wall, a glacier, some kind of barrier that I didn't even realize I had built, Natalie stormed right through it. My heart swells at the faith she has in me. I don't feel worthy of it, but every cell that's still part of me wants to become the kind of man she thinks I am.

I may have failed Susanna and Daniel, but I won't fail Natalie.

She presses a kiss to my shoulder and nuzzles into the crook of my neck. I rub her back until she dozes off, checking the heat of her forehead occasionally to see if the fever has broken.

An hour passes, and she wakes. She says nothing, just stares at the ceiling. It goes on long enough that I grow concerned she isn't actually awake. I didn't expect to discover anything about Natalie that would be a turn-off, but sleeping with her eyes open? That might make the list.

"Natalie?" I whisper, hoping she'll hear me and respond. "Are you awake?"

"Mm hm," she replies, and my shoulders instantly feel lighter. Okay, so she's not a creepy haunted doll. I'm relieved but still perplexed.

"Tell me what you're thinking."

She shrugs. "Mom and I moved around a lot when I was young. We once ended up in an apartment that had a skylight in my bedroom. When I can't sleep, I always think about that place. That skylight. Being able to see the stars was such a comfort."

"Really?" I've gazed at the stars many times but never found them to be particularly comforting or interesting. All I see is a bunch of blinking dots. "What do you like about it?"

Her reply is immediate. "The reliability. The way it makes my problems feel insignificant. Knowing that the stars will exist as long as I do, and long after."

I never considered this before, but I understand it. She's lost too much, so much that the most reliable presence in her life are the stars. Maybe I could be that steady presence in her life.

Or...an idea hits me.

With the way the house was designed, there's nothing above this bedroom. The third floor only consists of three rooms, with the attic above that. I wonder how difficult it would be to install a skylight directly above the bed.

"Isn't it boring for you?"

When I don't reply, she purses her lips at me.

"Lying here with me, doing nothing."

I put a hand behind my head. "Boredom isn't something I experience. There are times I'm impatient, but that's obviously different. When time is endless, there's less pressure to fill it." It took time to adjust to this, around five years or so. To resist the pull to be productive every moment of my existence. Now, I can enjoy the freedom of choosing how to fill my time. I'm able to appreciate the slow pace of the afterlife, especially with Natalie here. Silently lying beside her may seem dull, but I like watching her chest rise and fall, and the small movements of her body when she's fighting off a bad dream or trying to get more comfortable. I could do it forever and not get bored.

She looks wistful. "That sounds really nice. I wish I had the ability to just live and not obsess over all the things I should be doing."

I'm running my finger along the line of her jaw, savoring the softness of her skin. "I can help you with that. It's something I wish I had learned to do before I died." My finger travels down the length of her throat and reaches the top of her shoulder, where the elephant tattoo is peeking out from beneath the sleeve of her shirt. "What's the significance of this? The elephant."

She looks down at it, rolling up the sleeve and making the design entirely visible. "Oh," her chuckle is soft as blood rushes to her cheeks. "It was a silly act of rebellion, I guess. I was made fun of for being a chubby kid. There was one kid in middle school who liked to call me 'Nelephant.' He'd draw pictures of me with a trunk and tusks, and he and his friends would make that trumpet sound whenever I walked by. Fuckers were relentless."

I continue stroking her skin as she speaks, hoping my touch will keep her steady as she recalls these memories. Meanwhile, I'm fantasizing about throttling this boy she speaks of.

"Anyway, I started researching them, and I learned how intelligent and empathetic they are."

"Elephants?"

She nods. "They experience grief and joy, *and* they can detect the scent of water from miles away."

"Huh. I didn't know that."

"And their skin is extremely tough, but also sensitive." She shrugs. "I don't know. The more I learned, the more I felt connected to them. I started embracing them as a symbol, as a way to reclaim the word from my bullies and make it my own. A way to eliminate the shame and turn it into something powerful." She lets out a long, deep yawn. "When I decided to get a tattoo, I didn't want just one little design on my wrist or ankle. I went from none to a half-sleeve, and I knew an elephant would be at the center of the design. I found a tattoo artist nearby and...the rest is history."

"It's beautiful." My gaze follows the clean lines of the elephant's ears, then to the petals of the many flowers surrounding them. "Will you add color to it?"

"I don't think so. Sometimes I get the urge, but it looks exactly how I want it to look right now. Any changes to it could make it look worse, and I'm not willing to take that risk. Not with how expensive it was."

"Even if you might end up liking it more with color?"

She shakes her head, confidence clear in the lift of her chin. "When the grass is already green, why would I look for a greener patch?"

We talk about the cost of tattoos and how addicting they can be until Natalie nods off. At some point, deep into the night, her legs twitch, and she mumbles something that sounds like, "luffoo." I assume it's nonsensical sleep talk, and ignore it, but when it happens a second time, not ten minutes later, I wonder if she's awake. I look down, and her eyes blink open, but quickly fall closed once more. I'm not convinced she's fully conscious.

"Illuffoo," she says again, her breath hot against my neck.

"Natalie," I whisper, cupping her cheek, testing to see if she's awake. "I can't hear you, sweetheart."

Her hand strokes down my arm, her fingers landing on my bicep. "Love you."

Time stops. The world stops.

Did I...Did I imagine it? Or did Natalie truly just say that?

No, I know what I heard. That doesn't mean she meant what she said, though. Her eyes aren't even open anymore.

It meant nothing.

But what if she did mean it? What if she does love me, and the feeling is so consuming, so deep that the words slipped past her lips while unconscious?

The possibility of that doesn't scare me. It doesn't bother me in the slightest. In fact, I want nothing more than for it to be true. Because I love her too. Of course, I do.

I'm not sure when it happened, but at some point, this curvaceous, clumsy crumb-dropper became the center of my universe. I'm completely fucking gone for her.

Chapter 16
Natalie

I wake up with the sun streaming through the window, and a layer of crust trailing from my eye to my chin. "Ugh," I groan, turning onto my side, trying to wipe my face clean. A heavy arm curls around my waist, and a large hand squeezes my belly. My eyes fly open, and I instinctually curl inward.

"Uh-uh. None of that. Don't hide from me." Winston's gravelly voice has me clenching my thighs together. I push back against him, his hard dick poking me in the ass.

"*Fuck*," he growls, grinding against me. "Do you know what you do to me?"

I arch my back, placing my hand over his and guiding it to my breast, squeezing it with him. Using my other hand, I reach back and grab the back of his neck, pulling his lips an inch from mine. "Hm, can't say that I do. I think you should show me," I whisper, before leaning in for a kiss.

Then I remember how gross I felt the moment my eyes opened, and wince as I pull away. He sees it. "What's wrong?"

I rub my lips roughly, every muscle clenching in disgust

and embarrassment. "My breath must be awful. Run away. Save yourself."

Winston's long fingers wrap around my wrist and pull it away. "That's absurd. Come back here."

I duck my head and try to wriggle away, but he's too strong. I'm immobile in his hold as he pins me against him as we lay on our sides, facing each other. He smacks his lips together, his gaze lifting to the ceiling. "You taste the same as always."

"And that means?"

"Sweet. Warm. Like you."

My heart squeezes. How anyone can make barf-scented morning breath sound pleasant is beyond me. I'm assuming he's lying his tiny, delectable ass off to make me feel less self-conscious, but I think I'm okay with that.

His hand lifts to my forehead. "Shit." He sounds more than a little annoyed. I wonder if I'm the source as he rolls out of bed, releasing me altogether. "You're still hot."

"Thanks?"

He chuckles as he gets up, comes around to my side, and grabs the thermometer. "Your head. Open up."

My temperature is 100.4, which is a vast improvement from last night, but based on the way Winston's brows are pinched, it's not enough to continue fooling around. He kneels, his palm cupping my cheek as if I'm made of porcelain. "How do you feel?"

"I'm fine, really." It's not a lie. My headache is gone, and the nausea has subsided. I still feel like I'm sweating more than someone lying perfectly still should, and my skull feels like it's carrying a block of sludge, but other than that, I feel great. "I could go run a half-marathon right now." Okay, that's a lie, but he's overreacting. An elevated temperature isn't a big deal.

He grabs the glass of water off my nightstand and presses it to my lips. "Sit up and sip this slowly. I'm going to make you some toast."

I roll my eyes. "Fine, Sergeant. I'll have some water. You don't need to make me food, though. I'm not hungry."

My stomach chooses that exact moment to bellow in defiance. A cocky smirk plays on Winston's lips.

"How did you know?"

He chews the inside of his cheek. "Because I pay attention, Natalie. *Very* close attention." His eyes are an otherworldly shade of green as he stares at me. My heart beats in my throat, and suddenly this room feels comically small.

He leaves, and I take a breath for what feels like the first time in several minutes. If my temperature doesn't get back to normal and pronto, I'm going to need to take a butcher knife to all of these pillows just to keep myself sane. Until then, a shower should cool me off and calm my raging lady bits.

Knowing Winston will be back soon with toast, I make it quick, skipping the conditioner and body wash, and hitting only the basics—shampoo, face wash, and soap. Even luke-warm water feels too hot for me right now, so I turn the knob over to the blue side. The chilled stream stings my skin at first, but once I'm used to it, I let out a sigh of satisfaction.

I pat my skin down with a towel once I'm out, apply the various serums and moisturizers to prevent my skin from feeling like dragon scales, and scrunch some curling gel into my hair. I'm in the middle of removing the sweat-soaked sheets from the mattress when Winston returns with a tray over-flowing with food. There's a glass of orange juice, a steaming mug of tea, a stack of lightly browned toast, and four small jars of jams in various flavors. Above the plate of toast is a single yellow sunflower, its big brown middle and striking bright petals making me smile.

He looks at me with a sheepish expression. "I wasn't sure

how you like your toast..." he trails off. His gaze turns steely when he notices what I'm doing. "Are you changing the sheets?"

When I nod, he puts the tray down on the dresser and nudges me aside. "You shouldn't exert yourself. Let me do this." He shoos me toward the tray of food. "Eat your toast."

I go with the apricot jam, and I expect the first bite to make me moan with pleasure, but the opposite happens. The flavor bursts on my tongue, and it sends me to my knees. Tears fill my eyes and quickly overflow down my cheeks. I'm chewing and crying as I place the toast back on the plate. Winston must hear my sharp intake of breath, because he stops wrestling with the clean fitted sheet and pulls me against him.

"Tell me, Natalie. Is the toast not how you like it?"

His tone isn't mocking, but if I were truly crying over the state of my toast, I'd hope it would be. "No, that's not it at all." I'm mortified, though, because I didn't expect apricot jam to be the thing that shoves me into a flurry of memories of Mom. That's grief for you, though. Sometimes you see it off in the distance and accept its presence when it creeps in. Other times, it kicks your door down and knocks the wind out of you, leaving you writhing and confused on the floor.

"It's m-my mom," I mutter between sobs.

He pulls back to look at me, brushing a lock of hair behind my ear and wiping my tears with his thumb. My eyes fall closed at the tenderness of the gesture.

"Will you tell me about her?"

I sniffle as I nod, trying to catch my breath. His thick arms come around me once again, and I feel his lips press against my hair, followed by a deep inhale.

"She put half a tablespoon of apricot jam on my toast whenever I was sick," I begin, my voice shaky. "When I was younger, she tried to give me plain toast when I was sick, and I refused to eat it, or I pouted just enough to make her cave. I don't remember. But when she spread a little apricot jam on top, adding just enough sweetness to make it feel like a treat, she said my smile was brighter than the sun. It became a tradition after that. If I felt sick, she'd bring me apricot toast in bed."

Winston lets out an amused grunt and squeezes me tighter.

"I hadn't thought about that in years, because she hasn't made it for me in decades."

His scent envelops me, pine and woodsmoke and the natural spice of his skin, and it makes me feel safe. It's grounding, given how exposed and embarrassed I feel. "She sounds like a wonderful mom."

I swallow the lump in my throat. "She was."

He holds me until my tears run dry, then returns to making the bed as I eat a couple of pieces of toast. I take a sip of tea, and Winston glares at me when I politely refuse the rest of it. "The honey in it will coat your throat. It must ache after last night."

Last night? Ah, Pukefest 2025. It is a little scratchy, now that he mentions it. Failing to come up with a sassy retort, I slowly drink my tea until the mug is empty. Much to my chagrin, my throat does feel a little better.

We snuggle in bed for a bit, talking about everything and nothing. The silence between topics is easier than I thought it'd be. Comfortable. Like we've shared the same space for years.

At some point, I grab my phone to check my email and scroll through Instagram. "Did you turn off my alarm this morning?" I ask as I open my clock app.

"No. Why?"

I let out a frustrated grunt. "My alarm is a pain in the ass. It never goes off when I want it to, and I have no idea why. I've checked the settings, the volume, everything."

Winston holds out his hand like he wants to help, and a

laugh rips through me. "Seriously?" I say, giving him the phone. "You're going to provide tech support? Didn't you refer to my AirPods as ear sticks?"

He takes the phone and, without even looking at it, puts it face down on my nightstand. "I did, because ear sticks is a much better name, and no, I don't plan on fiddling with your phone applications."

"Then..."

He smiles, and it leaves me breathless. The dimple returns. "I will be your alarm."

"Excuse me?"

"I don't plan on spending my nights anywhere else, Natalie, and if I'm here, I can wake you up whenever you want. Just tell me what time."

"Winston, really, you don't hav–"

He makes an exasperated sound. "I want to."

Winston waking me up with a kiss sure does sound nice. Or a cuddle, or...other things. And I believe him when he says he wants to, but how long will that last? How long will *we* last? I don't want to ruin this moment we're having with The Talk, but deliberately not having it seems dumber than the return of flared jeans, so I swallow my fear and ask, "Should we maybe, I don't know, discuss what we are?"

"What we are?" he repeats the question, confused at first. His eyes widen a moment later in understanding. "You mean, to each other?"

"Yeah, I don't want to rush things, but I want us to be on the same page."

He nods, his gaze unfocused on the comforter as he thinks about this. My heart beats louder with each second that passes. Why is he taking so long to answer me?

"Well," he says, after what feels like ten minutes, but is likely about ten seconds. He scrubs a hand down his face, and I catch a flash of sadness in his eyes, I think, quickly replaced by an inscrutable expression making my stomach twist. "It's not really up to me, is it?"

That's definitely not what I wanted to hear. "What do you mean?"

He chews on the inside of his cheek, as if trying to find the right words. "I mean," he begins, then pauses. "I'm happy with the way things are, and admittedly, I know very little about how romantic couplings are labeled these days. I will defer to you, Natalie."

Ugh, why does he have to talk in code? Can't he just tell me how he feels? Granted, societal expectations regarding dating have changed since 1901, so I get it, but I'd rather hear his old-timey evaluation of what we are than figure it out all by myself. This is a two-way street, and he just pushed me into the middle of it, straddling the dividing line.

Maybe he's nervous to open himself up again, after how horrible things were with Susanna. Rest in peace, and all that, but thinking about how cruel she was to him makes me want to summon her spirit, grab her by the shoulders and scream, *Are you kidding me? Did you not see the wonderful man you had?* in her face.

He's not the only one afraid to get romantically involved again, though. I'm freaked out too. These feelings that I have for Winston—I wasn't expecting them. I wasn't expecting *him*. When he kisses my forehead, or pushes my hair behind my ear, or pulls me closer when our bodies are already flush from head to toe, I get these little painful pangs in my chest. They aren't unpleasant by any means. I'm not entirely sure what they are. All I know is that they make me want more of him. Of us. But whenever I feel them, I'm reminded of my limited time here.

This isn't my house, and Lindsay will want me out of here at some point. For that reason, I need to keep my head above water and not lean into those painful pangs. I can't let whatever this is go beyond casual sex. Maybe it already has, but even so, it can't go any further. We need to be smart about this.

"Okay," I finally say, "then let's keep things how they are. Fun. Casual."

His expression sours on the last word, but when I lean in for a kiss, his lips are just as hungry and intense as always. It doesn't take long for us to become breathless and start pawing at each other.

"Come here." Winston says with a chuckle as he removes my hands from his pants and maneuvers behind me, pulling me gently between his legs. His back is against the headboard, and he starts running his fingers through my hair. It feels so good, a sigh tumbles from my lips as I press my scalp deeper into his hands. At some point, he goes from brushing my hair to twisting it in a way that has me suspicious.

"What are you doing?"

"Braiding your hair."

A surprised laugh bursts out of me. "Why?"

He clears his throat, voice confident as he replies, "Because I'm spectacular at it."

"Do I want to know how you developed this skill?"

"I used to braid my sister's hair all the time."

"You had a sister?" I ask, ashamed that this is the first time I'm hearing about a sibling of his.

"Yes." In only one word, I can tell the mood has shifted. "She was the best person I've ever known. The only one in my family I liked being around."

I reach around to squeeze his hand. "We don't have–"

"It's okay," he interrupts. "She had cerebral palsy. Though, at the time, we didn't have a name for it. My mother did her best, but she was trying to raise three of us alone. I don't think she had the energy to be what Ginny needed."

"Three of you?"

"Me, Ginny, and my youngest brother, Harold. My father was an angry drunk, so he doesn't count. Was barely conscious when he was home. My brother and I helped as much as we could until we lost her."

"Lost...Ginny, or your mother?"

I hear him suck in an uneven breath. "Ginny. She went first. Only eight years old." His words are choppy, and his voice is a somber scrape as he continues. "My sorry excuse for a father was supposed to be watching her while my mom was at the market. He passed out while she was eating. Her respiratory system was already strained, and she started to choke. It didn't wake him up. Mom came home and found her dead."

"Jesus." Once again, I'm stunned into silence at Winston's pain. It's so much for one person to carry. Dying doesn't seem to have helped ease it, either. Time, maybe a little, but it's been over a century, and he can barely get the words out.

I don't know what to do to make him feel better, but maybe he'd take comfort in knowing he was a little less alone?

"I had two miscarriages," I blurt, immediately regretting it. Does he really want to hear this right now? Does he care? Do I have any right to shift the attention to my pain right after he's done exposing his? Unfortunately, the words are out there. I can't walk them back now. "With, um, Kyle."

His hands go still. I feel him shifting behind me. Then, his fingers crook under my chin, forcing my gaze to meet his over my shoulder. "Natalie, I'm so sorry."

I nod, my throat going dry. "It's okay. Really." It sounds like a lie, and it is. Most of the time, I work exceptionally hard to forget that period of my life was real. "Kyle got injured playing hockey in college. His dreams of becoming a professional athlete were shattered. It took him a long time to get past it, but once it seemed like he had, he became fixated on parenthood.

Wouldn't stop talking about it. Now, I realize, he never actually got past it. He swapped one obsession for another."

"He pressured you?" Winston asks, his jaw taut with frustration. No, it's closer to rage.

"No, well, not really." Looking back, he did pressure me, but I didn't see it as pressure at the time. Like a sweet, young idiot in love, I thought it was a green flag. Proof that he was the perfect man for me.

He wants kids that *bad? Obviously, he's a keeper!*

"The first pregnancy was a surprise," I tell Winston. "I wasn't ready, and we did everything right, but the morning-after pill didn't work on me because of my weight." It's been a while since I checked, but if the weight restrictions haven't been bolded and changed to size twenty-four font on the box of the morning-after pill, I'm ready to ride at dawn. "When I told Kyle, he was so excited, and it was contagious. I got excited, too."

A sigh slips past my lips. I'm feeling very tired. "We lost her at twelve weeks, and it broke me."

"How did Kyle take it?" My ex's name sounds bitter on Winston's lips.

"Not well." Reliving this is twisting my stomach, making it hard to breathe. "It was a week, maybe two, after it happened, and he was ready to start trying again."

"What?" Winston is aghast. "You're not serious."

I nod, trying to stop my lip from trembling. "My body wasn't ready, my heart was still in pieces. Kyle tried to convince me that trying would take my mind off the pain."

"Did you? Start trying again?"

Shame fills my chest as I nod. "At some point, I think I was too exhausted to argue. It was just easier to give him what he wanted and hope it all worked out." I feel Winston's fingers return to my hair, twisting the strands into a braid once again. I expect him to be rough, for the tension in his body to trickle out of his hands, but he's gentler than before. The repetitive motion settles my stomach. It gives me somewhere else to put my mind as I relive this. "I got pregnant again two months after my miscarriage and miscarried again after nine weeks. Me and Kyle never recovered."

I hear Winston wrap the elastic around my hair, the light snap of it breaking through the heavy silence. He grunts, the sound pained as he presses his cheek against the crown of my head. "My Natalie," he whispers.

I like the sound of that. Maybe a little too much.

His large hands engulf mine, the chill of his skin providing the relief my body always seems to need. He doesn't say anything, doesn't offer any of the platitudes I got used to hearing back then, and I'm so grateful for it. Winston understands loss better than most. He knows that, ultimately, this is a deep enough cut that words would never be able to reach it. Never even come close. Time is the only method of healing, and the scars won't fade.

He kisses my temple with so much tenderness I can't keep myself from crying. Winston moves down until our bodies are more aligned, my back pressed against his hard stomach. He caresses my cheeks every so often, catching the tears that continue to stain my cheeks, and I fall asleep in the arms of my ghost, my emotional closet now free of skeletons, feeling lighter than I've felt in years.

Chapter 17
Winston

Natalie rises from her nap after two hours, my arms never loosening from around her body. This sleep seemed more peaceful for her, which I'm thankful for, following such a somber admission. I considered prodding her for more information.

Did Kyle pressure you a third time?

Did he care for you properly after what you endured?

Was he the one to end the relationship, or was it you?

Ultimately, I already know the answers to these questions will disappoint and enrage me, and Natalie doesn't deserve to witness that side of me. She needs the level of care she's been starved of, and I intend to gorge her on it.

We go downstairs at Natalie's request, for a change of scenery, and snuggle up on the couch beneath one of her many pastel-colored throw blankets. Amid the dark wood and mostly black and crimson furniture, she has injected these jarring pops of brightness around the house. It's nice. If it were anyone else, I would be irritated. But this is Natalie. *My Natalie.* She can do whatever she wants, and I'll find it charming.

"Oh! Vyla told me Mapletown has its own Wi-Fi network. It's free for the entire town, and she gave me the password."

I watch as she looks between her phone and the TV remote, pressing several buttons and inputting letters. She cheers when a *bum-buhhhh* emanates from the TV as the screen turns red.

"We have Netflix!"

I don't understand the significance of this, but I refuse to be the asshole who takes the wind out of her sails. "Oh, yes. Finally."

She puts on a show about people who seem to be in a colorful state of purgatory, where they are unable to curse and are urged to apply morality to each choice they make in order to reach a version of heaven by a slightly different name. I pay attention to a certain degree, but it's difficult with the sweet scent of Natalie's skin filling my lungs. She giggles whenever my nose brushes against her neck or her scalp, but I can't stay away. "You smell so fucking good."

It's early afternoon when I press my palm against her forehead, encouraged by the subtle warmth of it, compared to the fire I felt this morning. When I take her temperature, Natalie squeals with glee when she sees it's 97.9.

She becomes a blur as she knocks the thermometer out of my hands, pushes me down onto the couch and climbs into my lap. I barely register what's happening until the soft tip of her tongue swipes against my lips.

"Slow down, sweetheart."

"No." Her voice is firm as her hips roll, my cock hardening quicker than my heart is beating.

"I'm better. My temperature is proof." She kisses me hard, and I can feel the hunger that's been building inside of her since we first touched those many days ago.

It mirrors my own. I've been desperate to fuck her since

long before that first kiss, but now that I know how she feels, how her pussy tastes, I need more. I need all of her. My concern still lies in her state of health, however. Before she came down with the flu, or whatever it was, she was overworked and exhausted. I also know that once I experience the euphoria of her cunt squeezing me until I come inside her, I may never be able to stop.

"Are you sure?" I ask, looking around the living room. There are no lit candles, daylight streams through the windows, and the only sound that fills the room is the banter between a demon named Michael and his tiny human friend, Eleanor, on the TV. There's nothing romantic about this setting. I go to push her off my lap so I can pull her upstairs, but the worry in her gaze makes me pause.

"Oh," she says as her face falls, "I'm sorry. I must've misread things." She looks around the room, as if desperate to avoid my gaze.

I'm such a fucking idiot. My sweet, beautiful Natalie thinks I'm rejecting her. That I don't want what she wants.

"Hey." I soften my voice as I grab her chin, forcing her to look at me. "You didn't. I want this." A rumble deep within my chest punctuates each word. "More than fucking anything. But your needs will always come before my own, and this is not a setting befitting what I've imagined doing to you."

I expect her to survey the room and agree with me. To demand that she's worthy of so much more. To ensure the mood is just right for her to even consider this. That's not Natalie, though. That was Susanna, finding the slightest excuse not to have sex, and to confuse Natalie with Susanna is a shameful mistake on my part. Natalie's rich brown eyes hold me in place. She doesn't need to look around, because she doesn't care where we are or what time of day it is.

Instead, she kisses me. Her lips are gentle as she plucks at mine. "Winston," she whispers into my mouth, "I want you to fuck me so hard that I forget what planet I'm on." Another soft kiss. "Can you do that?"

A breath lodges in my throat as my hands tremble. She's perfect. My dick throbs painfully as it strains against my pants, my need for her so visceral that my chest is already heaving. Not only does this feel like I'm on the verge of releasing one hundred and twenty-three years of pent-up sexual tension, but it also feels like, in many ways, this will be my first time having sex at all. Susanna didn't take my virginity. With those who came before her, sex felt good, but nothing beyond that word. And with Susanna, it wasn't even that. Somewhere, deep within my cells, I know it'll be different with Natalie. Better. Life-changing.

With my forehead pressed against hers, I nod. "As you wish."

When our mouths meet again, it's filthy in a way that makes precome leak from my swollen head. Our tongues are hot and eager as they slide against each other. I yank her t-shirt off, and groan at the sight of her glorious tits, bare for me. They bounce as she grinds against me, and my mouth waters at the sight of her hard nipples, the big circles of dark pink that make up her areolas, and as I trace the outline of one with my tongue, Natalie lets out a needy whimper that I never want to forget. Her skin is as delicious as her scent, a bit of sweat mixing in to add a pleasant saltiness.

She gasps as she grips my shoulders, arching her back and pushing more of her breast into my mouth. I take it, greedily sucking and biting her nipple as I pinch the other between my fingers.

"*Yes,*" she pants, her fingers running up the back of my neck and through my hair. "More."

I release her nipple and kiss along her chest until I reach

the other as I slip a hand down the front of her sleep shorts. She's bare here, too. And absolutely *soaked*.

A growl punches out of my throat as I slip a finger through her folds, meeting no resistance. "You're so wet, so responsive."

Another whimper as her mouth moves along my jaw, her tongue tracing the shell of my ear. "Ahh," she cries, "I n-need you, Winston." The next word is a breathy hiss. *"Please."*

I sink my finger deep into her core. Her walls flutter around me, and I have to focus on my breath to keep from coming this soon. A few thrusts, and I add a second finger. She's tight, but she can take it. Two fingers and my dick, however, are very different things.

Natalie's hands yank my suspenders off my shoulders, and she tugs at my shirt until I let her pull it off. When I return my attention back to fucking her with my hand, I add a third finger, and her legs jerk around my hips in response. I tip my head back so I can properly take her in, her eyes pinched shut in ecstasy, the puffy look of her freshly sucked nipples, the erotic jiggles of her belly...I've always found the female form to be pleasing to look at, but Natalie is out of this world. It's as if I created her in my mind, and in some puzzling twist of luck for a chronically unlucky man like myself, she landed right in my lap.

When her eyes flutter open, they land on my pants, and a frown curls her lips. She unbuttons my fly and pushes my pants and underwear down my hips as far as she can until she can wrap her small hand around my length, freeing it. Her eyes widen, pupils blown out, and something flashes across her face. Is it fear? It's gone so quickly, I can't be sure.

"Jesus," I hear her mutter under her breath. "Uh, I didn't, well, I wasn't expecting. I mean, I've used plenty of dildos of various sizes, but this... You—"

Ah, it was fear. I suppose I should be flattered, but I need

Natalie to be relaxed and eager before we proceed, not afraid. Fear is the opposite of what I want her to be feeling. "You can take me. I know you can," I promise her. "We'll go slow, okay?"

She nods, the furrow in her brow easing at my words.

"If you want to stop, it doesn't matter when. You say the word, and it ends."

She swallows, leaning into my touch like a pet as I cup her cheek. "Okay."

I reach for her pussy, prepared to continue stretching her when she grabs my wrist. "No. I need you now."

"Yeah?"

Everything in me screams to protest, to insist we slow down to prevent causing her even an ounce of pain, but the way she's looking at me, like she'll die without my cock filling her up, the words never come out.

I guide the head of my cock to her entrance, at first just gliding it back and forth, mixing my precome with her sweet nectar.

"Oh god," she cries, her nails scraping against my chest. Her hips slam down, eager to reach me. I'm not even inside her yet, and I feel a deep tingle at the base of my spine. I stroke my head against her clit, focusing on the friction and where I've learned she likes it most.

Grabbing her hips, I slow her movements. She looks down, pouting, a flash of fury in her gaze until she sees what I'm doing. Spreading the swollen lips of her pussy, I push inside, just enough to feel her tight channel clamping down around me.

A choked gasp rips from her throat as we lock eyes.

"Breathe," I remind her.

She nods, her hands coming up to squeeze her tits as I feed her another punishing inch.

It comes out of nowhere. Rips through me violently

without warning. My body seizes up, the feel of her core, so slick, so hot, and so good (too good) for me that I lose control of my body and come. And come. And come. Black spots flicker at the corner of my vision as I clutch her body to mine, holding on to her like a tornado is on the verge of tearing me away. I hear distant noises, low and gravelly, that I assume must be coming from me, but the sound is so far outside my body that I can't be certain.

"I've got you," Natalie whispers, her hand in my hair and the other stroking across my back.

Realization dawns.

Shit.

Did I really just come without being fully seated inside her?

I'm mortified. This is not what I promised her. I told her that her needs would come before mine, and I've failed. What a pathetic excuse for a man.

"I'm sorry," I mutter, my head hanging against her chest. "That was not—"

"Shh," Natalie interjects, lifting my chin enough to kiss my forehead. "Winston, you haven't had sex in over a century. Did you really think you'd be able to last?"

Honestly, yes. At least, that's what I'd hoped. The dozens (hundreds, actually) of fantasies I've had about fucking Natalie never included premature ejaculation. But—

She laughs, pinning me with a look of affection that tells me I'm taking this too seriously. I take in the halo of light around her face and shoulders, the drop of sweat running down her neck and between her heavy breasts, and the reverence beaming from her every pore. There's enough time for us to get this right, and there will be instances where our sex is sillier than sexy, or clumsy at first, or wherein one of us is too in our own head to come. Perfection isn't the goal of sex. Not for me, anyway. It's intimacy. A closeness with Natalie that only we can experience whilst our bodies are connected. That's all I want, and it's happening right now.

I laugh with her, softly nipping at the hollow of her neck. My stubble must tickle her there, because her giggle grows louder, wilder. A calm settles over me at the break in the tension. I can fix this. My needs have been met. Now is my chance to focus on hers.

With a renewed sense of determination, I say, "I just need a minute to recover." My chest is still heaving, and I'm surprised to find my cock is still hard as it rests against Natalie's mound. There's come all over her lower belly and in the soft curls above her cunt, and the sight of it triggers a primal groan deep within my lungs. She looks filthy, and like...mine. I want to cover her body in it, force her to let it dry on her skin so that every step she takes outside this house, passersby will smell it on her and know that she belongs only to me.

She reaches between us, collecting a handful of my seed from where it's coating her belly, and wraps her hand around my length, using it to lubricate me. My dick throbs in her grasp, and I can't seem to make sense of what I'm seeing or feeling. I've never remained hard like this before, and it's not as if I only came a little. I've created a mess between our bodies with my seed.

Just as I suspected, it's different with Natalie. Better than I ever could've imagined.

She guides my fat head back toward her clit, and sets a steady rhythm, stroking me while rubbing my cock against that sensitive, swollen nub. I'm entranced. Natalie is using me to take what she needs. Part of me wants to take over, but soon, she's writhing against me as shallow gasps escape her lips. I use my hands and mouth on her chest, biting the underside of her breast softly before easing the pain with my tongue.

When her movements become erratic, I take my cock from her hand and guide it back inside her cunt. She's practically dripping now, and it slides in easily, but only a few inches.

"Winston," she moans, her hands coming to the back of the couch, on either side of my head. "More." She's begging now, and I can deny her nothing.

I watch her wince the deeper I go, and I have to remind her twice more to breathe. She's taking me so well. "Almost there," I vow, running a thumb over the hood of her clit, then tapping it gently, just once.

That's what does it. Her walls convulse around me as her body falls forward against my chest. She doesn't even realize it, I don't think, but she's impaled herself the rest of the way on my cock with that small movement. We're hip to hip now as she bounces up and down and her body quakes in my arms, her cries and the wet squelch of her cunt echoing through the house. I remain still, biting the inside of my cheek until I taste copper, trying to be what she needs while she rides out her orgasm. I also want to make sure she's not in any pain.

When her moans soften into panting breaths, I pull back to pepper her face with kisses. "You're so beautiful. So perfect, Natalie." I brush the hair off her face, stroking along the pinkest part of her cheeks. "Are you okay? Any pain?"

Her eyes finally open, and they're filled with so much warmth my heart skips. She shakes her head.

Brushing my nose against hers, I whisper. "I won't move until you're ready, okay?"

She bites her lip. That magnificent plump lip that's even more swollen from my kisses. What she does next, I don't see coming. Natalie's hands settle back on my shoulders, and she lifts herself up, then slams herself back down.

We moan together, the sensation of it too much for both of us.

"Fuck," I shout when she does it again. "Sweetheart, you are ruining my resolve."

"Ah, you're so," she cries, tears streaming down her cheeks, "s-so fucking deep."

The slap of our bodies gets louder as I shift my hips up to meet her. I feel her teeth sink into the base of my throat as I grip the round globes of her ass, trying to make this time last for her. To make it unforgettable. Then I remember where she likes my touch the most, where she *needs* it most.

I reach down to stroke her clit, but before I can, she's coming around me, hard, and fast, a silent scream keeping her lips parted wide. "Again? So soon?" I kiss the tears off her cheeks as I continue to thrust, and she holds on tight despite the limpness in the rest of her body. Grabbing her by the ass, I flip our bodies until she's on her back beneath me, her right leg straightened and her foot next to my ear, the flush of her skin stealing the breath from my lungs.

"Yes, Winston," she whimpers, her gaze pleading as her other leg wraps around my hips.

I smile, press a kiss to her brow as I whisper, "Don't worry, love. I'm not done with you yet." I feel her heel pressing into my ass as I begin to thrust, warmth building at the base of my spine and spreading throughout my limbs at this new angle, and how much deeper I'm able to go like this. I could live here, I realize, in her tight heat and vise-like grip around my cock. She must feel it too, because her moans get louder, more guttural.

My mind is a fog as I drive into her, my balls slapping against the skin of her ass. Everything inside me coils tight, the air around us crackling.

"W-Winston." It's a plea, I think.

I answer it by moving faster, harder, until my orgasm tears through me and I'm filling her cunt with my come.

It becomes impossible to hold myself up any longer, so I let my weight sink into her.

She lets out a contented sigh as she pulls me somehow closer, more flush against her body.

It takes us a while to come down. Several minutes, an hour, I have no fucking idea. But when we do, I push onto my forearms to ask, "How do you feel?"

She lets out a breathy chuckle, unable to hold her eyes open. "Amazing."

I get to my feet, then grab a washcloth from the hall bathroom, running it under warm water. When I return, I run it over Natalie's cheeks, down her chest, stomach, and clean the mess of come that's dripping between her thighs. I'm not sure what compels me to do it, but my teeth sink into the fleshiest part of her inner thigh, and she tries to kick me away with an "Ouch! You dick."

I regret nothing, kissing the red mark I left, while hoping it takes years to fade. Like this, with her legs parted wide, I can see every inch of her pussy, and I'm unable to look anywhere else. It's too beautiful. Too pink and engorged. A masterpiece worthy of replacing the Mona Lisa. I study each dip and curve and practically every follicle of hair that can be found on this part of her body. She is... *God,* a miracle that must've fallen from the fucking sky. I toss the washcloth aside and haul her into my arms.

She squeaks in surprise as her arms wrap around my neck. "Where are we going?"

I adjust the arm beneath her knees, ensuring she's comfortable with the way I'm carrying her. "Upstairs."

She looks puzzled. "For?"

I know how little she expects of others, and I'm determined to show her how much higher her standards should be. I can't help the smile that's curling my lip. She must be able to see how excited I am. "I'm drawing you a bath."

Chapter 18
Natalie

My body is wrecked. A mess of loose limbs and dark red marks from his bruising grip and wicked mouth. I've never felt so utterly satisfied. When he carries me bridal style up the stairs, my mind doesn't take me to that dark corner of self-loathing about my body and how heavy I am and how I look to him from this angle. It can't, because my mind is empty. He fucked me so well that I couldn't recite the alphabet if I tried.

Winston places me on my feet inside the bathroom attached to Penelope's bedroom. My legs feel like jelly, and it takes a minute of holding on to Winston before I can stand on my own. This is not a room I've seen. Since the bedroom hadn't been touched after Penelope's passing, I assumed the same was true for her bathroom. But it's massive and surprisingly clean. Not a speck of dust to be found on the toilet seat or the support bars on either side of it, the sill of the oval-shaped window overlooking Mapletown forest, the walk-in shower, or the oversized tub that could fit at least three Winstons.

"How long have you been plotting to run me a bath?" I ask,

knowing that Lindsay certainly didn't bother to clean this room before she left me here. What he says next stops my heart.

His cheeks flush as his gaze travels down my naked body. Shy Winston is about to peel back another layer of himself for me. "Since the first time we spoke, and I heard the weariness in your voice." He nods. "I saw how defeated you were, in the way gravity was pulling you toward the ground by your shoulders. I thought, this woman needs a long soak in a cloud of bubbles." He chews on the inside of his lip, hesitant to continue. When he does, he says, "What I didn't expect was that I would be the lucky one to run it for you."

I scoff. "You feel lucky to pour bubble bath into a pool of hot water?" It can't be *that* much fun. "I would say you need to get out more, but..."

His lips twitch, and for a second, I wonder if I've offended him. Something flashes across his face. I can't tell what. When it morphs into amusement, I let out a breath I didn't know I was holding.

"One day, you'll understand. For now, get in the tub, sweetheart."

I shiver at the authority in his tone. He holds out his hand, and I take it, letting him guide me into the tub, his strong arms ready to catch me if I stumble. The water's so hot it stings my calves, but the deeper I sink into it, the quicker my body adjusts, and soon I'm moaning as the tension leaves my muscles.

I wait for the feel of Winston's calloused fingers against my skin, but it never comes. A needy whine escapes my lips at the sight of him leaving the room. He dims the lights, and his tight ass flexes, my mouth filling with saliva.

"Where are you going?"

He reaches me in a single stride, grabbing my chin between his thumb and pointer finger, tilting it up. My gaze locks with his. His green eyes dart down to my lips, and it's like he becomes hypnotized. I open my mouth to break his trance, but before I can, he says in a low rasp, "If you think I'd abandon you like this, naked and soaking wet, you've underestimated my obsession with you."

My stomach flutters, and I wonder if this is just him engaging in some innocent post-sex flirting, or if there's any truth to his words. We've come a long way since that first conversation in the driveway, where he scolded me for inviting Mark over, but *obsessed?* Could that really be how he feels? The term isn't exactly a synonym for love, but it's adjacent to it, right? If Winston behaved in a toxic manner, I'd say no. And, admittedly, he got a little territorial when Dominic dropped me off. And before I knew he lived here, I guess it could be argued that his penchant for making himself invisible and watching me was stalkerish.

On the other hand, Winston is the first romantic partner that's ever made me feel precious, that my needs are important. The sex is amazing, the best I've had, but more than that, he makes me laugh. I feel safer in his arms than anywhere else. If that's how Winston defines his obsession, couldn't I say the same about him? If I were to add those factors together, wouldn't the more appropriate term be lov–

No. I can't go there. Not yet. After Kyle, I swore I wouldn't lay my heart bare until I was sure about how the other person felt. I also have no idea what's going to happen when Lindsay decides to reclaim Caraway Manor for her own use. We decided to keep this casual, so that's what we're going to do. There are too many unknowns to make any serious declarations.

Winston kisses the tip of my nose and leaves, and I sink deeper into the heat of the water. He returns quicker than I expect, fully dressed, apart from his bare feet.

"Boo," I say with a dramatic pout. When he starts rolling up his sleeves, exposing his thick, veiny forearms, my mouth falls open. I wouldn't be surprised if drool spilled out.

He notices, then laughs as he comes to kneel behind my head.

The second his hands are on my shoulders, I melt. My hands grip the sides of the tub, my knuckles whiter than milk as his thumbs dig into the knots on my upper back. It hurts, but in the best way. He moves up my neck and into my scalp, then down the base of my spine. My eyes remain closed the whole way, moaning, my core clenching around nothing.

His lips close around my earlobe, moving down my neck. "Those little noises you make drive me fucking crazy." It's practically a growl, and when his teeth graze my pulse, my hips buck in the water. I suck in a breath as I watch his hand move to the front of my body and slip deeper beneath the bubbles. He parts the lips of my pussy and swipes his thumb across my clit. Despite the time that's passed since we had sex, I'm still oversensitive—not enough to have me pushing his hand away, though.

I don't even notice his other hand squeezing my breast, because he sinks two fingers inside me and I'm so wet, my body taut like a bowstring, that I'm arching into his hand, sending water splashing over the sides of the tub.

"Yes," he grits, pressing rough, bruising kisses along the column of my throat.

"W-Winston," I gasp, my nails digging into his arms as I hold on for dear life.

There's a steady rumble deep within his chest, and I feel it vibrate against my back as he adds a third finger, hooking into me and reaching that place deep within my pussy that sends a sharp buzz throughout my body and has my feet kicking up out of the water. I'm close. I can feel it crawling up my spine with every thrust.

The bump of his palm against my clit has my thighs quaking, my grip tight around his wrist as I hold him in place. "More," I keen in a low voice I don't recognize. Hot tears sting my cheeks, a stark contrast to the rapidly decreasing temperature of the water. My body is on fire as Winston pulls me slowly up the first hill of the rollercoaster. The anticipation, the tension, it's almost too much to bear knowing how close I am to the rapid descent into euphoria.

"You want more, Natalie?" His breath hitches against my ear. It sounds as if he's as close to coming as I am.

I nod. "Please." I'm begging, whimpering as I continue to buck against his hand.

"I'd do *anything*, hand my soul over to the devil, just to see you come again."

When he pulls his fingers from my cunt, I want to scream in protest, until those three fingers start rubbing my clit, circling it. I unravel almost instantly after that. My vision blurs as my hips jerk against his hand and water sloshes onto the tiled floor. The sound that fills my ears is the roar exploding from Winston's throat. His head is pressed against my cheek, his tight grip on my breast painful, but in a way that extends my orgasm, a slower wave that I ride for what feels like a very long time.

When our breathing returns to normal, Winston hauls me out of the tub, wrapping a towel around me and sweetly rubbing my sides as he kisses across my cheeks and eyelids. I look down at his pants and laugh at the wet spot. "What was the point of getting dressed, exactly?"

He grins as he pulls me against his chest, not caring how wet my skin still is. "You're just jealous because I never have to do laundry."

I nod. "Damn. That *is* unfair."

"Nothing about life is fair, and I'll never understand why our kind assumes it should be. Being alive is mostly monotonous, with the occasional chaotic break to keep us from losing our fucking minds."

I pull back to look at him. Is he really that cynical? "Then what's the point of all this? Why do we keep going, do you think?"

He brushes a lock of wet hair behind my ear. "I don't know. Maybe because, in this whirlwind of tedium and confusion and unspeakable pain, there are moments when everything makes sense. When it feels like time stops just for you. You, and, if you're lucky, the person you'd die to protect. We don't rise each day seeking fairness. It's the search for wholeness that keeps us going." He clears his throat. "It is for me, at least."

Winston undresses, tosses a few towels around the tub where the water is splattered across, and we make our way back across the hall, into my bathroom. He pushes the towel off my body and pulls me into the shower, where he makes me come two more times with his mouth before the water runs cold.

I'm sated, relaxed, and my body is begging me for a nap when my phone rings. My heart stutters when I see it's Lindsay. Not that I dread talking to my closest friend, but the idea that one of these days, she's going to call and say, "Hey, I've decided I'd like my house back now," sends me into a sticky web of anxiety.

Winston sees the name flash across my phone, and his lips form a grim line. He must have the same fear.

"Hey Linds," I say, trying to sound delighted and not at all nervous to talk to her.

"Nat! Girl, guess what?"

I don't want to guess. This game sucks for anxious people.

There's absolutely no way to win, and the only thing it makes us better at is catastrophizing. "What?" I finally ask.

"I'm taking Friday off, and we're going to have a girls' weekend!"

What? This Friday? That's two days away. As long as I've known Lindsay, she's been a meticulous planner. Spontaneity is not her thing. "Is everything okay?"

"What? Of course! Couldn't be better. I just need a break. From work, from life, from disappointing *men*, i.e. men." Her tone is jittery, and a little manic. There's something she's not telling me. "So I figured we'd have a good ol' fashioned sleepover, and you can show me this bar you're working at now, and we'll hit the town! Sound good?"

What can I say? *No thanks, Linds. I really appreciate you giving me a free place to stay, but you're not allowed to come visit because I'd rather spend the weekend having sex with my ghost boyfriend in every room of the house you own.* "Sounds great. I can't wait to see you," I tell her, dodging the impatient, frustrated look Winston's giving me.

"Okay. I'll text you when I'm on my way. Byeee."

The phone disconnects, and Winston and I exchange a knowing, panicked glance.

"Lindsay's coming up this weekend."

He runs a rough hand through his hair. "Well, shit."

Chapter 19
Winston

Natalie paces across the small rug in her bedroom, nibbling on her thumbnail. "We need to figure out how to approach this." Nervous energy floats off her supple body, and my fingers twitch at my side, eager to smooth the crease in her brow. She put her loose t-shirt back on, and nothing else. Her blonde curls are dry and wild, and my gaze lingers on the pastel purple tips of her small toes. "The order of operations."

I cross my arms, leaning back against her headboard, willing myself to pay better attention. "I'll follow your lead, of course."

"If she gets here on Friday afternoon, maybe I can rush her out the door for an early dinner. Pizza. Yeah, pizza."

"Pizza is a good idea." This feels like a two-way conversation, but it isn't, really. I know nothing about Lindsay, other than the fact that I find her annoying. Natalie needs to work this out on her own, and I'll provide as much support as she'll willingly take.

"Then, at dinner, I can ease her into the existence of

monsters," she continues. "Likely, there'll be one or two working at Crust Lust, so that'll help. We'll be in public, so she won't be able to lose her shit. There will be time to answer her questions, of which, she'll have many."

"Then what?"

"She'll probably want a stiff drink. I'll take her to the bar." She blows a strand off her forehead. "I can't believe I'm not on the schedule for that night."

I knew this already. She writes her schedule down on a notepad that she sticks to the fridge. I had many plans for her Friday night off. All of them filthy.

Fucking Lindsay.

"At the bar, we'll have drinks, and after her second, she'll be buzzed but not drunk. Perfect time to tell her about you."

I snort. "Why does she need to be buzzed to find out about me?"

She rolls her eyes, putting a hand on her hip. "Babe. Come on. Learning that monsters freely wander about town is not the same as learning a centuries-old ghost lives in your house, had a close friendship with your late grandmother, and is currently fucking your friend."

A fair point. I nod. "Right. Wait until she's buzzed." I'm not offended by the way she labels our relationship. It seems reductive, but she stated clearly that she wishes to keep this "casual." She has to know it's more than that, though, right? It always has been. Since the first kiss, I've belonged to her in every way that matters. I thought, by the way she looks at me when my cock is buried deep inside her, that she feels the way I do. That nothing matters outside the pocket of space our bodies occupy when we're together. Maybe I'm wrong. Maybe I'm just the first man who gets her off and doesn't treat her like an afterthought.

My fist clenches against my ribs. Once Lindsay's visit is

over, I'll talk to her about this. It's a discussion that's long over-due, and we should be on the same page. Lindsay better allow my Natalie to stay here. Otherwise, I might set the house ablaze and blame it on a newly discovered spider nest.

"What about the termites?"

She scrunches her nose and growls. "Shit! I forgot about the termites. That should rank third among earth-shattering news I need to deliver, don't you think?"

"Yeah, probably. She knows termites exist, so that works in our favor." I come to stand in front of Natalie. She stops pacing and instinctively leans her head against my chest. My arms wrap around her, and I revel in the feel of her beating heart against my sternum. "Everything will be fine. Lindsay will understand. You've got this."

We spend the rest of the evening getting organized and cleaning the house in preparation for Lindsay's arrival. Natalie doesn't seem any less nervous, but cleaning seems to be a productive distraction for her, so I simply keep an eye on her as she moves from room to room, stopping her with a glass of water when she seems thirsty, and forcing her to put the antibacterial wipes down for a dinner break a moment before her stomach demands to be fed. She chose breakfast for dinner, which includes my famous French toast. It seems to be her favorite.

We're cleaning different areas of the kitchen. Natalie is wiping down the shelves inside the fridge, and I'm putting the clean dishes away while her small black speaker plays the greatest hits of a man named Hozier. For such a happy person, my Natalie's taste in music is awfully melancholic. We move around each other seamlessly, without words, kind of like a dance. It's as if we've been sharing this space for years. That is, until I find a plate with crusted red sauce on it and go to place it back in the sink. It's at this same moment that Natalie takes the bowl full of ice water from the fridge to dump in the sink, slamming it into my stomach. The dirty plate shatters on the floor, and the water splashes onto both of us, drenching our shirts equally.

This is the kind of situation that would normally send me into a fit of rage. The carelessness of it, paired with the preventability, would cause me to erupt. I'm shocked when it doesn't, and even more so when I feel my lips curve into a smile, matching the one on Natalie's beautiful face.

Laughter bursts out of us as we shake the freezing water from our skin and clothes. She wrings out her T-shirt, shaking her head. "Well," she says, pushing a wet strand of hair off her cheek, "I *was* working up a sweat, so at least that's taken care of."

She always sees the upside, and I have no idea how she does it. My mind simply doesn't work that way. Every experience I have serves as confirmation that I'm better off alone, as far from other people as possible—Natalie being the exception—and the more time passes, the deeper this theory burrows itself into my psyche.

Natalie is the opposite, never considering that her troubles are caused by her proximity to others. She's stubbornly cheerful, like a weed intent on reaching for the sun, but in a way that makes me want to be more like her.

I try to push away the nagging thought of what I mean to her, but it's next to impossible when I discover more of her quirks that are so cute I want to lock her inside this house for a week and not let her out of my sight. The way she closes one eye to aim when she throws a napkin or anything remotely resembling a ball into the trash bin. The childlike grunt she lets out as she's searching for the most comfortable position in bed before falling asleep. The scent of her skin in the morning—so warm and fruity and *her*.

She's still far messier than I'd like, but when she spills salsa on her shirt while we're eating the tacos I prepared, or when I find flattened popcorn beneath the throw pillows on the couch, annoyance is not the dominant emotion that registers anymore. It's amusement.

Taylor Swift is even starting to grow on me. Natalie blasts it as we work, and I must say, the weaving of her tales of heartbreak is...impressive. Eloquent. Undeniably catchy. When Natalie catches me singing along to "The Man" as she passes me sweeping the staircase, she chortles, and I'm grateful that's where the mockery ends.

Once Natalie's Thursday night shift comes around, the house is mostly clean. The parts we know Lindsay will occupy, that is. Natalie plans to take a trip to the market tomorrow morning in order to restock the fridge. While she's gone, I've been tasked with alerting Ethel about our upcoming guest, and checking to see why the dryer is taking at least three cycles to dry Natalie's clothes.

Ethel takes the news well, mostly because she happens to be in a bright mood today. Natalie plans to keep Lindsay far from the garden to avoid any potential unpleasantness.

Grabbing the toolbox from its designated shelf in the basement, I make my way into the laundry room next door. Once I clean out the filter and disconnect it from the power source, I set about taking it apart to get a deeper look.

By the time I've cleaned the lint filter housing, the dryer drum, ensured the dryer vent is clear, and screwed the parts back together, Natalie is an hour from her shift being over. I panic at the state of my dirty clothes and lack of a plan for what to cook for dinner, when my gaze lands on her full laundry basket sat atop the washer. On top of the pile is a pair of midnight blue, high-waisted panties. My pulse quickens. These clothes haven't been cleaned. This is the pair she put on last night before bed. The pair I shoved down to her ankles in the middle of the night so I could feast on her pussy. Now they're just *here*. Unattended.

I check over my shoulder, despite knowing she's not home yet, before pressing the soft cotton against my nose. My eyes fall closed as her warm, sweet musk fills my lungs. I stuff the underwear into my pocket, hoping she has enough pairs that she won't notice one is missing. Or wait, this is the second pair I've pilfered, isn't it? Oh well.

Modern women must have vast collections of undergarments, right? Clothing is cheaper than it was in my day. I know that. A new pair of underwear is, what, thirty cents? If she makes a fuss, I could find a way to sell some of Susanna's old jewelry on the internet to pay her back.

I drop the underwear in my room in the attic before shifting into mist and floating downstairs to the kitchen. The fridge and cabinets are mostly bare, but we have the ingredients for chicken lasagna, so that's what I make.

Natalie bursts into the kitchen with a wide, toothy grin as I'm taking the lasagna out of the oven. "I got you a present!"

"Is that so?"

She hands me a blue and white polka dot bag with blue tissue paper sticking out of it, bouncing on the balls of her feet.

When I pull out the matte black box, I stare at the photo on the top, confused.

"It's a phone!" She takes the box from my hands and rips it open, tossing the spare cords, plastic sleeve, and twist-tied accessories on the kitchen island. "Well, barely a phone, compared to the others out there. They practically gave it to me for free." The phone is a small silver square, and I'm surprised when she unfolds it into a rectangle. She powers it on and starts pressing the small buttons. "You can't connect to the internet, but you can make calls and texts. I figured that's all you'd be interested in doing for now. You can upgrade later if you want, once you master the basics."

I force a smile, hoping she can't see through it. "This is a lovely gift, but"—I clear my throat, softening my tone—"what would I need this for?" She's the only one I care to speak to, and when she's not here, she's at work, unlikely able to chat anyway.

She nods with a knowing expression. Not hurt by my question, which is a relief. "This way, I can send you a warning text next time another man is driving me home, so you don't get spooked."

I scoff, offended. "I was *not* spooked." Furious, bloodthirsty, seconds away from committing a serious crime, yes, but not spooked.

"Or if I'm running late, or if I'm bored at work, or if I just want to tell you my legs are sore as hell from the way your gigantic dick almost split me in half." She kisses my cheek, and I forget why I thought this gift would be another item collecting dust in the study.

"I'll never tire of hearing that." I hold out my hand, palm up. "Okay, show me how to use this machine so I may hear more about my dick."

She doesn't hand it over. Instead, she takes a seat at the counter while I fix her a plate of lasagna, and tinkers with the phone between bites. Once the basic settings are in place, she shows me how to type using the number buttons and pulls up the only contact saved in the phone.

"That's my number. Send me a message."

It's...difficult. I struggle for several minutes. Penelope had a large computer she kept in the study, and a cellular phone of her own, but I never attempted to use them. There was no need. With each button I press, I worry I'm about to accidentally call 911 and be forced to explain that there's no emergency at Caraway Manor, just a ghost attempting to use technology for the first time.

By the time Natalie's almost done with her meal, I manage to successfully send my first text.

Hello, sweet Natalie. Sincerely Yours, Winston

Natalie: YOU DID IT! I'm so proud of you! 🥰

We do the dishes together, shut down the house, and make our way upstairs while pawing at each other's clothes. I fuck her against the wall, then once with her sitting on the edge of her dresser before we make our way to the bed. She falls asleep sweaty and relaxed, with her cheek against my chest. Being with her, whether it's having sex or just lying next to her, is *easy*. Comfortable. As if we've been doing this for as long as I've been dead. I stare at the ceiling, measuring with my eyes while I figure out how to install a skylight in Natalie's room without her knowing.

The next day, Natalie is abuzz with anxiety as she waits for Lindsay to arrive. She receives a text around lunchtime from her saying she's about an hour away. There's nothing I can do to calm Natalie, so I follow on her heels, ready with antibacterial wipes in hand to clean any last-minute messes my Natalie makes.

"What if she freaks out and, I don't know, brings a priest here to exorcise you from the house?" she asks, her voice higher pitched than normal.

"Is Lindsay even religious?" She doesn't strike me as someone with the fear of god in her.

"No," she replies with a frown. "But what if this is the thing that sends her in that direction?"

She's babbling now as her anxiety goes into overdrive. I step into her path and take her face in my hands.

"What if–"

I don't let her continue. Instead, I lean down and silence her with a kiss. Her lips are frozen at first, but it doesn't take long for her mouth to move against mine, and for her body to sink into my embrace. I lick into her, tasting the deepest corners of her mouth. She lets out a needy moan that has my cock throbbing painfully. When I pull back, her gaze is heavy-lidded, and her lips swollen. She's impossibly beautiful.

"Did you do that to shut me up?" she asks with a playful smirk.

I run my hands up and down her arms. "It was more to calm you down. The shutting up was an added bonus."

She shoves at my chest, her soft chuckle filling the air and wrapping around me like a blanket.

We go through the plan a few times, since it seems to give Natalie an outlet for her nervousness. But the plan is obliterated when Lindsay arrives red-faced with tears staining her cheeks.

Chapter 20
Natalie

"Fuck men," Lindsay says through gritted teeth. "Fuck every single overpaid, mediocre one of them. There isn't one man on this entire goddamn planet worthy of anyone's time or attention."

I rub her shoulder as Vyla puts a gin and tonic in front of me and a martini in front of Lindsay. This is the second drink for me and the third for her. I had to quickly make her aware of the existence of monsters in Mapletown in the car between the house and the bar. She showed up at the house, sobbing, tossed her bags inside the front door, and grabbed my hand. There would be no pizza in our immediate future. She wasn't hungry. The only thing she wanted to do was drink her sorrows away.

I had no choice but to follow along and look for breaks in the conversation to dump my three pieces of news. To my shock, she didn't seem to care much about the first piece.

"You mean, like, werewolves and shit?" she asked as we pulled into the parking lot of the Fast Glass.

"Yeah, and lots of other species of monster. They're real,

and they live here. The owner of the bar is a zombie," I explained. "But he *doesn't* eat human brains, so don't worry."

I don't think she believed me at first, since she nodded and said, "As long as none of them hit on me and then ghost me immediately after, whatever. It's cool."

When we went inside and I introduced her to Vyla the orc and Rizlan the dragon behind the bar, her eyes widened to the point I was ready for them to pop out of her skull and roll across the floor. She took a handful of deep breaths, shook their hands with a tight smile, and plopped onto a stool at the bar, eager to order her first drink. After Vyla sauntered away to retrieve the glasses for our drinks, Lindsay turned to me and whispered, "Wow, monsters. Okay. I'm good." And that was it.

"Is it Billy? Or someone new you're seeing?" I ask Lindsay.

She lets out a sardonic chuckle. "Billy. No, he's too busy *not* being a deadbeat loser with his new girlfriend. Guess who finally decided to become a fucking grown-up? Not that I'd be into him anyway."

I believe her. She can barely stand Billy, but it's always weird to see an ex move on, especially when they start acting the way you wanted them to act with someone who isn't you. "I didn't realize you were dating anyone."

Lindsay shrugs. "Nothing serious. I reactivate my dating apps every few months, go on some horrible dates, and turn them off again. There was just this guy..." She gulps her martini, winces as the drink slides down her throat, and smooths her slick-straight ponytail. "It was casual, until it wasn't. I'm such a moron, Nat," she whines as she drops her head into her hands. Then she peeks over her hands with a sheepish look on her face. "He's twenty-five years old. Why did I–"

I press my hand to my mouth to avoid a spit take. "I'm sorry. Twenty-five? You were dating a twenty-five-year-old?"

It's not funny, but I can't help but laugh. Linds is such a buttoned-up, no-nonsense mom and corporate badass, I'm blown away by the slip-up in her everyday rigidity. I'm proud of her. "Oh my god, does that mean he never had a Myspace page?"

A surprised laugh tumbles out of her as she nods. "Never knew the cutting betrayal of being bumped from a friend's top eight."

"Well, clearly, you're better off."

"Know what else?" She pauses, looking around us to see if anyone's listening. "He didn't know who Madonna was."

I smack the top of the bar, aghast. "You are kidding me."

"He put on some EDM club cover of 'Like a Virgin' and when I told him the original was better, he had no idea what I was talking about. It devolved into a twenty-minute education of her impact on pop music." She shivers. "It was *chilling*."

She lists a dozen more examples of aging herself in the presence of this manchild, but when I catch her staring off into the distance, biting her lip, it's clear why those moments weren't enough to make her end it.

"Sex was good then?"

"Yeah." A swoony sigh bursts out of her. "It melted my brain. I truly believe that's what happened. That hairless fuckboy with three percent body fat dicked me down so well that it killed the part of my brain responsible for critical thinking." She's laughing too, now, and the dark cloud above us feels like it's finally cleared.

"Well, brain-melting sex will do that to ya," I say with a nod. Is this a good segue to letting her know about Winston? I certainly have my own sexcapade stories to share as of late. After looking at the bloodshot state of her eyes, I decide against it. This is about her. She needs me to be there for her right now. I lean close to her ear, "I'm going to need explicit details."

She slows her drinking as she fills me in on the many positions they tried. Each one sends a throbbing ache into my joints as I wonder how Lindsay managed to execute them without breaking a hip. Particularly, the Golden Gate.

"A decade of yoga," she replies with a wink.

I need to start exercising.

"The best was when he took charge." She looks wistful, devastated, as if she'll never find another sexual partner that can meet her needs. The reason she's so devastated is that this Gen-Z shithead love-bombed her for weeks, got her addicted to the athletic sex they had, and then ghosted her. She facepalms. "I'm so embarrassed. You'd think I haven't been walking this blue marble fifteen years longer than he has."

"Was this your first time being ghosted?"

Amazingly, I have yet to experience this particular brand of torture. But when you don't put yourself out there, you don't get rejected.

"No," she grumbles, chewing on her olive after draining her glass. "This is the first time I cared. That's the difference."

"I'm so sorry, Linds."

Vyla comes over and drops her elbows on the bar. "Settle a bet for me, pretty babies." She gestures to Rizlan as he waits by the kitchen for plates of food to be ready. "We're trying to figure out what you are," she looks at Lindsay pointedly. "Rizlan thinks–"

"Ugh, seriously?" Lindsay groans dramatically. "Even in a fucking monster town? My dad is second-generation Italian American, and my mom was born in Korea. Okay? Jesus." She's definitely buzzed, because her words are starting to slur, and she's not aware of the amused look Vyla shares with Rizlan.

Normally, she'd be delighted to have the opportunity to mess with a well-meaning person (in most cases, a white person) when they try to guess her ethnic background. But that's not what's happening.

"Cool," Vyla says with a patient smile. "Not what I was meant, though."

I put a hand on Lindsay's forearm. "Linds, she means ancestral monster line." I explain the requirements to enter the town, and that she must have some kind of monster blood in her since the house was in Penelope's name and was able to pass it on to her.

"I'm betting you're a witch." Vyla says, then, louder, "Rizlan thinks you're a werewolf. Can you please tell him how extraordinarily stupid and wrong he is?"

Rizlan saunters over with a crooked smile. He's, well, I wouldn't describe him as traditionally handsome, but you *cannot* miss him in a crowd. His features are striking and rough and a little terrifying. I'd be nervous to be near him if I hadn't already learned he's a ridiculous softie. Whenever we need a bouncer, Rizlan plays the role like the Meryl Steep of Mapletown, but those who know him well know that his look is the only tough thing about him.

He watches Lindsay with interest, his gold eyes sparkling as he looks her up and down.

"How could she be a werewolf without knowing?" Vyla asks, incredulous.

"Lots of weres shift later in life than expected," he says. His rich voice is rumbly and warm, despite the shiver it sends through me. He also has a subtle accent that I can't place. Nordic, if I had to guess. The man could narrate erotic audiobooks and make a fortune. I'd tell him as much if I weren't worried it could be taken as sexual harassment, and I'm not going to risk losing the first job I've truly enjoyed in years. He's so tall that he has to bend at the waist to lean on the bar, which he does, next to Lindsay. "Perhaps it hasn't happened for you yet?"

She chokes out a laugh. "I'm in my forties, man. If I were part wolf, I think I'd know by now." If she notices the way Rizlan is ogling her, she doesn't point it out. Her focus is on Vyla. "A witch, though. That's a possibility."

I gawk at her. "Really? What makes you think that? And *why* are you just telling me now?"

She chews on the inside of her cheek, thoughtful. "I have this vague memory of Dad telling me about his nonna, and how she'd have herbs drying all over the kitchen, and she'd recite things under her breath while cooking. How she'd break out these old books and teach him rituals for good luck."

I know I'm staring, but I can't help it. There are a million questions running through my head.

She jerks back. "What? It's not like he taught me any of this shit. I have zero magical powers. I can't even wrap a present without using nine pieces of tape."

"What about Penelope? Did she practice any magic?"

Lindsay shakes her head. "Not that I know of."

Vyla unrolls her impressively long, textured tongue and waggles it at Rizlan. "Ten bucks, dingus."

Rizlan rolls his eyes playfully as he pulls out his wallet and drops two five-dollar bills in her palm. "Innocent mistake." He pins Lindsay with a heated gaze. "I sensed a wildness in you. Guess I was wrong."

Lindsay finally picks up on the flirtation, and she smirks, but holds up her hand. "I'm incredibly flattered," she lets her gaze linger on Rizlan's sharp jawline and wide chest, "but I'm not open for business. Maybe never again."

He nods, patient and mostly unbothered, before heading back behind the bar and talking to Vlad the vampire at the far end.

I never get my chance to tell Lindsay about Winston. We have two more rounds—my last is a water, and Lindsay's is a Long Island Iced Tea—before walking home. I'm not drunk, but I'm still in no shape to drive, so Lindsay stumbles and I hold her up on our long walk up the hill to Caraway Manor. Anything I tell her now, she likely won't remember, so I promise myself I'll tell her tomorrow over coffees and breakfast burritos at Hot & Steamy Coffee Bar.

I text Winston on the walk home that Lindsay still doesn't know. That he'll have to remain invisible until tomorrow.

> Winston: I refuse to meet the morning sun without feeling your lips on mine. Sincerely Yours, Winston.

A fluttering warmth spreads throughout my stomach, and I don't even try to hide my smile. Lindsay is singing "Creep" by TLC to herself between hiccups, and has no idea what I'm doing. I didn't think this giddy feeling was possible for someone my age, but holy shit. The butterflies are there, and they're multiplying by the second.

> I miss you too. Meet me in my room once Lindsay's asleep?

> Btw, you don't have to add a signature to each text. I know it's you.

> Winston: What is "Btw?" Sincerely Yours, Winston.

> It means "By The Way."

Winston: I see. Regardless, I won't adhere to the shorthand ribaldry of your generation. It's embarrassing. How are you not embarrassed?

Whatevs, old man.

Winston: Do not disrespect me, young lady. I'm not above punishing you.

My pussy quivers at the idea of Winston landing a firm hand on my ass enough times to leave a mark.

Mmm. I'm not above begging for that.

Seconds pass as I wait for his reply.

Winston: Come home right now.

I chuckle as I bite my bottom lip, buzzing with anticipation.

When we make it home, Lindsay kicks off her shoes haphazardly in the entryway and staggers up the stairs. I carry her luggage, pulling out a pair of pjs and her toiletry bag, leaving them on Penelope's bed. My brows lift in confusion when I find her washing her face in my bathroom.

"Linds? I put your stuff in your grandma's room. I changed the sheets this morning."

She looks at me in the bathroom mirror. "Dude, no. Nonna died in that bed. I figured we'd share yours."

I can practically hear Winston's disapproving groan behind me. It's not ideal, and I'm more than a little frustrated, but I'm trying not to judge. Some people are weirded out by death and their proximity to it. I understand. Plus, she's heartbroken and needs comfort. She drove all the way up here from Boston for the comfort she can only find in me. I'd be a shitty friend if I denied her that.

We take turns in the bathroom changing, brushing our teeth, and going through our respective nighttime beauty routines. Lindsay takes an ibuprofen, chugs a glass of water, and covers her eyes with a sleep mask. I play on my puzzle app to pass the time until I hear Lindsay's light snores. Then I tiptoe out of the room and down the hall to the study. I'm not sure why I assume that's where he'll be. The only plan we had was to meet in my bedroom. But I know he's here. I know he's watching.

My hand is still wrapped around the door knob, the door letting out a final pitiful creak before it's closed when a pair of strong arms wrap around my middle, hot breath against my ear. "You are so fucking beautiful," he rumbles.

I try to turn in his arms, but his grip is like a vise. My hand reaches back to cup the side of his face. "I'm sorry I took so long. I didn't expect her to want to sleep in my bed."

His dick is a hard steel pole against my ass. My breath hitches when he thrusts against me. His hand squeezes my breast, then moves down to my stomach. Another squeeze. Then, his fingers slip beneath my boxers. I didn't bother with underwear, since I knew we'd have this sneaky playtime, and also, I feel like I'm missing a few pairs, and clean underwear is hard to come by until I do a load of laundry.

"What is it, sweetheart? Are you lacking in attention?" He asks. I'd find it patronizing if his voice weren't so gravelly and low. "Do you need my touch?"

The part of my brain that's desperate to avoid the insinuation that I'm needy or clingy wars with my need to come. Being seen as clingy is a turn-off for most, if not all men, right? I think of Lindsay, being ghosted after falling hard for that twenty-five-year-old. I can't see Winston's eyes since he's behind me, but the sound that escapes his lips, and the way he's gripping my body, doesn't seem like he's turned off. If anything, he seems hungry to provide what I want.

But what I need from him is just release. Not anything more, right? If it's just sex, I shouldn't worry about pushing him away. Our needs are perfectly aligned. I want to come, and he wants to make me come. Why am I so terrified by the thought of him breaking my heart?

I nod, trembling too hard to offer a verbal response.

"Let me take care of you."

He walks us backward until we're both sitting in the oversized chair with the high back. His favorite. Where I always find him reading, or drawing in his sketchbook. He settles my body between his muscular thighs, pulling my back flush against his chest. His fingers graze my nipples through my t-shirt, and my breath turns into shallow pants. Winston's touch is slow, agonizing, and sends an electric current straight to my clit.

"Please," I whimper. He rewards me with a hard pinch of my nipple. It hurts, but the pleasure covers it like a blanket, and I arch my back, needing more.

His hand moves even slower, down my belly, stroking lovingly across it, then down the center of it, then lower, and lower, until his middle finger swipes along the wet seam of my pussy. He does it again, from the bottom of my entrance, all the way up to my clit, before circling it.

I cry out, and his free hand covers my mouth.

"Shh. You need to be quiet, Natalie. You don't want Lindsay to hear, do you?"

I shake my head, desperate to do what he says, not only because it would be a disaster for Lindsay to hear me, come in here, and discover that I'm getting finger fucked by the free-loading specter living in her house, but also because this dominant side of Winston is so hot I can barely keep myself from falling apart in his arms.

"Good. You're so good for me, sweetheart." His mouth is hot on my neck as he kisses and sucks my sensitive skin, continuing to whisper praise against my throat. I feel his pointer finger and middle on either side of my clit, and when he starts to move...

"Oh *god*," I mewl against his palm. Two strokes later, and I'm coming, my vision blurring as my body jerks in his hold.

"Let it out, my love. Bite my hand if you need to."

I can't focus on the endearment, on how I haven't heard it before now. My body is on fire, and I'm trying to escape it and bathe in it at the same time. The only thing I can do is sink my teeth into the fleshy skin in front of my mouth until I start to come down.

Winston's hand leaves my mouth, and I hear him chuckle. His hands roam my body, caressing and rubbing as he kisses my temple. When my breathing returns to normal, he shows me his palm. It's bleeding, and the surrounding skin is an angry red.

It feels like a stone drops into my stomach. "Oh. Oh, Winston. I'm so sorry." I pull his hand closer to my face so I can examine the bite more closely.

"It's okay, Natalie," he reassures me. "I'll be healed in under a minute. Quicker, if I shift into mist and back."

I get off his lap and wait. He sits there, his lips parting as his green eyes linger on my tits.

"Well?"

"I'm not going to shift. I want this mark to stay as long as possible."

I shouldn't like the sound of that as much as I do, but fuck it. Winston is bringing out a new side of me, and I...like it.

He's still sitting in the accent chair, male pride and arrogance curling his lips into a smirk. It's then that I realize there's something we haven't done, that I've been looking forward to doing, and there's no better time than right now.

I lower to my knees in front of him, pressing his thighs open as I unzip his pants.

"Natalie, what are yo–"

Reaching up, I pull his suspenders off his shoulders, and tug on the open waistband of his pants. "What does it look like I'm doing?" I ask through my fluttering lashes, feigning innocence.

He brushes a lock of hair behind my ear. "You don't have to do this. Really."

Yet, he's not stopping me, and I don't want him to. "I know I don't."

His dick is throbbing and hot in my hand when I free it from his underwear, whitish liquid pooling at the tip. I've had him inside me, but now, it's close up and *perfect*. It's thick and pink and mostly straight, with a vein along the underside and a fat mushroom head that I want to lick like an ice cream cone. It felt amazing inside my pussy, and my mouth waters as I lower my lips to it.

Unable to resist, I press kisses to his inner thighs and the neatly groomed hair above it, teasing him. Building the tension.

He throws his head back against the chair, groaning, "Fuck, Natalie." His grip tightens on the arms of the chair, knuckles white.

I quickly grow tired of the teasing, mostly because of the way his dick twitches against my lips. I run the flat of my tongue along the underside, tracing the vein. Then, I swirl my tongue around the head before taking him into my mouth, sucking hard.

He lets out a low grunt, guttural, as his fingers tangle in my hair, tugging until my eyes lift to his.

I wrap one hand around the base, the other massaging his

large, heavy balls as I continue to lick and suck and take him in as deep as my throat will allow.

"Your fucking mouth, Natalie." His words are reverent despite the tautness in his jaw. "You're perfect. Made for me."

My mouth moves faster, and I suck harder, keeping my stroke steady.

"Fuck! I'm so–" he grits. "I'm clo–"

He explodes on my tongue, his hot seed sliding down my throat. It's sweet. Sweeter than I expected it to be, and I can't seem to get enough of it as I lap at the rest still spilling out of his cock.

It takes a minute, but when it hits me, I'm so taken aback, so baffled that I stagger to my feet, forgetting my surroundings and the need to remain quiet when I shout, "Winston, why does your come taste like salted caramel?"

Chapter 21
Winston

Natalie and Lindsay leave shortly after they wake up. They take Natalie's car to the coffee shop for breakfast, and this is presumably where she will reveal my presence in the house, and our romantic situation. Not that I know what she'll say, or what label she'll choose to apply to us. We didn't discuss it, and I didn't want to push. This scenario is precarious enough without forcing the relationship talk on Natalie when she's fighting off an alcohol-fueled headache.

If it were up to me, Natalie would tell Lindsay that we're madly in love and planning a future together in this house, so kindly fuck off back to Boston.

Last night was life-changing. Natalie's mouth, so hot and tight around my cock, it ruined me. Not for other women, as there will be no other women for me. She ruined me for other women ages ago. It doesn't matter how many centuries my soul remains tethered to this plane. She is it. She ruined me for...life, perhaps? Because I'm not sure I'll be able to think of or do anything else until she wraps her soft lips around my cock again.

I had no answer for her when she revealed the flavor of my come. It's bizarre, but I can't say I'm upset. Natalie said it was her favorite flavor of ice cream, and if that's how my dick tastes, she'll be more tempted to gobble it on a regular basis, right?

My heart beats erratically when I hear two cars pulling into the driveway. They must've stopped by the bar to pick up Lindsay's car. I hide in the study, knowing I'll have to be summoned before I reveal myself, and I'd rather not be creepily waiting in the foyer when I make myself visible.

"Winston," Natalie calls out. I hear her hang up her purse on the hook by the door, and suppress a groan of annoyance when I hear the plop and the jangle of a purse and keys being tossed on the floor. Lindsay's, no doubt. "Can you come down here for a minute, babe?"

I take a breath, stroll out of the study, and down the stairs. "Hello, Natalie. Ah, Lindsay, it's such a pleasure to finally meet you." When I reach the bottom of the stairs, I hold out my hand, offering my most winning and least sarcastic-looking smile.

She glares at me, then down at my hand. Eventually, she shakes it, touching me with as few fingers as she can get away with. "Hi."

No smile. No pleasantries.

I try to see it from her side, and I suppose I would be wary of me too.

Remain friendly. Don't be yourself.

"I'm not sure if Natalie told you, but I became close friends with your grandmother, Penelope. She was a wonderful woman. I'm sorry for your loss."

Her gaze remains stony. "Yeah, she told me." She blows a hair off her forehead, and when she notices Natalie looking at her expectantly, she forces a smile. "I also hear you and Natalie have gotten close as well."

Natalie looks relieved as she comes to wrap her arms around my middle, but I'm not fooled. Once Natalie's back is turned, Lindsay's face twists into a scowl.

"Okay, I'm going to shower," Natalie says, pushing up on her toes to kiss my cheek. "I feel disgusting."

I pull her against me, my palm splaying over her lower back. "You are the opposite of disgusting." I inhale the skin of her throat. "Delicious."

She giggles while playfully pushing my chest.

"I'm so glad you two are finally meeting," she says, ascending the stairs. "My two favorite people."

"Yeah, it'll be great for us to chat," Lindsay replies. "Get to know each other."

A lump forms in my throat once the bedroom door closes, and I hear the shower turn on. Lindsay crosses her arms over her chest, stomping toward the kitchen. I don't ask where she's going. I simply follow along, bracing for whatever she's about to say.

She pours herself a tall glass of apple cider I made from scratch. I rock back and forth on my heels, hating the silence, which is a new feeling for me. Most of the time, deep in silence is where I'm happiest. That's changed since Natalie's arrival. But this is different. Lindsay clearly doesn't like me, doesn't approve of our relationship, and I just want her to scold me and get it over with so I can go back to focusing on the woman I love and making her smile.

"Did Natalie tell you about the termites?" I ask, gesturing to the empty rectangle where the cabinets used to be.

She nods. "Yeah, she got the number for the pest control company in town. I called. They're coming out tomorrow after-noon to give me an estimate."

Her tone is chilly, her words clipped. I'd appreciate her unwillingness to engage in small talk if she weren't such an important person to Natalie, and didn't have such obvious disdain for me.

She sits at the counter, her different-colored eyes leaving me feeling unsettled as she steeples her fingers against her chin. "You know this is going to end badly, right?"

I focus on the loose thread inside my pocket, tugging it, wrapping it around the tip of my finger until it grows numb. "No, I don't know that."

Lindsay rolls her eyes. "Okay, let me spell it out for you. Has Nat mentioned Kyle at all?"

I nod. "She has. I know about her miscarriages, and that he wasn't worthy of being within a twenty-mile radius of her, let alone date her."

"And you know about her mom, I'm sure."

I nod again. "Yes, I do." For a moment, I feel confident. I know Natalie, and I'm acing this test Lindsay is giving me.

The sneer she gives me, however, tightens my stomach. "Look, Winston. It's Winston, right?"

My jaw tics. The clarification is intentional, an attempt to make feel small. I need to let it go. "Yes."

"Natalie is one of the kindest, most generous people I've ever known. I love her. Love her to bits, and the last thing I want to see is her getting caught up in another relationship with a guy who can't give her what she deserves."

That's it? *That's* where she thinks she's got me? "I'm aware of how much Natalie deserves, and I plan to give her everything. She's the only one who matters to me."

"Aww, so sweet." Sarcasm. "Kyle was great at spewing all kinds of sweet bullshit in Natalie's ear, too. But do you know what he did after her second miscarriage?"

My stomach twists. That's an answer I don't have.

When I say nothing, she continues. "He convinced her that the reason for both miscarriages was because Natalie's body wasn't in good enough shape, that she wasn't strong enough to carry their babies to term. That it was her fault. He wanted to act as her personal trainer, forcing her to push her body to its physical limits while she was in the process of healing from one of the most traumatic events someone with a uterus can experience."

A shiver rips through me, and I don't realize how tightly clenched my fist is until I feel something drip from between my fingers onto the floor. Blood. This likely plays into the discomfort she experiences when I touch her belly. Not the entire reason, but certainly part of it. It all makes so much sense now.

"He was a hockey player, and apparently, he was on track to be drafted into the NHL. When he got injured and his career prospects disappeared overnight, Natalie gave up everything to keep him emotionally afloat. She got into nursing school. Did you know that?"

I didn't.

"She was so excited about it. I think she got through one semester, maybe two, before she dropped out. Kyle was too much of a ballsack to take himself to therapy, but had no problem destroying his girlfriend's future so he didn't have to be alone with his thoughts. She took a job close to home that had more flexible hours, abandoning her dream."

If I could spew fire from the depths of my throat, I would.

"That bullshit happened before the miscarriages, and after...she still stuck by his side." She pins me with a cruel glare. "Do you know what happened then?"

I shake my head.

"He dumped her for someone else. Younger. The new girlfriend was pregnant within three months." Lindsay gets to her feet and comes around the kitchen island to stand in front of me. "So forgive me if I'm a protective of her. She's been through too much shit to settle again. Natalie puts everyone's needs before her own. It's part of who she is, but she deserves to be taken care of for once. Treated like a damn queen." She jerks back to look at me. "And you, no offense, seem like another black hole looking to suck her in."

"How?" I ask, disgusted by the comparison. "I've treated her with nothing but care and respect. She means the world to me. I'm not Kyle." Anger escalating, my voice raises. I know I should calm myself, but I can't keep it in. My jaw tense, I spit, "You know nothing about me."

This is a waste of time. I couldn't give less of a fuck what Lindsay thinks of me. She hasn't been here. She hasn't seen Natalie and I together. We're *supposed* to be together. I don't care how trite the thought feels once it settles in my mind. It's the truth. There's no one I have ever, or will ever, love more than Natalie. I may not deserve her, but I have every intention of making her feel loved and supported and cherished every fucking moment she continues to exist.

I spin on my heel, ready to storm into the shower and wrap Natalie in the safety of my arms when Lindsay says, "You might think you're different, but you're not. Can you support her financially?"

Financially.

Well, I don't technically have an income, but there are other things I provide for her. "I cook her meals," I tell Lindsay.

"Who pays for the groceries?"

I open my mouth, but Lindsay interrupts before I can speak.

"Let's say she rents the house from me, or, fuck, let's say I just give her the house for free. Do you think she can afford the repairs, utility bills, and property taxes of this place on her own? On what? The tips she makes from the bar?"

The blood in my veins feels ice-cold.

"Can you give her a child? She may not have been ready to

be a mom when she was with Kyle, but it's been a dream of hers as long as I've known her."

No. I can't give her that. I didn't even realize she wanted a child. Wouldn't she have told me?

"What happens if Natalie is seriously injured or is diagnosed with a terminal illness? She told me you can't even leave the fucking property."

"That...is true," I admit sheepishly. My throat is so dry I can barely speak. "I can't leave." I feel like such a fool. Why hadn't I considered any of this before now? Were we truly so wrapped up in the lust we feel for each other that none of this crossed our minds?

"If you can't leave, how do you expect to visit her in the hospital—god forbid she ever ends up there? Or take her to doctor's appointments if she can't drive herself?"

The tinny sound of Susanna's voice plays in my head.

How do you expect to carry yourself like a member of high society when you can't even hold a fork properly?

Why are you such a constant disappointment? It's embarrassing. I don't even like being seen with you in public.

Do you really think I pursued you because I loved you?

How could you delude yourself into thinking someone like me *could love someone like* you?

"I can't," I mutter quietly. To myself, to Susanna, and to Lindsay. "I don't know." The room is starting to feel small, and my breaths are coming out in short, uneven puffs. "I need to repair the fence. Tell Natalie I went to repair the fence." I drop my phone on the counter in the kitchen, then storm outside without looking back.

Chapter 22
Natalie

The vibe is off when I get out of the shower. Lindsay seems tense, but also smug, and Winston is nowhere to be found. Lindsay tells me he went outside to repair a fence, but I'm guessing it was an excuse to get away from her. She can be direct and come off as rude. If anyone can handle rude directness, however, it's Winston.

I don't take it personally when he stays away until nightfall. In fact, it's really sweet that he's giving me and Lindsay space to hang out. He knows she's hurting, and she wanted a girls-only sleepover, and he's giving us that.

Whenever I mention Winston, whether it's talking about the house, or me gushing over how amazing he is, her mouth forms a straight line, but that's okay. I'll melt the ice between them soon enough.

I find him in the kitchen as Lindsay is getting ready for bed, and sneak a few long, passionate kisses before I head back upstairs to go to sleep.

The next day, Ivan, kraken shifter and owner of Maple-town Pestbusters, shows up at two-thirty on the dot. He has a sharp, assessing gaze and a warm blue tint to his skin. Lindsay gives him a wide berth, though it could be just as much about the bugs as the fact that he sleeps underwater, wrapped in his own tentacles. When he hands Lindsay a quote after surveying the house, her jaw flops open.

"Six thousand dollars?" she asks, aghast. "Are you kidding me?"

Ivan smiles widely, somehow unaware of Lindsay's mood. "Not kidding at all, ma'am. And I'll need all living creatures to vacate the property for three days while the fumigation is in process."

Lindsay's gaze tips to the sky as she lets out a frustrated huff. "Fine. I'll pull it from my emergency savings. How soon can you start?"

He pulls his phone from his pocket and starts scrolling through his calendar. "I can start on Tuesday, if you'd like."

Lindsay turns to me. "Would you be able to find a place to crash this week? From Tuesday to Friday?"

My heart lurches at the thought of being away from Winston for three days. This issue needs to be fixed, though, and I can't ask Lindsay to delay it for such a selfish, silly reason. I nod. "Of course. Vyla's tight with the owner of the Pebblebrook Inn. I'll see if she can get me her contact over there." I shoot a text to Vyla explaining the pickle I'm in. She replies about an hour later, telling me she has a spare room at her place, and I should stay there instead.

Are you sure?

Vyla: Of course, I'm sure! You can repay me by putting in a good word with your pretty friend.

I chuckle.

> She's straight, I'm afraid, and determined to stay single forever.

> Vyla: 😂😂😂 That's a bummer, but I accept. You still owe me a favor.

> Fair enough.

Lindsay and I head into town for lunch before she leaves, and I bring the leftover pizza home for myself. We hug in the driveway, and she thanks me for being there for her. For giving her the slumber party she needed.

"Just promise me something, okay?" she asks, squeezing my shoulder.

I nod.

Her gaze shifts toward the house. Winston isn't watching us from the windows, but I know she's about to say something about him. "Pace yourself, okay? With Winston."

A laugh bursts out of me. Surprised. "What do you mean?"

"I know you guys are all over each other, and don't get me wrong, it's adorable. The insane lust phase of a new relationship. I've been there." She lowers her voice. "It's just... It's been a while since you've done this, and I want to remind you that this phase doesn't last forever. I don't want to see you hurt again. I love you, and you deserve the best."

At first, I'm amused. The idea that she sees me as this love-struck tween who doesn't know how to navigate a relationship is comical. As I watch the taillights of her car fade down the steep driveway, I start to feel incredulous. Lindsay shows up for one weekend and thinks she knows my relationship better than I do? I know she has good intentions, but the *nerve*.

When I turn to go back inside, a realization halts my tracks. How well *do* I know my relationship? Am I even in one? It feels like Winston and I are more than just fuckbuddies, but we haven't explicitly shared that either of us wants more. A warmth fills my chest when I think about how Winston is with me. How he holds me like I'm the most precious thing he's ever encountered. The romantic things he whispers when he's deep inside me. The tender way he cares for me after the sex is over. He did my laundry when I puked all over my clothes when I was sick. Then he braided my hair. Those are signs of something more, aren't they? I've had fuckbuddies before, and none of them behaved that way.

It's upsetting that I don't have a clear answer. The only thing I feel is unsure. Unsure how he feels. Unsure where we're headed. Unsure there's even a place for us to go.

We need to talk about this. I'm not going to let Lindsay get in my head.

I find Winston sitting on the couch in the living room, staring vacantly at the TV, which isn't on. "Hey," I say, sitting next to him and putting a hand on his knee. "We should talk about something."

He doesn't turn to look at me. His gaze drops to the hand on his leg. I expect him to wrap his big hand around mine and entwine our fingers, but he doesn't. He remains perfectly still, and something inside me twists in panic. I suddenly feel like I've lost control of the situation, of my emotions, and I wonder if I ever had it to begin with. Has Winston always had such a powerful hold over me? When did it go from being about just sex to what it is now? The confusion and worry swirl together, causing my palms to sweat, and out of nowhere I blurt, "Winston, I love–"

"You want to end this," he interrupts, not a question. He straightens his spine and faces me, a somber expression pulling at his features. "I think it's the right choice."

The words don't register. They don't make any sense, especially considering what I was about to reveal. "I, what?"

He nods, his gaze dropping to his lap. There's something off about his posture, or, I don't know. He doesn't look like himself. "I heard Ivan and Lindsay. You're going to stay at Pebblebrook Inn this week for three days while the house is being fumigated."

"That was the plan, but Vyla is letting me stay at her place instead," I say, panic rising in my throat. "Is that why you're being weird? Because I have to leave for three days or risk being poisoned to death?"

He presses the palm of his hand against his eye, as if trying to ward off a headache. "No. No. Of course that's not why. I'm just trying to be realistic here. We've had fun, haven't we?"

My eyes sting with tears as a crack forms in my chest. I try to swallow the tears as the floor feels like it's being ripped out from under me. "Y-Yeah."

"I agree. I've had a wonderful time with you, Natalie." He exhales, the sound heavy and dark. "But it's starting to feel like there might be something more between us, and we'd be lying to ourselves if we thought it could last."

I feel my lips tremble, so I look away, training my gaze on the coffee table.

Be strong. Be strong. Be strong. Don't crumble.

"Why would that be a lie? I don't understand."

He looks at me like the answer should be obvious. Like I'm an idiot for not seeing it. "This isn't your house, Natalie." His expression tightens. "What's your plan? To convince Lindsay to let you live here? Then what? You pay for everything with your meager wages while I do nothing, taking up space on a property that I can never leave?"

He says it like it's all so clear. So simple. That this was always meant to end for the aforementioned reasons.

Would've been nice of him to let me know.

"I guess I hadn't thought that far ahead."

I spot his hand hovering above my shoulder, but it never lands. He pulls it back, as if touching me would burn him. A million miles between this and how he was not even twelve hours ago.

Where the fuck did this come from?

"I won't be selfish with you, Natalie. You m–" his voice wobbles. He bites the inside of his cheek, and after what feels like too many seconds pass, he continues. "You mean too much to me to keep you here. Your future is brighter than this house. This town."

My voice is shaky and quiet. "I like this town." I wanted to settle down here. This town feels like home to me, or at the very least, a place that could feel like home someday in the near future.

"You have goals. Professional and personal that I can't help you reach," he explains. I have no idea what he's talking about. "In fact, being with me would prevent you from reaching those goals. Fuck, Natalie"—he lets out a choked laugh—"I'm not even alive."

My hands are clammy, and I can no longer sit still. I get to my feet and stand in front of him. "I don't care about that!" I shout. "I want to stay here, in Mapletown. The job I have is the one I want." What personal goals is he referring to? I don't even remember discussing any personal goals with him. Other than being able to grieve the death of my mom in a healthy way. "Eventually, I wanted to adopt a dog, or a cat, but that was off in the distance, and it was just an idea..."

He gives me an odd look that I can't decipher.

"Why are you looking at me like that?"

He scrubs a hand down his face. "Regardless of what your goals are, we're on the verge of something more than sex. I feel it, and I think you feel it too."

I reach for his hands, but he pulls them away, his gaze turns cold and distant. "I do. I do feel it." My voice is pleading.

"You deserve a man who can take care of you. Who can contribute more to your household than just cooking your meals. Putting the financial strain on your shoulders isn't fair, and I won't do that."

I think about all the married couples who work so much they barely see each other. Or the exhausted parents whose focus is entirely on their children and barely have enough energy to steal five minutes together without a kid's wailing cry slicing through the moment. Or the couples whose love died years before, and they can't hold a conversation anymore without being reminded of everything they've come to resent about the other.

Compared to them, what Winston and I have seems pretty goddamn magical. What we have is easy. It's tender and comfortable. With him, I've become a version of myself that I actually like, and I haven't felt that way in a long time.

"I won't get in the way of you finding the man who truly deserves you. A man who has a job. Who isn't anchored to a pile of wood and nails. Who has a fucking heartbeat, Natalie."

"Why are you doing this?" I ask, unable to stop the tears from falling. "You're pushing me away. Why? Because you're scared?" My sobs are loud and wet and shake my shoulders.

He says nothing. Just stares at me for a long time. His gaze is distant and guarded.

For a moment, I think he's going to take it all back. The flicker of hope in my chest has me reaching for his hand, and this time, he lets me take it. "Please, Winston." I swipe at my cheeks and eyes, trying to clear my vision so I can hold his gaze. "Did Lindsay say something to you? Because she doesn–"

"No." His tone is firm, unyielding. "This has nothing to do with Lindsay."

"I don't want this to end. Why are you doing this?"

It looks like it shatters his insides to release my gaze, but he does, pulling his hand away. He rubs his temples, and I wait. Hoping he'll come to his senses. Hoping he'll remember what we've built, and how much we make sense.

"Natalie," he says, finally. There's an edge to his voice that I haven't heard since the first night we met, when he spoke to me like I was a bug he intended to squash with his boot. "Don't you realize what you're doing?"

I don't know what he's talking about. I search my mind, my memories, and find nothing. Asking him to clarify terrifies me. The words never come, so I just shake my head.

He sighs, his gaze swirling with pity, and my stomach sinks. "You're doing the thing you never wanted to do again."

I shiver, the word, *No*, playing over in my head as the room feels like it's shrinking around me.

"You're begging me to stay."

He doesn't need to continue, but he does. A final twist of the knife.

"Even though I've already left."

What Kyle said to me. He's actually using my biggest regret as a weapon against me. Things move in a patchy blur after that. I hear myself say, "Okay. Fine. I'll go." I'm in my bedroom, tossing unfolded clothes into my suitcase. I don't remember entering the bathroom, but my toiletry bag is full at my feet when I text Vyla, asking if I can come over tonight.

I'm in my car when she texts back, asking if I'm okay, telling me she already made the guest bed, and she can't wait to have a sleepover with a human.

> Vyla: I already bought six bags of Doritos. How many bags do you typically eat per meal?

I don't really eat Doritos. Is that what you thought humans eat? You've seen me eat at the bar.

Vyla: The only overnight human guest I've had is my ex's twelve-year-old daughter.

Vyla: Whoops! That's my bad. You don't have to eat them if you don't want to.

With the way I'm feeling right now, I'd gladly pair a bag of Cool Ranch with a bottle of Rosé for dinner.

Vyla: I gotchu covered, Normie!

I wish I could laugh at Vyla's antics, but I don't have it in me. Not with everything that just happened.

Winston and I may have exchanged final words, or a hug, but I don't remember. What I do know is that when Mom died, I was certain my heart had been broken so irrevocably that I'd never be able to smile again. Why does this feel worse?

* * *

The only times I return to Caraway Manor during the following week are to let Ivan and his team inside, and to lock it up three days later once they're done. I don't go inside, and I don't peek my head around the house toward the garden either. Ethel deserves a goodbye, and I feel bad that I didn't give her one, but I think if I saw her face, the truth would spill out of me, and I'd end up in the fetal position until Winston discovered me. I'm not prepared for that level of embarrassment.

I let Lindsay know that I'll be staying at Vyla's until further notice via text, and she's more than fine with it. It seems odd, given her initial concerns about having a house she owns sit there unoccupied while she lives so far away. Though, maybe knowing Winston is there is good enough for her. It's not like he'd let anyone break in and start stealing things.

Part of me hates him. A big part. I also feel foolish and manipulated. Is this how Lindsay felt with her baby boy toy? I suppose it's better that Winston didn't ghost me, but the jarring rejection when I was starting to fall in love and thought everything was fine still cuts me deep. The ache in my chest that used to be a warm, happy place filled by Winston and his ridiculous rules, his boyish grin, and the safety I felt in his arms throbs. I can't help but rub the spot, trying to soothe it.

I've been through heartbreak before, and just like then, I was sure I'd never recover. I will, though, right? It won't always be like this? I won't always be on the verge of collapsing into a puddle of tears and insecurity and broken shards of unrequited love, will I? I'm not sure I can take a lifetime of this. I can barely get through an entire day.

Vyla has been an exceptional shoulder to cry on. She hasn't mentioned Winston at all, but she lets me cry when I need to, and attempts to distract me the rest of the time with tales of her sexual pursuits, gossip about Dominic and his ex, and her favorite show, which is a sitcom on an app I've never heard of about a group of twenty-something monsters trying to find themselves while living next door to each other in a fictional monster town. Basically *Friends*, but with beasts I never knew existed until a month ago.

When I call Lindsay to vent, she listens, offering me kind words, promising me I'll be okay, that I'll find someone worth my time and energy.

"Winston *was* worth it," I point out.

"And yet..." she trails off. I can't argue with her.

Winston was worth it, until he destroyed me.

* * *

A week goes by, and then another. It's embarrassing to admit, but I check my phone several hundred times a day, just in case Winston sent me an *I'm sorry. I love you. Please come home* text. He never does.

I create a steady, joyless routine of waking, working, eating, and sleeping. I sleep a lot. My body clearly needs it, and during my waking hours, I do my best to look and act normal, but I'm not fooling anyone. Dominic offers to help any way he can. Vyla randomly picks me up and swings me around in a tight hug during our shifts, just to see if I'll crack a smile. I do. It's impossible not to, and I'm grateful I've made such a great friend here.

She also keeps my pint glass filled with fresh apple cider, my new favorite drink. The cider king seems to have noticed as well, since he keeps dropping off gallon jugs for free, winking at me before he leaves.

Lindsay checks in daily. She sends me gift cards to the few restaurants in town, reminds me to stay hydrated, and assures me that it can't get any worse than this. As much as I appreciate it, it reminds me of Winston, and when he'd take one look at my lips and press a full glass of water to my mouth, ordering me to drink.

When I cry myself to sleep each night, I can't tell if the tears are for Mom, Winston, my current lot in life, or all three.

On the morning of the 5K race, I show up at the volunteer tent ten minutes early with a large, salted caramel latte in hand. The sky is a bright haze of clouds, making it hard to decide if my sunglasses are necessary or not. I'm cozy in my fitted navy-blue joggers and gray hoodie, and let out a contented sigh when the wind whips around me, kicking up fallen maple leaves around the entrance of the tent. This is the best time of year and somehow feels even better in Mapletown.

"Natalie," Mayor Crane says with a warm smile. "Lovely to see you. How are you doing?"

I nod, trying to smile. "Great," I lie. "Excited for the race to begin."

She puts a hand on my arm and gives me a knowing look. "I know you're not okay, but I need you to hear me. First of all, heartbreak is an inconvenient bitch, and I'm sorry you're going through it. Please keep in mind that I'm a witch, part of a coven, and a member of the most powerful family of witches in the country." She lowers her voice, looking over her shoulder. "If you'd like a hex put on someone, turning their dick into a shriveled banana, turning their carpets into sheets of Legos, unleashing a curable but messy illness on them and everyone they care about, you let me know, okay?"

I laugh, thanking her with a hug. She squeezes me back, and I feel an overwhelming sense of belonging, for the first time in, maybe ever. "Was there a second of all?"

"Ah, yes," she says. "I've said this before, but you're welcome to stay here for as long as you'd like. The zoning laws require property to be transferred to and from those with monster blood, but I'd be happy to make an exception for you, should you ever decide to buy real estate."

"Oh," I say, honored. "I'm probably a few decades away from that, but I really appreciate it."

She pats me on the shoulder. "What I meant was, you have the town's support. You're one of us, regardless of your boring normie blood."

I'm not sure I've ever received such a wonderful compliment. I ride the high of feeling at home among the monsters of Mapletown throughout the race, cheering on the runners, offering cups of water, and breaking down the tent long after the race is over.

It was a nice few hours to forget the pain slicing through my middle. But it all comes crashing in on me once I'm back in my room at Vyla's place. And the next thought I have—one I know I shouldn't have and certainly don't want to have—is whether anyone has made Winston feel as loved and supported as the people of Mapletown have made me feel. The likelihood of that is tragically low, and as furious as I am at him, my heart squeezes on his behalf, wishing I could be that person.

Chapter 23
Winston

Time goes by in a blink, or it trudges on like spilled molasses. I don't know, nor do I care. Nothing matters anymore. My Natalie is gone. It's what I intended, but the last thing I wanted.

If I had let her say...what she started to say, I would've said it back, promised her forever, and as long as I treated her with even a hint of kindness, Natalie wouldn't have left my side. She would've felt beholden to me, and I won't do that to her. I won't let her know that my universe is in her eyes, her smile. I'll never go a day without her filling my mind, but she deserves to be cared for in ways that I can't.

She deserves this kindness, because of how much she freely gives to others. My suffering is my burden. It's for the best. I know that.

Hopefully, she's happy, smiling that wide, sparkly grin of hers, lighting up the sky with it. I hope she's applying for nursing school, adopting a cat or dog or lizard, whatever she wants. Finding a man who can give her the child she deserves. The life she deserves.

I'm not sure I'll ever be able to forgive myself for breaking her heart. Replaying it, I have no idea how I got through it. With each word, with each savage lie, I put more distance between our bodies, a brick, and then another, laid in the wall I erected separating our hearts.

What I didn't lie about was that she deserves better. That's always been true. I'm not enough for her. I'm a poor, prickly ghost who spent his final years alive pretending he was a member of the upper class, and the century thereafter pretending to enjoy being alone. Bullshit. All of it.

Being alone was only enjoyable until I knew what it was like to be with Natalie. The companionable silence we shared in between the wild laughter and the intimate moans. Now that I know how full life can be, I can't go back to how it was before.

I try.

I make the rounds, tidying, dusting the shelves, and sweeping the floors. Then I go outside, checking the exterior of the house, and the fence that runs along the edge of the property, looking for repairs. I've been avoiding Ethel since Natalie left, and she knows it.

When I spot the bright red lips and dark brown hair, I spin on my heel, pretending to head into the forest, but it's too late. She's spotted me.

"Winston! Come here, would you?"

I keep my stride short and slow, delaying this as long as possible.

"How are you, my dear?"

"Fine, Ethel," I say quickly. "Thank you for asking."

She's trimming the ends of a pile of flowers into sharp diagonal points. Next to the flowers is her blooming strawberry patch, the berries a striking bright red beneath the warm sun. "And your lovely wife?"

The word is like a bullet lodging itself in my chest, the tissue necrotizing around it. "Uh, Natalie is doing well, I assume."

That last part has her gaze lifting to mine. "You assume?"

"She's gone, Ethel," I say in a single breath. "I fucked it up. I fucked it all up. I told her to leave, and she left." Everything spills out of me. Every emotion and thought and plea I held back in Natalie's presence that last day we spoke, it erupts from my mouth. I fall to my knees, pressing my palms and forehead into the rich soil. "She's not coming back. I told her to go, and she's never coming back."

Ethel's voice is muffled, but I feel her hand on my back as she says, "There, there, dear. Where did she go?"

I try to organize my thoughts and lay it out chronologically for her from the beginning, but my voice is cracking on every word, and my mind is a pile of mashed potatoes. I doubt what comes out of me is more than Natalie's name and how much I love her.

Ethel's hand remains steady on my back, rubbing comforting circles. She tells me that Natalie will come back, and "never say never!" but it's not true. I've lost the only person I've ever truly loved, and the worst part is that if given the chance, I'd do it again.

Natalie is a beautiful, brilliant woman with a heart full of courage, not lacking in pain, and still, she trusts so openly. I used to see this as a weak quality, but in reality, it's the opposite.

Her heart breaks, and she puts it back together herself. Then she offers the entire thing to the people she deems worthy, trusting they'll handle it with care.

I can't say I've ever been that brave. In fact, I'm a fucking coward. The only brave thing I've done is let her go. Give her the space to pursue her goals and let the right man find her. I stepped out of the way, allowing her to be found by the one who will not only cherish her the way I did, but fill in all the gaps I never could.

My fingers are stained brown as I dig my hands into the soil. I end up on my side, and when a whiff of strawberry hits my nose, the last scraps of my resolve are torn away. Suddenly, I'm pulling myself closer to the strawberry patch, desperate to keep the scent in my lungs because it's hers. It's not the same, but it's close. The closest I'll ever get.

It's better than lying in the shower, running my nose along the faded tiles in an effort to breathe in the leftover tendrils of her shampoo, which is what I've done every day since she left. Natalie took the bottle of shampoo with her, otherwise, I would've spent our days apart rubbing it into my skin, little by little, until it was the only scent my nose could register.

"No, Winston," Ethel says from somewhere behind me. "You'll see her again. You'll smell her again. You'll get to hold her again. Don't worry."

I didn't realize I'd mentioned her scent aloud, but it makes sense. She's everywhere, despite the lack of her presence. It's too late. She's in my cells, my bones, the follicles of my hair, and that'll never change.

I'm not sure how it happens, but I end up in the middle of the strawberry patch, clawing at the velvety green leaves and the ripe berries themselves. But it's not the same. Not nearly.

"Not the same. Not at all the same," I hear myself mumble incoherently.

A wave of anger hits me, and I let it take me, closing my fists around the roots poking out of the ground around my head. A voice deep inside my head urges me to pull. I know I shouldn't; I just can't remember why. If I can't have Natalie, why would I allow this fraudulent scent source to continue to antagonize me?

"Not the same!" I shout. "It's not the same."

My cheeks feel wet, and my eyes are stinging, but I don't realize I'm crying until Ethel wraps her arms around me and pulls my upper body into her lap, wiping my cheeks. "It's okay, doll. It hurts now, but you'll be okay."

She's talking to me, but I'm not listening. I can't stop pressing my nose against the berries until they pop. Juice explodes up my nose and across my cheeks, and I breathe it in. But it doesn't soothe the hollow ache inside me. "Not the same. Not her."

"No, it isn't."

I continue to rip the roots, squeeze the berries, rip and squeeze, rip and squeeze, until the entire strawberry patch is obliterated, and I look like I committed murder.

"Not her. Not the same."

Ethel continues to rock me, petting my hair, generously ignoring the destruction I just made of her beloved garden.

* * *

Some odd days later, I hear the front door swing open, and I feel my heart shoot up into my throat. Could it be *her*? My sweetheart. My Natalie.

I'm working on a new sketch and forget to leave the sketch-book in the study before becoming mist and shooting down to the first floor. A disappointed sigh tumbles out of me at the sight of Lindsay.

"You," I seethe. "What are you doing here?"

She shoves her oversized sunglasses atop her head, and her face scrunches like she's just swallowed something vile. "Trust me, this is the last place I want to be."

I cross my arms over my chest. "Then why the fuck are you here?"

She pulls a stack of papers from the large bag on her shoulder and throws them to the floor. "Why am I here? Because I'm never going to sell this fucking nightmare of a house. That's why!"

The only reason I bend down and gather the scattered pages is because I like the sound of that—her misery, and my house remaining mine. I sit down on the first step and attempt to put them in order.

"The zoning laws in this town are bullshit!" She shouts, throwing her hands up. Her heels clack loudly as she storms into the kitchen, returning a moment later with an open bottle of clear liquor, pouring the booze down her throat as she walks. Her face scrunches in disgust, and it takes her a minute to swallow and keep it all down before she resumes talking. "I can't sell the house to anyone outside the town limits unless they have monster blood, or unless the mayor approves. How the hell am I supposed to list this place with requirements that rigid? I've never met the mayor. I don't even live in this state."

I'm inclined to pity her, to say, "there, there," even. But I don't, because the memory of her listing the ways I'm too much of a loser to be with Natalie is still fresh. Still, I can't ignore the power she has over the place I call home.

"What happens now?" I ask.

She shrugs as she takes a seat on the floor, and I hear her crying softly. "Got me. It's not like I can rent this place out with you here. No matter how much I beg you, I know you'll scare the shit out of any potential tenants I let move in. And *I* certainly don't want to be your roommate."

I laugh. "The feeling's mutual."

"Even if I wanted to level this place, I'd have to pay for that, and I can't afford it. If I turn off every utility and just let the place rot, I'd still have to pay the property taxes, which I can't afford." She hangs her head in her hands.

"Why can't you just rent the place to Natalie? You won't make as much as if you'd be able to rent out every bedroom, but it's better than nothing."

She whirls on me, smacking my knee with the back of her hand. "Because this is the last place she wants to be after you broke her heart, you dick!"

My patience—what little I had of it—dissipates. "Are you fucking kidding me? You got exactly what you wanted! Natalie isn't with me. I'm not dragging her down anymore."

Lindsay stares at me, her gaze intense, assessing. It only adds to my anger.

"You might think you know her better than anyone, but you didn't get to see the side she showed me. She's not this fragile dove with a broken wing. Have you considered, for just one goddamn moment, that maybe she's actually stronger than that? Stronger than you, even?"

She remains silent, as if waiting for me to continue.

"Do you have any idea how brave it is to trust new people after your heart has been torn to ribbons? And how many times has her heart broken? Yet she continues to trust. Continues to believe that she can find happiness in the presence of others."

Lindsay winces, as if I slapped her.

"I can't speak for you, Lindsay, but my heart has been chewed up and spit out endless times, and it's only reinforced my belief that other people aren't worth the trouble they come with. My heart has only gotten harder, while hers gets softer." I suck in a breath, realizing that adrenaline is pumping through my veins and my entire body is shaking. "Although, I think I've spent enough time in your company to know that you're just as unpleasant and difficult to be around as I am, so maybe take a moment and reflect on your low opinion of Natalie. She's stronger than both of us, better than both of us, and you don't know what the fuck you're talking about."

I shift in my seat on the steps, and my sketchbook slides down onto the main floor, between me and Lindsay. Her hand darts out faster than mine does, and she flips it open as my heart climbs its way up my throat.

"What do we have here?" she says, tone awestruck.

She studies each page, and I wish I could read her mind. Other than the widening of her eyes, her expression gives away nothing as she takes in page after page of drawings of Natalie. There's nothing in my sketchbook but her because there's nothing else that has so thoroughly captured my interest. There are drawings of just her face when she's smiling, of her profile when she's looking out the window and the sun casts shadows across her cheek and down the delicate column of her throat. I've drawn portraits of her sleeping peacefully, of her naked with her juicy thighs spread wide and her face twisted in lust. She fills the pages just as much as she fills my mind.

I don't expect Lindsay to burst into laughter, but that's what happens.

I'm ready to throw her stack of papers in the air and storm back to the attic when she puts a hand on my arm.

"Wait, I'm sorry." She fans her face with the sketchbook, trying to cease her laughter. After a moment, she says, "You know what, Winston? You're right."

"I'm...I'm right? About what?"

She shakes her head in what looks to be wonder as her different-colored eyes size me up. "I don't know what the fuck I'm talking about. See, I thought you were a horny old man taking advantage of my very vulnerable friend, and the idea of you fucking her in the bedroom I once slept in before I got my period, I'll be honest, it freaked me out."

I'm offended for so many reasons, but I also can't figure out where this is going. "I died when I was in my late thirties. I haven't aged a day beyond that, so I'm not an old man."

"That wasn't the case, though, was it?" She asks, ignoring my comment. "You weren't in it for just the sex." Her gaze narrows. "You were in love with her, weren't you?"

"No," I correct. "I *am* in love with her. Present tense."

She searches my face, looking for something, and I squirm under the focused attention.

"Are you done staring at me like that? Jesus."

Another moment, then she nods. "Yup. I see it now. You're telling the truth." She chuckles as if this whole ordeal is amusing to her, then lets out a gasp that echoes all the way up to the third floor. "Oh my god." Her hands clutch the sides of her head, her eyes wide in horror. "Oh, no. No. No. No. No."

"What?" I demand, growing impatient. "What the hell is wrong now?"

"Winston." She reaches out, squeezing my shin, unshed tears filling her eyes.

I bat her hand away, disgusted by the physical contact. It's not Lindsay that disgusts me. She pisses me off, but I think I'd have this reaction if any woman other than Natalie laid a hand on me.

"This is my fault. All of it." Her eyes dart around the foyer, as if she's likely to find the solution to her problems thumbtacked to the wall. "Y-You ended it because of me. Her broken heart is my fault." She starts crying again as she folds in on herself and goes back to muttering, "No, no, no."

I don't conceal my scoff. Of course, this is her fault. She should've minded her own business.

"Winston, oh god. I'm fucking awful." Her sobs are louder now. "This whole thing was supposed to bring us closer together. We'd grown apart the last few years, and it haunts me that I wasn't more supportive when she was caring for Rita in her final days. I knew this wouldn't make up for me being a shitty friend, but I was hoping it would, I don't know, mayb—"

It's getting harder for her to speak, the tears big and fat as they dribble down her cheeks onto her shirt.

"Then go apologize," I interrupt. "This is no longer about me, so if you don't mind…"

"Uh uh. No way, buddy," she says, wiping her drippy nose on the used tissue she pulls from her purse. "We need to fix this together. I might have been the conductor of this ten-car-pileup, but you played your part in it too."

I pause, sitting back down. "What do you have in mind?"

A smile stretches across her face, dimples forming on both cheeks. "Have you never watched a rom-com? This is the part where a grand gesture is needed."

How vague and unhelpful. "Have you forgotten that I'm a penniless dipshit?"

She holds up a finger in protest. "I never used the word *dipshit*."

We brainstorm ideas, based entirely on examples from movies she's seen. None of them seems right for Natalie. What we keep coming back to is the house.

"I know I seem like a greedy piece of trash," she says, "insisting I sell this house that was just handed to me. But it's not like that. I have a kid, Winston. Do you know how expensive children are nowadays?"

"No idea," I tell her honestly. "It's just you? Where's the father?"

She grits her teeth and makes a stabbing motion with the pen in her hand. "He's useless. Rarely utilizes his visitation, so I'm basically a single mom. It's up to me to save for college, and potential injuries or illnesses and,"—her face crumples and the tears resume—"my baby just came out as trans, and I want to make sure they, she? *she* has the money for all the gender-affirming care she needs. I have no idea what insurance will cover, probably nothing by the time she needs it." Lindsay's shoulders heave, and for the first time, I feel like I can see the expectations she has for herself, impossibly high, stacked on her shoulders. "Billy, my ex, doesn't even know she's trans, and based on, well, everything, he's going to be an asshole about it, so I'm on my own. I just…" Her gaze returns to mine. "I want her to be exactly who she is, authentically herself, and not have to worry about what it'll cost to make that happen, you know?"

I nod, a tightness forming in my chest.

"I make decent money, but Boston is expensive. Selling this house would've given us a solid nest egg for whatever she needs."

It's not a comfortable feeling—agreeing with Lindsay, but she's right. Her child should come first, and if she needs costly medical care, selling this house is the best way to get it.

"But even if I could sell it," she adds, "I'd still be kicking Natalie out with little notice. And who knows how much I could even get for it?" Resigned, she heaves a weary sigh and shakes her head. "You know what? Just take it."

She starts shoving the loose papers at me.

"Take what? The house?" I ask, perplexed by this sudden turn of events. "You need the money for your kid."

"I can't sell it, remember? The zoning laws? Also, even if I could, it would probably take years to get to know the right people and the right resources to get the word out there, and I don't have the time or the money to cover the repairs it needs beforehand, or schlep back and forth to Boston every time I need to meet with a realtor."

I stare at her, blinking slowly as a seed of yearning is planted in my gut and begins to grow.

"If I can't sell it without having to shell out thousands of dollars up front, I'd rather you have it. Take it, please. And I'll do whatever else I can to help you get back with Natalie."

A thought. My body recoils at it, fights against it, but it

sinks its teeth in so deep that the words fly out. "Come with me. I think there's a way for both of us to get what we want."

Chapter 24
Natalie

Another week later...

Halloween Night

I'm finishing my third apple cider and vodka of the night when "Monster Mash" starts blaring over the speakers. I've always loved this song, but hearing it sung loudly by this particular group of beauties and literal beasts is a whole other vibe. The stacked empty glasses and beer bottles clink against each other on the tray I'm carrying, and I worry I'm about to be surrounded by broken glass, which would be a catastrophe, and I'm already in a sour mood.

Halloween in Mapletown isn't like Halloween anywhere else. Since the town is filled with monsters, most people don't wear costumes here. The attire is closer to New Year's Eve, or a wedding, where the dress code is black tie optional, and if you decide to wear a costume, fuck it, that's okay too.

However, there are still buckets of candy in the center of

every table, and at each end of the bar, because, as Dominic says, "We may be monsters, but we're not cruel." There are autumn-themed cocktails that Rizlan made up, and he, Vyla, and Dominic are behind the bar pumping them out at record speed.

I'm wearing my fanciest dress, an A-line orange chiffon dress with little white flowers all over it. A white petticoat beneath it makes my skirt puffy, like the 1950s spit me out in the middle of the forest just for this grand soirée. I also have a white faux-fur shrug in my cubby in the back room, but it's way too hot to wear it in here. The crowd is thick, and the bodies in here are sweaty as they move together in raucous glee to every Halloween-themed song Vyla put on her party playlist.

I volunteered to bus the tables, since it allows me to keep my body moving while minimizing the possibility for socializing. Not that I find talking to the Mapletown residents a chore under normal circumstances, but my heart is still in a million pieces, and I'm just not in the mood.

That doesn't seem to stop the eager demon—Fitz, maybe? Or Ferris? Something with an F—from following me around the dance floor like a lost puppy and peppering me with the basic rundown of first date questions. The fact that I'm working doesn't seem to slow him down. He's nice, I guess, but that's all. Everything about him is nice. Nice face. Nice eyes. Nice hands. Nice height. But I feel nothing.

I can't stop thinking about Winston. My grumpy ghost and his obsession with bookmarks. His intensely green eyes, bizarrely different shades based on his mood. They were dark when I first met him, a deep hunter green. Toward the end of our time together, however, they were more of a rich, sparkly emerald.

Why did he end things between us? It still doesn't make

sense to me. The sharp turn from constantly hovering around me to the chill in his voice when he reduced what we had to a fling that could go no further, I can't figure it out. What the hell happened?

And why the fuck hasn't he called or texted me to apologize?

Though, he did warn me that he's an asshole, did he not? I guess I should've believed him.

I sigh wistfully, but Fitz/Ferris doesn't notice. "Are you close with your parents?" he asks.

It's an innocent question, but I'm in no condition to spew the whole sad story of how my dad left when Mom was pregnant, how I never met him, or how I lost Mom to cancer just a few months ago to him right now, nor am I interested in picking that scab. I'm barely holding it together as it is.

"I'll be right back. Bathroom break. Maybe I'll catch you later," I tell him with a tight smile as I drop my tray on the bar and head to the restroom.

Inside, I find Mayor Crane, her chief of staff, Ezra, and Vyla huddled in the corner and passing around a fat joint. The skunky smell of weed fills the air, and I let my nose carry me closer, silently begging for a contact high to lighten my mood.

"She tasted like an orange creamsicle," Vyla says with an unhinged giggle. "Are you sure your mom had nothing to do with that?" she asks the mayor. "Are you *sure* sure?"

"Yes, Vyla, I'm sure," the mayor replies in a serious tone, but grinning widely. "The flavor spell was for peens only. That's not something I would've forgotten, considering she cast it when I was thirteen."

My ears perk up. "Flavor spell?"

"Natty!" Vyla shouts, as if just noticing me. "When did you get here?"

Ezra exhales a cloud of smoke from the side of their mouth, looking very much like a pirate. "She's been here for twenty minutes."

"More like two," I clarify.

Ezra looks down at the joint in their hand, eyes wide. "Shit, this is good weed."

Mayor Crane takes a puff, then coughs several times. Once her airways are clear, she says, "We're talking about the flavor spell my mom cast when she was mayor. Vyla's trying to convince *me*," she turns to Vyla, "who was in the room when she recited the spell, what was said, but she's wrong."

"Huh. What was the spell for?"

Vyla chuckles. "You don't know?"

I smirk. "I might," I say, licking my lips at the memory. "But I want to be sure."

Vyla starts telling the story, but the mayor interrupts her, insisting she can tell it better. "My mom is and always has been a staunch defender of women's rights. Huge feminist. She was an activist, bra burner, protest marcher, etc. The lack of equal rights in this country appalled her, so when she was elected mayor, she used what power she had over this tiny scrap of hidden land, and...leveled the playing field, in her own unique way."

Ezra and Vyla are practically cackling, pride and admiration shining in their eyes.

Mayor Crane looks amused as she shakes her head. "The spell she cast makes every penis within the town borders taste like the favorite ice cream flavor of the person sucking on it."

My mouth waters as my jaw drops, and I come close to drooling on the bathroom floor. "That's why!"

Vyla points and laughs at me. "Ahhh, our little Natty has had a taste!" Despite knowing the owner of the penis I've tasted, and being high off her ass, she doesn't mention his name, which I appreciate. "What did it taste like?"

I feel the blood rushing to my cheeks. "Salted caramel."

"How is your mom these days?" Vyla asks the mayor. "I feel like it's been ages since she came to visit."

"That's because it *has* been ages," she replies. "Both of them are in Amsterdam at the moment. They've been there for most of the year. Not sure where they'll head next. Maybe to see Uncle Henrik."

Did I hear her correctly? "Moms?"

Ezra nods. "She has two of them. Ursula and Tova."

"Quite possibly the two coolest names I've ever heard," I tell the mayor. "I've never heard the name Tova before."

Mayor Crane takes another puff and adds, "It's a Swedish name."

"Yup," Vyla says, "the most powerful witch in Mapletown fell in love with a Swede."

"My grandparents were *not* happy, but my mom never gave a shit about the opinions of others, so that didn't stop her."

"Good for her," I reply, envious. If I weren't such a people pleaser, maybe my whole life would've turned out differently. Maybe I'd be happier, or at least in less pain.

My stomach aches from laughter by the time I leave the bathroom. It's a good feeling that gives me hope. That maybe, someday, the sharp soreness in my chest will dull, and I'll be able to smile regularly again.

I make my way toward a messy table with a handful of empty cocktail glasses. Before I reach it, a hand wraps around my wrist. When I look up, I'm shocked to see Lindsay standing there, for once the most underdressed person in the room, wearing jeans with a hole at the knee and a green hooded sweatshirt. She chews on the inside of her cheek, looking more nervous than I've seen her in years. Lindsay Abbadelli is not a nervous person. When she enters a room, she commands it. Not this time, though.

"Linds. What are you doing here?"

"Hey, Nat," she says, her voice timid. "Can we talk? Outside maybe, where it's not so loud?"

I nod, my stomach twisting anxiously as I let Dominic know I'm stepping out for a minute.

When I find her outside, she's standing on the edge of the parking lot. I'm not sure why. She's not even near her car. I look at her, glancing around. Puzzled. "What's up?"

The air is chilly, and even without a steady breeze, goose bumps race across my bare skin. It's about forty-seven degrees, and the skies are clear. Perfect Halloween weather. I wonder if the kids of Mapletown still go trick-or-treating. Do they wear costumes? Or child-size formal wear? Oh my god, how cute would that be?

Lindsay lets out a heavy breath, pulling me back to the here and now. "First, I want to apologize to you, for so many things." She holds out her fingers, counting. "For losing touch with you over the last few years, for not being there when Rita was near the end..." She huffs a shallow breath, as if she's in the middle of a cardio workout. "For projecting my bullshit when I forced a sleepover with you out of the fucking blue,"—another quick breath—"and most importantly, for meddling with you and Winston. I never should've pressured him to back off, and I never—"

"Excuse me?" I jerk back, hands suddenly shaking. I had no idea she spoke to Winston. The events over the last month suddenly become crystal clear. I step toward her, an unfamiliar sensation growing in the pit of my stomach. "You pressured him? What did you say?"

"Right," she says, her shoulders hanging lower as she shifts her weight between her feet. "Look, it was totally uncalled for. I know that. But I had just gotten ghosted, and you had just told me about the existence of monsters, and the last fucking thing I expected when I came up here for the weekend was to discover that not only did you have a boyfriend, but you were already living with him in my house."

The feeling continues to grow, but eases in intensity, just slightly. Rage. That's what it is.

"None of that excuses my behavior, but I just want you to understand my mental state when all of this came out." She rubs a hand across her forehead, trying to get her bearings. "I was bitter, and jaded, and so over men that when you told me there was this guy, this one hundred and twenty-something year old guy who was obsessed with you and showering you with orgasms, it immediately reminded me of the situation I was in, and it also seemed seriously shady. As your friend, I questioned his motives. I was trying to figure out what he was getting from this arrangement. I promise I was only trying to protect you."

That's what does it. That last sentence. I explode. "What makes you think I need protecting? I'm not a young, impressionable girl, Linds. I'm in my fucking forties."

She tilts her head, examining me with a pitying expression. "Come on, Nat. Look what happened with Kyle."

"What about him? That was a million years ago."

Lindsay fidgets with the string of her hoodie. "I watched him treat you like shit, over and over, and when I thought you'd leave, that surely you wouldn't tolerate another second of it, you stayed and let him do it again. You gave up your entire life, your entire future to be his babysitter, and you got nothing out of it. I didn't want you to fall back into old patterns."

I'm appalled. Not about what she's saying about Kyle. All of that is true. I put up with far too much for far too long, but the audacity of this woman I trusted, whom I considered one of my closest, if not my best friend, stepping into my life and causing absolute chaos in the name of shielding my heart?

"You wanted to become a nurse, you wanted kids, and it made sense to put all of that on hold when you were taking care of Rita, but you were finally getting back on your feet, and I didn't want Winston to do what Kyle did and railroad your potential."

When I don't say anything, Lindsay rushes to add, "You have to admit that you and Kyl–"

"I don't give a fuck about Kyle. He's in the past, and this has nothing to do with him." I clench my fists, letting the fury that's boiling my blood simmer over. "What makes you think those are dreams I still want to pursue?"

She looks around the parking lot with a scoff. "You can't seriously want to be a bartender for the rest of your life, do you? In this tiny–"

"What's wrong with being a bartender? If I'm making enough to cover my bills and feed myself, why do I have to scrape and push for more? Not everyone is built to climb a corporate ladder, okay? Not everyone wants to become a manager, or a vice president, or a chief of whatever the fuck simply because they're good at their jobs." My fists start to unclench, and I realize I'm verbalizing thoughts I've had for years but could never articulate. "Some people are happy to remain right where they are, and that's okay."

She kicks a rock, looking like the girl I met in college. Weird and direct and brimming with sass. I hate that things are strained between us, but if we're going to continue this friendship, I need to press on. She needs to know these are my boundaries and I won't let her cross them again.

"I want to know why you thought you could breeze into my life after years without much contact, pretend like we were the same people we were a decade ago, and destroy the best thing that's ever happened to me."

"Again, I'm sorry about the last few years. I feel terrible about it."

"You don't even know me anymore, Lindsay. You have this warped idea in your head of who I was and that, in spite of the time that's passed, I haven't changed at all.

"Do you have any idea what it's like to watch your only remaining parent slowly die in front of you? Do you know what it's like to watch them age fifty years in the span of a few months because of the cancer that's ravaging their body? And the chemo that's trying to fight it off? Do you—" My voice breaks, and I have to swallow a sob. "The woman who brought me into this world, who changed my diapers. I had to look into her eyes as I changed hers, knowing that she was fully aware of what was happening, and filled with shame that she no longer had the ability to do it herself. I felt honored to do it. To care for her during her most vulnerable time."

She sniffles, but I don't look at her. I can't. The pain is too much.

"She was all I had left in the world, and I remained by her side until the very last breath left her body. Do you know why?"

She doesn't answer me.

"Because that's what love is. Devotion. Family. That's what you fucking do for the people you care about. And I don't care that Kyle turned out to be an asshole and left me for someone else. I don't regret what I sacrificed for him. When I was by his side, guiding him through that difficult time in his life, it felt right. Being his rock was what he needed me to be. I would've done the same for you."

Lindsay nods, taking a tentative step in my direction. "I know. You love without caution, and it's never about whether they deserve it. The people you choose to keep close are the ones who are lucky enough to bask in your light." She uses the sleeve of her sweatshirt to wipe the tears from her cheeks. "Winston is actually the one who made me see how brave that is. Here I was, worried you couldn't protect yourself without my help, and you're braver in love than I'll ever be."

The mention of his name makes my heart squeeze. "Did you know that Winston has lived longer than us, longer than most, and no one has ever truly loved him?"

Shock fills her gaze. "What?"

I nod. "He had a terrible childhood. It's not my story to tell, but he's been through some dark shit, Linds. A lot of it. To the point where even Arya Stark would be shocked."

Lindsay chuckles quietly. "Really, Nat? Still with *Game of Thrones?* No one cares about that show anymore."

"But it was the most popular show in the world when it was on."

"Yeah, but that was years ago, hun. You need new buzzy dramas to reference. Have you seen *Severance?*"

I roll my eyes. "I can't afford all the streaming channels."

"I'll give you my login," she offers.

"This isn't the point!" I shout, frustrated by the derailed conversation. "Tragedy after tragedy hardened Winston. It made him think he was made wrong, and chronically undeserving of love. But when we were together," I explain, "being on the receiving end of my affection, even for little things, it's like he was starved of it, and once he knew how it felt, he was so much lighter."

"About Winston," she says, her lips twitching. "I know I fucked up royally, and I don't expect your forgiveness. But if you give me a chance, I'll put all my effort into making things right between us. You're the best friend I've ever had, Nat.

These last few years without you have been miserable. I don't want to lose you again."

It's a nice offer, and I believe her when she says she's sorry, that she'll work hard to change, but the betrayal is still too fresh. I shake my head. "I don't know. I'll think about it."

"I understand," she says with a solemn nod. "It's just...I need you to come with me right now."

"What?"

"There's something you need to see, and if you still don't forgive me after you see it, that's okay. I'm not giving up on this friendship."

"What do I need to see?" I look around, confused, and honestly, a little wary.

"It's not here," she says, a smile playing on her lips. "You have to follow me."

My curiosity is begging me to follow her, but I can't just disappear. "Linds, I'm working tonight. Can we do this tomorrow?"

Vyla's booming voice shouts from the doorway. "Dom says you've got the rest of the night off. Happy Halloween, Natty Baby!"

"Wait, seriously?"

Rizlan pops his head out. "Yep. Have fun, Normie. See you tomorrow."

My stomach flutters as I follow Lindsay toward the forest. Not just in any direction, either. She's leading me toward the tree line that separates the property between the bar and Caraway Manor.

Winston.

I feel my heart pound erratically, so loud I wonder if Lindsay can hear it. The woods are silent apart from the cool breeze whipping through the trees, the crunch of leaves under our feet, and the soft trill of creatures nestled in the safety of the forest. We've been walking for about six minutes when I notice a glow coming from up ahead and the beat of a song I can almost place.

Lindsay blocks my view, for the most part, but when we reach the clearing and she steps aside, the breath dies in my throat. It's a dance floor, surrounded by strand after strand of twinkly lights. It's freshly laid flooring with a glossy finish, and in one corner of the large square is a folding chair with a Bluetooth speaker on it, playing, "I Will Follow You into the Dark" by Deathcab for Cutie.

Winston stands in the middle, his shirt and pants freshly pressed, his light brown hair neatly swept off his face, and his hands shoved in his pockets. Though he's standing tall, his gaze is anything but confident. I know this look well. It's shy Winston, and man, have I missed him.

"Natalie," he says, his green eyes trailing down my body, then back up to the bodice of my dress.

My cleavage looks bomb in this dress, so the ogling just makes me smile.

"You look..." He doesn't finish his sentence, just extends his hand and waits for me to take it. "May I have this dance?"

I remember Lindsay's presence, and when I lock eyes with her, she looks like she's on the verge of squealing.

"I can take a hint," she says, turning to leave. Before she goes, she says, "Have fun, you two."

Winston chuckles, and I'm so caught off guard by the warmth he exudes while watching Lindsay leave that I let him guide me onto the dance floor and settle into the strength of his embrace.

We remain quiet for a while. Maybe too long. Neither of us knowing who should go first. I take the leap. "I have a lot of questions."

He nods, that boyish look lighting up his face. "I believe I have answers."

"Did you make this dance floor?"

He nods, the blood rushing to his cheeks.

I move on to the one that's clawing up my throat, the most desperate to be asked. "Why am I here, Winston? I thought you didn't want me anymore."

He lets out a pained grunt. "There has never been a second when I didn't want you, sweetheart. Not since the moment I became aware that you existed."

"So then..."

His gaze softens as he looks over my shoulder, toward the forest, as if gathering his thoughts. "Those things I said, that last day... I didn't mean any of them. Well," he amends, "I did mean that I don't deserve you, and never could. But the shit I said about our relationship being about sex and on the verge of something more—that was a lie."

"Why was it a lie?"

"Because it already *was* about more than sex." He chuckles, shaking his head in awe. "From the very first time I touched you, I knew I could never live without you."

"Then why would you end it?" I ask, my skin growing hot despite the chill in the air. "Why were you acting like such a heartless asshole that day? Reminding me of my lowest point with Kyle. Couldn't you sense that it was about more than sex for me too?"

His green eyes dart back and forth between mine, searching for the truth, maybe. "Fuck," he says under his breath. "I'm sorry about that. All of it. I only played that card because I knew it would hurt you enough to get you to leave, and I was afraid that if you remained next to me for another heartbeat, my resolve would weaken, and I'd beg you to stay."

I hate that he's right. It worked like a charm.

"Yeah, I could tell you felt the same about me," he continues, "but I was too afraid that I was wrong to believe it was real. I think about the life I lived, who I was before I died, and..."

"And what?"

"You do deserve someone better than me, Natalie. You're beautiful, and kind, and you love so fiercely and trust with your whole body. I've never seen anything like it. I've never been on the receiving end of love like this. It didn't feel real. You seemed too good to be true."

"That's bullshit!" I shout, surprising him with the volume and firmness of my voice, no doubt. "You cook my meals, you clean the house—the house that you built, by the way—you rub my shoulders when they're sore, you take care of me when I'm sick, you braid my fucking hair." I chuckle softly, still amazed that I landed this man, and annoyed that he can't see his worth. "And all of that is without mentioning how incredible you are in bed."

His cheeks flush, and he averts his eyes, as if embarrassed.

"When I say *incredible*, I want you to understand what that means, because there are a lot of men who don't know how little they'd have to do in bed to be considered incredible, so this is very important. Are you listening?"

He nods, his gaze dropping to my lips.

"You seek consent, you check in with me regularly, you put my pleasure before your own. You pay attention. It's so overlooked and underestimated, but it goes such a long way."

His chin is lifting, clearly enjoying my praise. "What else?"

"I can't speak for others, but my favorite thing, what means the most to me, is what happens after. When both of us have come and our bodies are at their most relaxed. Most sated." I stroke a finger along his jaw. "You clean me up with a gentle touch, and then you hold me like I'm a rare jewel, delicate and beautiful and unlike anything you've ever encountered."

He gives me an odd look, like I'm missing something. Like it should be as clear as the night sky above our heads. "Because you are, Natalie."

I close the distance between us until his forehead rests against mine.

"Sweetheart," he says, voice thick with emotion. "This is it for me. My life didn't begin until you came into it. Dead over a hundred and twenty years, and you were the one who made me feel alive. I fucked up by letting you go. I shouldn't have. But if you give me the chance, I will spend the rest of our days killing spiders for you, cleaning up your crumbs, stocking the study with bookmarks, and braiding your hair." Then a whisper, a plea. "Please, Natalie. Let me show you that I can love you better than anyone ever could."

I want to say yes. I want to forget about the last month we were apart and go back to how things were. But nothing about our situation has changed. How can we move forward with so much still stacked against us? "It's still Lindsay's house. How can we—"

"No, it isn't."

I pull back to look at him. "What do you mean?"

He smiles. "I traded the house for the last of my worldly possessions from when I was alive. Nothing that mattered to me, just stuff that my father-in-law thought was valuable, and gave to us as wedding presents."

I'm having trouble forming words. Or coherent thoughts. "What did you trade?"

"Susanna's wedding ring, as well as mine, some jewelry of hers, and a painting her father won at an auction. He was a big art collector and was always adding pieces he thought were a good investment."

"Holy shit. And Lindsay sold them for you?"

He nods. "Yeah, friends of hers from Boston who

connected her with a jewelry dealer and an art dealer. I didn't expect them to be worth much, if anything."

"And?"

His grin is so wide I can practically see all his teeth. "Ended up being five hundred thousand, give or take."

I push out of his arms unintentionally, shocked and bewildered and having no clue how to process this news.

"So Lindsay sold the house to you?"

He shakes his head. "To us. Your name is on the deed too."

I launch myself at him, in utter disbelief that the thing that's been hanging over both of us, following us from room to room inside that house, is finally gone. He spins me around, laughing as I squeal with excitement.

When he sets me on my feet, I lean into him. The solid wall of his chest keeps me steady, calming my nerves. He's home. Here, in his arms, I have everything I need.

I want to kiss him, shove him to the ground, and ride his cock on the dance floor in the middle of the forest, but...the future. There are still questions that need answering.

"What if I die and my ghost doesn't come back here?" I ask, articulating a fear that was shoved down so deep beneath all the other shit that I didn't realize how strong it was. "What if we aren't reunited in death?"

He presses a soft kiss to my cheek, tucking a lock of hair behind my ear. "Then I will pay every last cent I have to the witch who swears to bring you back to me, in my arms, where you belong."

He makes it sound so easy. I wish I felt as sure as he does.

"If that doesn't work?"

"Sweetheart, it will," he says, cupping my cheek. "Do you know how I know?"

"How?"

"Because I won't stop searching for you until I find you. It doesn't matter how long it takes. Until the sun burns out and the world is bathed in darkness.

"Luckily, it won't take that long. We will find each other again just like we did this time, because this is how our stories were always supposed to end. You and me. I'm keeping you for the rest of time, Natalie. I will not accept anything less."

The reverence in his gaze, the tenderness in his touch, I let them draw me in until our lips meet. It begins softer than it ever has, with feather-light kisses, quick pecks and brushes of our mouths together. His embrace is cold, but it doesn't matter because I've never felt warmer or more at ease. It's like our bodies recognize, at the same exact moment, when we decide that there will be no more hiding our feelings. His tongue swipes against the seam of my lips, seeking entry, but also forgiveness, trust, and faith that I'll give it all right back to him. And I do.

Hunger grows as our grip on each other tightens, and soon, my chest is heaving against his, my pulse racing, and my tongue dipping into the deepest parts of his mouth, learning him unlike anyone ever has, or ever will. It's filthy and passionate and I'm desperate to get him naked.

"Winston," I whimper into his mouth.

"Yes?" he asks, panting. His fingers are tangled in my hair, and his other hand is on my belly, a loving squeeze that sends a jolt of heat down my spine and directly into my clit.

"I love you," I say, my eyes filling with tears. "I love you so much."

His eyes grow wet as he rubs the tip of his nose against mine. "I love you, too, Natalie. My perfect, beautiful miracle."

We slow dance through another two songs. "Like Real People Do" by Hozier and "Simply the Best" by Billianne.

Winston laces his fingers through mine and presses a kiss to my hand. "Come on. Let's go home."

Fireflies blink around us, providing enough of a glow to safely make our way through the forest back to Caraway Manor. All is quiet as we cross the yard. He guides me through the side door, and upstairs, a sly grin tugging at his lips as we reach my old room.

"What's that look for?"

"You'll see," he says in a low rumble. He opens the door and puts a hand over my eyes. I feel his hard chest against my back as he walks me deeper into the room. "Okay, I need you to lie down, and keep those eyes closed."

"Okay," I say, giggling with excitement.

He keeps his hand over my eyes, but loosely, as I sit on the edge of the bed and lie back.

"Don't open them yet." I hear his boots shuffle around the bed, and the mattress dipping under his weight as he lies down beside me. His finger brushes against the back of my hand before our fingers lace together. "Okay," he whispers, "open your eyes."

I suck in a breath at the sight of millions of stars filling the sky just above my bed. "A..." I stammer. "A skylight? You installed a skylight?"

His response is proud laughter.

"Why?" I ask. "If you didn't know I'd ever come back, why bother?"

He sighs heavily, all traces of humor now gone from his voice. "I knew you might not forgive me, or want to be with me after what happened, but once I started clearing the spot where I wanted to install it, I knew it was the right decision whether you came back or not." He uses his free hand to rub his chest, right where his heart beats. Or used to, that is. "I figured, this way, I'd still get to stare up at the same stars as you. That, if this was all I had left of you,"—he turns, his gaze locking onto mine—"it would be enough."

I pull him in for a kiss, savoring the coolness of his skin and the safety within his arms. When we untangle ourselves, panting slightly, I lean my head on his bicep as his arm curls around me. We lie silently together, gazing through the glass to the heavens above. It's as if we're the last two people in the universe. Who knows. Maybe someday we will be. When that day comes, I might not even notice. As long as I have Winston, nothing else matters.

Epilogue
Winston

A month later...

"Why does the mayor need to be here, again?" I ask Natalie as she nervously paces across the rug of our bedroom, fuzzy green socks covering her feet. Taylor Swift is playing, but it's not having the calming effect it usually does on her.

"Do you think we should dust the living room again? She probably won't want to do it in there. I don't know how these things work. Do you think we'll do it outside in the garden? It's probably too cold for that."

"Do what?" I step in front of Natalie, blocking her pacing path.

"The seance or whatever. Remember? I put it on the calendar on the fridge. Mayor Crane is coming over to see if she can communicate with Thomas, Ethel's husband."

I nod. I do remember seeing this, and dreading it. There's no need for people to be in my house. Ever. No one but my Natalie. I cross my fingers, hoping the mayor will want to conduct her witch business outside. "Come, my love." I place my hand on her shoulders and guide her to our bed. "Now, lie back."

She follows my command, then lets out a contented sigh as she looks up at the puffy clouds through the skylight.

"Better?" I ask.

"Much. This always does the trick."

She turns on her side and nuzzles into my neck.

"Thank you again for installing it. It's perfect. No notes."

My chest puffs at her praise. I must admit, it was Lindsay's idea, and it was a brilliant one. After selling the painting and Susanna's jewelry, she offered to split the five hundred thousand with me as a peace offering for breaking us up. I couldn't accept. Knowing that her child would have such a better life with enough funds set aside, I refused. She countered with one hundred thousand. That, I accepted.

As with everything else, my mind drifted to Natalie, and how hard she'd have to work to save even a fraction of that. I may be dead, but I'm no deadbeat. The money immediately went into Natalie's savings account, and she spoke to someone who understands modern finances, who then moved it into another account that will accrue interest over time. It was all I could do to ease the financial burden that Natalie carries by being the sole breadwinner, and I'm glad to have had the opportunity. She did, however, take about eight thousand out of the hundred to buy me a laptop and replace various appliances.

With the computer, which I still find extremely difficult to use, I have been looking for remote work as of late. In fact, I applied to be an online moderator for Reddit.

Natalie laughed when I told her about that job application.

"Do you think I'll be good at it?" I asked her.

"Oh yeah," she replied, kissing my jaw. "You'll silence those incels quicker than they can post conspiracy theories."

"Remind me to call Linds after the seance is over. She's dying to hear all about it."

"I will," I promise her. They have grown closer since Lindsay apologized. Lindsay is even seeking to learn more about her grandmother's interest in witchcraft. She has made it known to Natalie that she wants to meet more of the witches in town, see if they'd be willing to teach her things.

The doorbell rings, and Natalie shoots out of bed, shoving her feet into her boots as I quickly wrap her puffy coat around her shoulders before she throws the door open.

"Hi, Natalie," the woman says. She has dark skin that seems to glow when the light hits her a certain way, and her posture is so perfect, there are moments I wonder if she's actually a statue. She and the person with her are bundled in wool coats and thick colorful scarves.

"Mayor Crane," she says. "Thank you so much for making a house call. I really appreciate it."

"My pleasure. You did have a favor to call in, and I'm impressed you chose to use it for this."

I clear my throat, making my presence known.

"Mayor Crane," Natalie says, cheeks flushed. "This is Winston Duffy, my–"

"Husband," I add. We're not technically married. Not yet. Natalie doesn't seem to care if we make it official or not, and I suppose neither do I. But that will not stop me from referring to her as my wife. The sound of it in my head and on my tongue makes me feel complete.

"Nice to meet you, Winston." I watch her lean close to Natalie, and I think I hear her say, "Salted caramel, was it?"

And Natalie's laughter is a loud, surprised cackle as it fills the house.

I follow Natalie, Mayor Crane, and her second-in-command, Ezra, outside toward the garden. It has snowed a few times, but not heavily enough to accumulate. The grounds are frozen and solid beneath us as Ezra lays out a large square blanket with thick black symbols in the center. She opens a briefcase and places candles, tied bundles of leaves, and other such oddities in particular spots on the blanket. While she does this, Natalie and the mayor sit on the corners, crossing their legs.

"I wasn't aware we were entertaining guests," I hear Ethel say in a tight voice.

This is my cue. I'm Ethel's designated de-escalator, tasked with calming her down and reassuring her that none of these women are here to see Thomas. "Ethel, hello. We have a very special day planned for you."

A smile breaks through the stiff and wary expression on her face. "Is that so?"

"Come along, dear." I guide her over to the blanket, and Natalie introduces Ethel to Mayor Crane and Ezra, explaining their purpose.

Ethel's eyes immediately fill with hopeful tears. "You mean... Truly? I might get to see my Thomas?" She looks to me for confirmation, and when I nod, her body starts to shake as she attempts to fan the tears falling down her cheeks.

Natalie places a photo of Thomas, taken from one of Ethel's photo albums, in the center of the blanket. There are many strange things that occur next. The women join hands from where they're seated around the blanket, closing their eyes. The mayor asks them to hum and recite some phrases in a language I don't understand.

Then, Mayor Crane takes the lead, and starts muttering more phrases on her own, while the rest remain silent with their hands clasped and eyes closed. A reddish cloud appears in the middle of the blanket, hovering two feet off the ground.

Lightning cracks inside the blood-red orb, thunder echoing, while still contained inside of it.

Ethel's face is open and filled with longing as she remains locked on the cloud.

"Ethel," Mayor Crane says, her voice at least two octaves deeper than when she arrived. "Speak to Thomas. He needs to hear your voice. Mine won't be able to summon him."

She stammers at first, but then, through tears, Ethel says, "Thomas? Are you there, darling?"

Mayor Crane gives her a nod, encouraging her to continue.

"I'm here, Tommy. At our house on the hill. You should see the garden. I've spent a long time getting it just how I like. You simply must see the height of the sunflowers. Oh, Tommy, you would just die. And–"

"Ethel, baby?" a deep, hoarse voice calls from somewhere inside the cloud. "Is that you?"

It feels like minutes pass, with Ethel confirming that yes, it is her, and the voice asking again where she is. Eventually, a face appears. I expect it to be inside the cloud, but it's not. A gray mist forms at Ethel's right side, then shifts into a man about my height wearing a military uniform, with a rugged face that matches the photo.

Ethel leaps from the blanket and jumps toward the mist, becoming mist herself in the process. The two of them become a colorless haze as they kiss passionately and talk over each other, exchanging *I love yous* and other intimate words I feel uncomfortable listening in on.

I take a step back, giving them privacy. I expect the others to do the same, but the three of them lovingly gaze at the newly reunited couple, never getting enough. Mayor Crane utters some more unfamiliar words and closes the circle, as she calls it, letting Ethel know that even though Ethel's spirit remains tied to the grounds, Thomas's spirit is not, and if she ever finds herself in the garden without him, she can simply call his name into the ether, and they'll find their way to each other.

Ethel and Thomas start to leave, the mist fading with each step they take toward the tree line, but Ethel stops, her form turns corporeal, and she races toward Natalie, throwing her arms around Natalie's neck and almost knocking her to the ground. Natalie's expression is nothing short of shocked as she pats Ethel's back.

When Ethel releases her, she cups Natalie's face and presses a kiss to her wind-bitten cheek. "You," Ethel says. "This is all thanks to you."

"What do you mean?" Natalie asks, puzzled.

Ethel's gaze lands on Mayor Crane. "To think, there was someone in our very own town who could bring Thomas back to me. I never would've known if you hadn't shown up." A tear spills down Ethel's cheek. "Thank you, dear."

Natalie's bottom lip trembles as she nods at Ethel, too overcome with emotion to reply.

As Ethel and Thomas leave, hand-in-hand, I pull Natalie into my side and kiss her temple as Ethel's words play in my head. Natalie really has expanded our world. She's our link to a community I didn't want but clearly need. She's changed everything.

When the mayor and Ezra leave, Natalie can't seem to wipe the smile from her face as we stroll back to the house. "What is it?"

She shrugs, leaning her head on my shoulder. "I'm just glad it worked out for Ethel. Being able to see Thomas will be such a huge help, especially on her more difficult days."

"Why did you use your favor on Ethel?" I ask. "Isn't a favor from the mayor kind of a valuable thing to keep in your pocket?"

She considers this briefly, then shakes her head. "Nah. I

don't need any favors. Besides, how can I deny a broken woman the chance to find the one person who makes her whole again? There's no favor that could even touch that."

I crook a finger under her chin, tilting her face up to look at me. "You're a fucking miracle, Natalie."

We grab Natalie's mother's urn from where we left it, just inside the living room, and head back outside. I wrap my arm around her, rubbing her arm in an attempt to keep her warm. We reach the wooden bench swing on the edge of the garden, and I pull her into my lap as we sit down. "You still want to do this? We can wait until the weather is warmer," I offer.

She turns to face me, the brown of her eyes reminding me of rich soil, of flowers that will soon be in bloom, of warm days and cool nights with her body tangled with mine, of a long and blissful future with my beautiful wife.

"No, I want to do it today, but we'll spread more of her ashes in the spring, then the summer, and the fall. I want her to experience each season in this very spot." She surveys the garden, then her gaze pans out further, over the entire property. "Near this house and on this land, where my life began again."

She shifts her body until she's off my lap and seated beside me. After letting out a deep exhale, she opens the top of the urn and looks at the ground beneath our feet as she starts talking to her mother. She introduces me, and I feel my cheeks heat as I wave awkwardly. I know her mother's spirit is not here, certainly not beneath the frost-covered grass, but nerves tighten my stomach, regardless. I hope, wherever she is, she approves of me.

Natalie goes on to sing my praises, most of which I don't agree with, but I remain quiet. This conversation is not for me. If she wishes to describe me as "better than a book boyfriend" for rubbing her feet at the end of a long shift at the bar, then so be it.

Once she's said all she wants to say, she removes the glove from her hand and reaches inside the urn, pulling out a fistful of ashes and spreading them on the ground in front of us.

We walk back to the house, and I stop her at the side door, stroking along her cheekbone. "I'm not sure I'll ever deserve you."

She lifts onto her toes to press a kiss to my lips, and I feel it all the way down my spine. "You know, I feel the same way about you."

My brow furrows. "That's ludicrous. I'm the lucky one in this equation."

She rolls her eyes. "Really? This argument again? Why can't we just agree that real love, love that sticks, is when both parties feel like they got the better end of the deal?"

I lift her into my arms, and she lets out that adorable little squeak. "Because you're wrong. I will not budge on this point."

"Why are you always so stubborn?" she asks playfully, pinching me along my ribs.

"I've always been a stubborn asshole, Natalie. This shouldn't come as a surprise to you."

She wraps her arms around my neck and runs her fingers through my hair. I halt my steps, unable to keep myself from leaning into her touch. Her hands are like magic on my skin, and I never want her to stop touching me. When I open my eyes, she's looking up at me through her long lashes. Her smile is warm, and her deep brown eyes pull me in, reminding me that there's nothing in this universe that will make me feel as safe and steady as her. My sweetheart. My Natalie.

Her hand cups my cheek. "You're not so bad."

Also from Ivy

<u>ALIENS OF OLUURA</u>

Saving His Mate

Charming His Mate

Stealing His Mate

Keeping His Mate

Healing His Mate

Enchanting Her Mate

(This series isn't finished. There's plenty more to come!)

<u>STRANDED ON EARTH</u>

Her Alien Bodyguard

Her Alien Neighbor

Her Alien Librarian

Her Alien Student

Her Alien Boss

<u>THE CURSED COMPOUND</u>

Alliance with the Alien Pirate

(This series isn't finished. There's plenty more to come!)

A Note From Ivy

May 30, 2024, was my birthday and also the day my mother died. She battled leukemia for nine months, and it was a brutal, devastating fight until the very end. We were incredibly close and losing her broke me.

At the time, I had several WIPs on my desk, including the second book in my Cursed Compound series. But the motivation to write a Happily Ever After just wasn't there. I tried for months, and whenever I sat down at the computer, the words just didn't come. The trick to getting me writing again was choosing to write a story just for me. Something I could get lost in and never want to leave. I've felt this way with all the books I've written, but sometimes, not until I'm about halfway through it.

This needed to be different. What I kept coming back to was the movie *Casper*. As an elder millennial, I'm not ashamed to admit that Devon Sawa was responsible for my sexual awakening with that movie, and shortly thereafter, *Now and Then*. A classic.

But I was always desperate for what came after Kat's epic Halloween party, where Casper became a Real Boy until the clock struck ten, floated her above the dance floor, and whispered, "Can I keep you?" Did they grow old together inside that creepy mansion? Did he ever get more time in his corporeal form?

And that's how *Adored by the Grumpy Ghost* started to

form in my mind. I wanted to live in a world where the spirits of the dead stick around, not just for unfinished business, but because they choose to. I wanted to believe that two people destined for each other could find their way, without the obstacles of time and pulse keeping them apart. There was also a big part of me that needed to articulate the pain I was in, not knowing how to go through life with such a significant piece of my heart gone.

There are lots of little details about Natalie's mom that mirror mine. My mom couldn't get enough fruit juice after her diagnosis. She loved it. She also offered to get me a glass of water when she was bedridden in the hospital, two days before she passed. That's just how she was—always putting her needs last.

This book helped me fall in love with writing again, in addition to healing my broken heart. I never planned on publishing this story, but the deeper I got into it, the more I thought others would enjoy it.

Let's be real; Winston is hard to resist. I was picturing a hybrid of Nick Miller, Wednesday Addams, and a cat when I wrote him. You can see it, right? I needed him to hate everyone else but melt at Natalie's feet. That's exactly what you want from a grumpy hero.

But where there's a grump, you can always find a steady ray of sunshine, and no matter how much he spoiled her, Winston wouldn't feel worthy of keeping her. I know a lot of you hate third act breakups (I'm sorry!!) but it had to be done. Knowing how much life she still had ahead of her, Winston wouldn't want to keep her tethered to him or the house. She's the reason he became his best self, and that version of him is as selfless as she is. Hopefully you enjoyed the groveling at their reunion.

Since this is book one, let's look ahead to the next story, shall we? My plan for Mapletown Monster Mates is to make them interconnected standalone novels. You can read them in any order you choose. I'm also hoping to expand the world to the other Monster towns across the U.S. But the next book will focus on...Lindsay and Dominic!

They didn't meet in book one, but get your hopes way up, because their meet cute is going to absolutely blow you away.

Thank you so much for reading. Book 2 is coming soon!

Xoxo
   Ivy

P.S. There are some incredible creatures I must thank for getting me through such a rocky stretch of life. To Dad, you're the coolest pirate on the high seas, and I'm glad we could lean on each other through this nightmare. Mom would be proud of us. To my amazing husband, you let me take as much time as I needed to process this loss and lump around until inspiration struck. You're the hero I always write. Thank you. To my dogs, Clover and Ruby. Roo, you helped me take the best depression naps ever. Clo, you got me moving even when I didn't want to. (Oh, my dogs can read. It's very impressive.) To my brilliant and lovely PA, Nikki, I hate sharing this loss with you, but I'm grateful it brought us closer. Thank you for your endless support. I love you.

To my editors, Chrisandra and Jenny, thank you for being so flexible with my chaotic timelines, and for shining my words up like a brand-new penny. To Rouge and Bri, for my beautiful covers. To Lindsey, for the gorgeous sprayed edges on my special editions. To my inspiring author peers and the incredible artists I worked with to bring this story to life, I appreciate you all so much.

About Ivy

Ivy Knox has always been a voracious reader of romance novels, but quickly found her home in sci-fi romance because life on Earth can be kind of a drag. When she's not lost on faraway worlds created by her favorite authors, she's creating her own.

Ivy lives with her husband and two neurotic (but very cute) dogs in Chicago. When she's not reading or writing, she's probably watching *What We Do in the Shadows*, *The Fall of the House of Usher*, *Bridgerton*, or *The Good Place* for the millionth time.